CATWAD

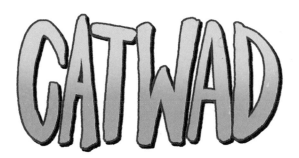

HIGH FIVE!

FOR KRISTEN LeCLERC.
I COULDN'T DO IT WITHOUT YOU.

ISBN 978-1-338-68222-9

10 9 8 7 6 5 4 3 2 1   21 22 23 24 25

Printed in the U.S.A.   40

First edition, April 2021

Edited by Michael Petranek

Book design by Katie Fitch and Cheung Tai

HIGH FIVE!

Jim Benton

AN IMPRINT OF

SCHOLASTIC

THE NEW HOBBY

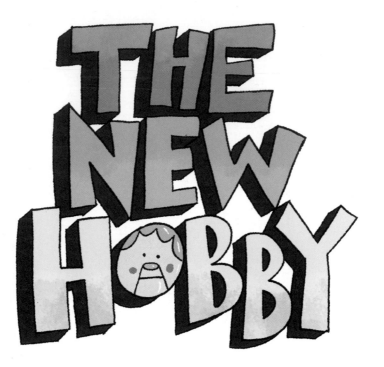

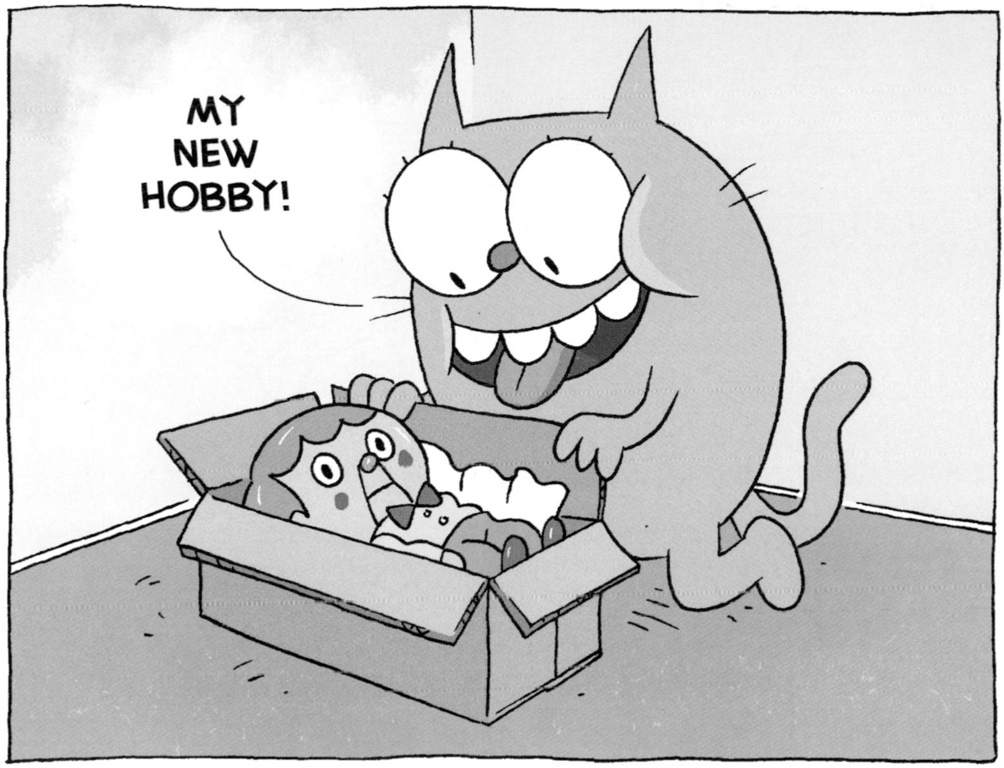
MY NEW HOBBY!

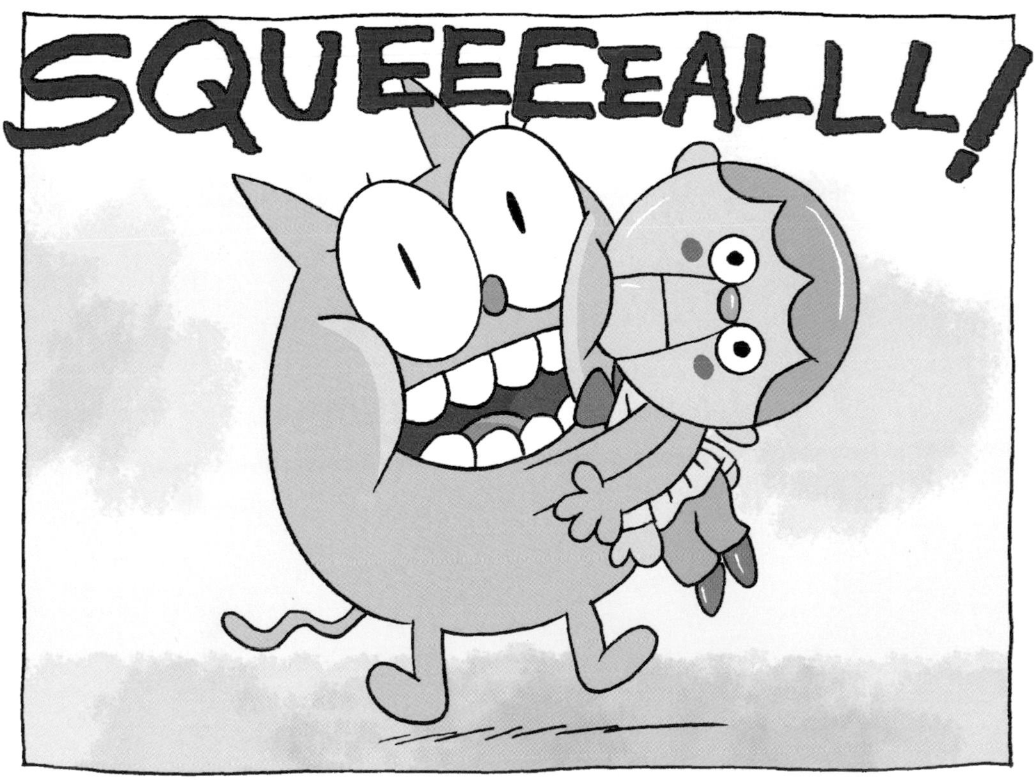
SQUEEEEALLL!

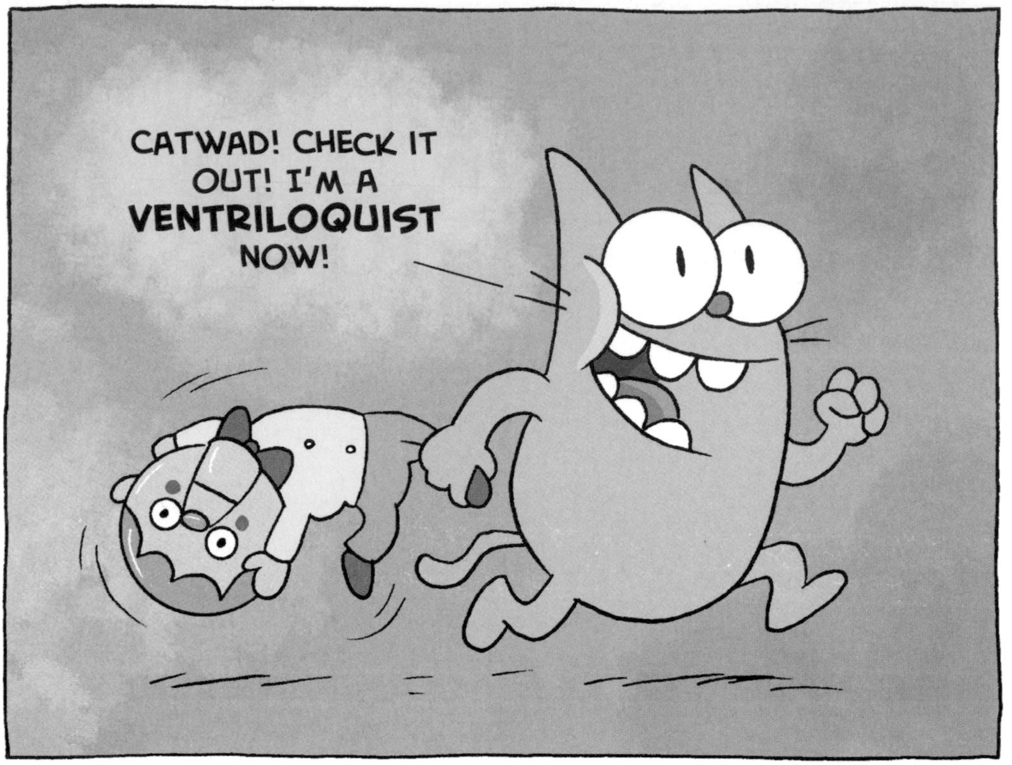
CATWAD! CHECK IT OUT! I'M A **VENTRILOQUIST** NOW!

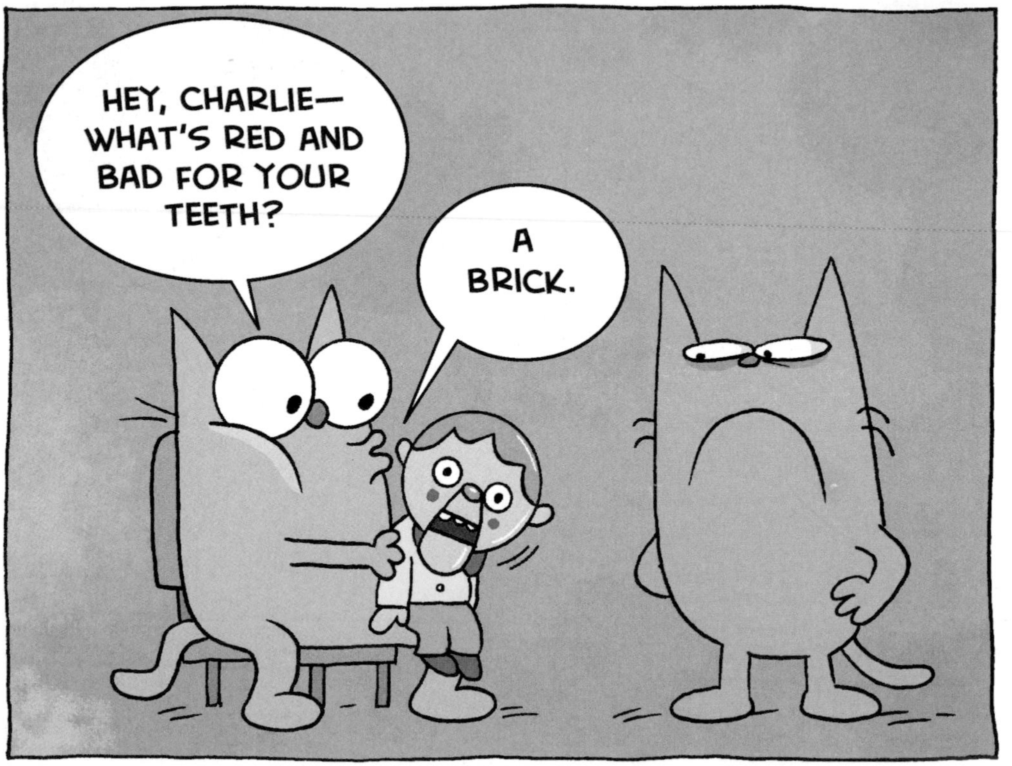
HEY, CHARLIE— WHAT'S RED AND BAD FOR YOUR TEETH?
A BRICK.

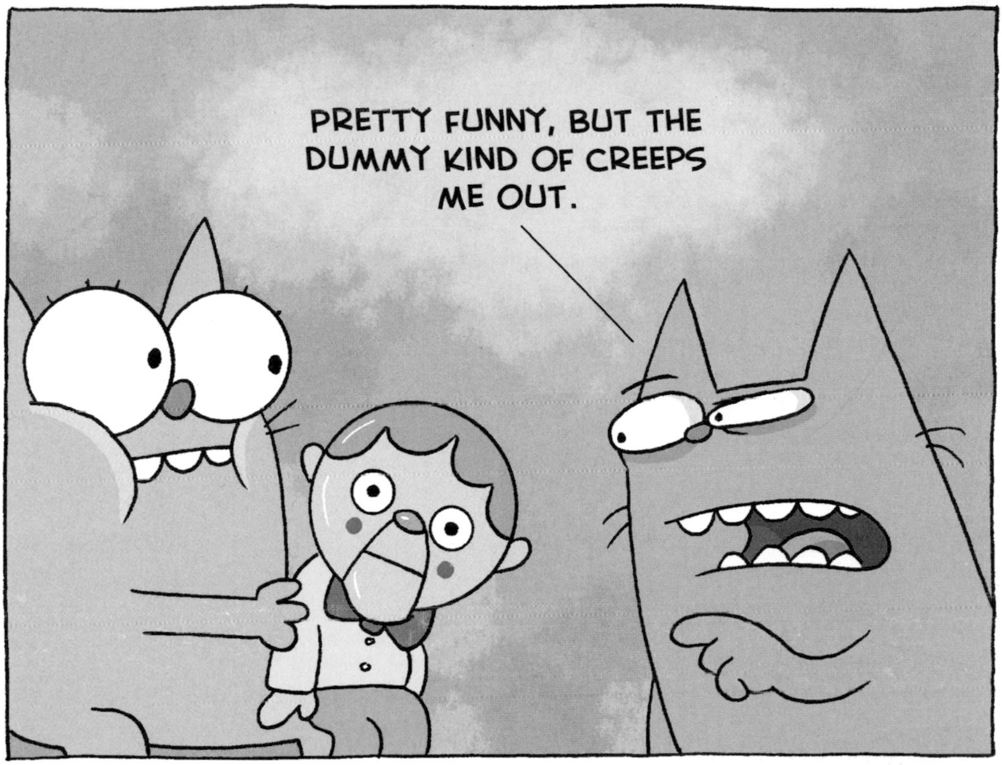
PRETTY FUNNY, BUT THE DUMMY KIND OF CREEPS ME OUT.

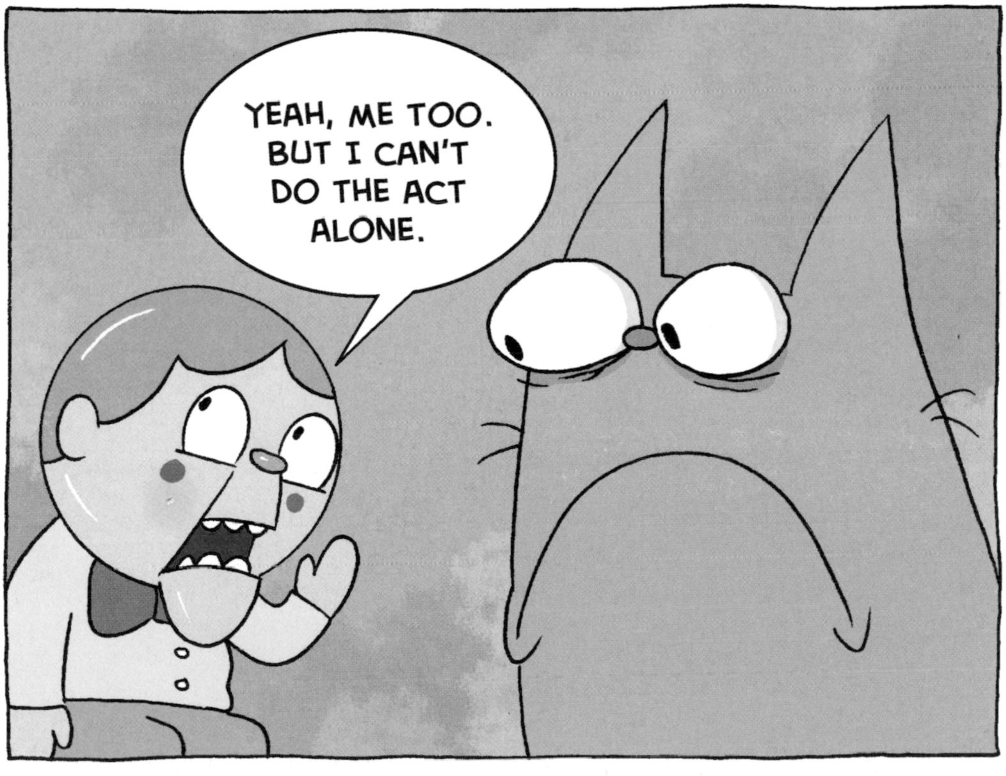
YEAH, ME TOO. BUT I CAN'T DO THE ACT ALONE.

SOCCER

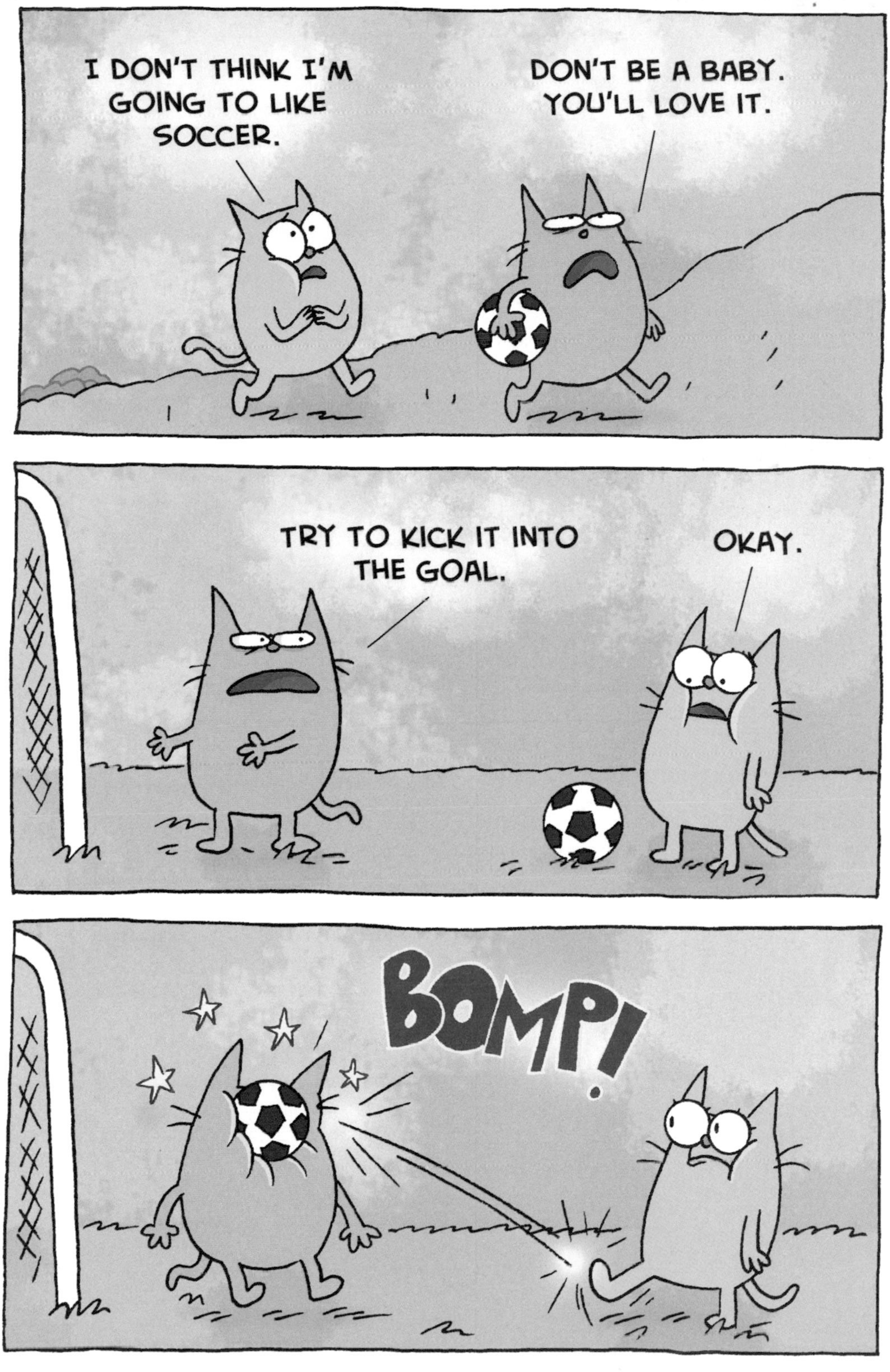
I DON'T THINK I'M GOING TO LIKE SOCCER.
DON'T BE A BABY. YOU'LL LOVE IT.
TRY TO KICK IT INTO THE GOAL.
OKAY.
BOMP!

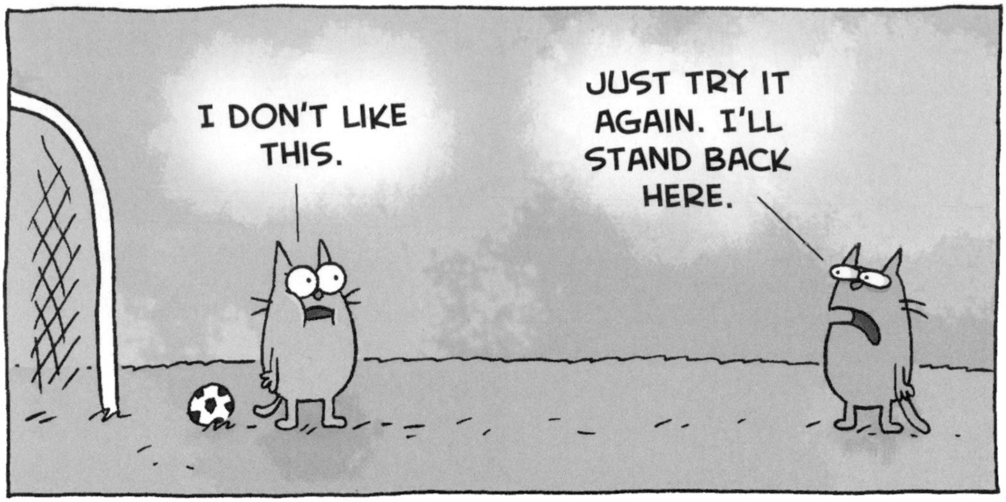
I DON'T LIKE THIS.
JUST TRY IT AGAIN. I'LL STAND BACK HERE.

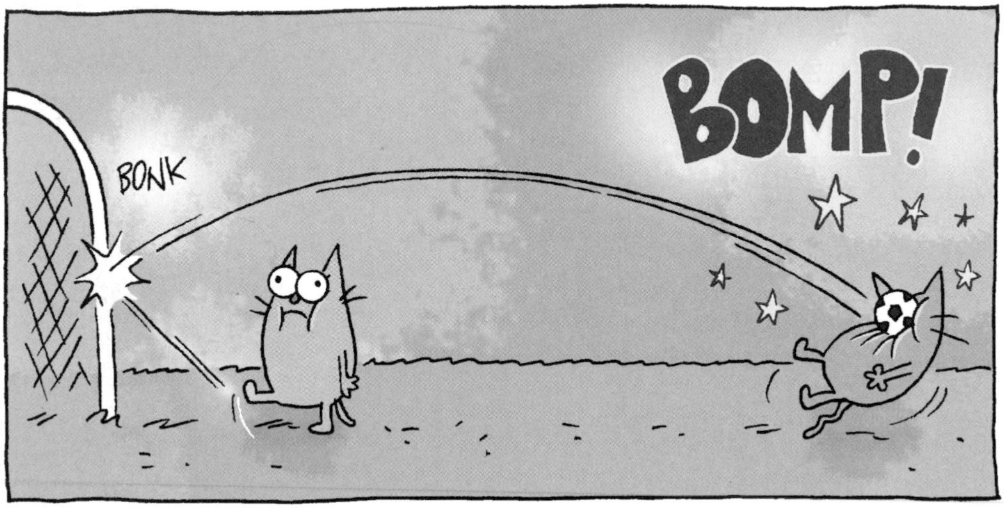
BONK
BOMP!

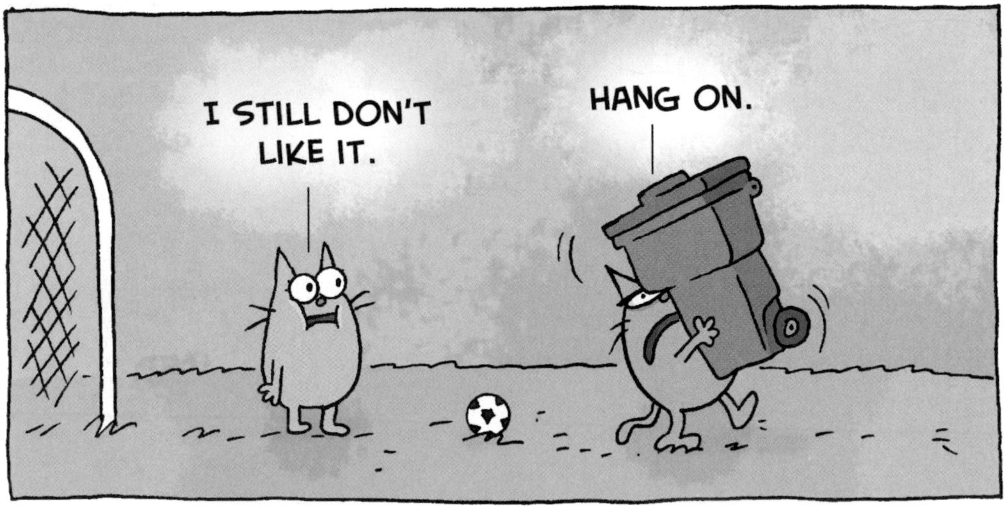
I STILL DON'T LIKE IT.
HANG ON.

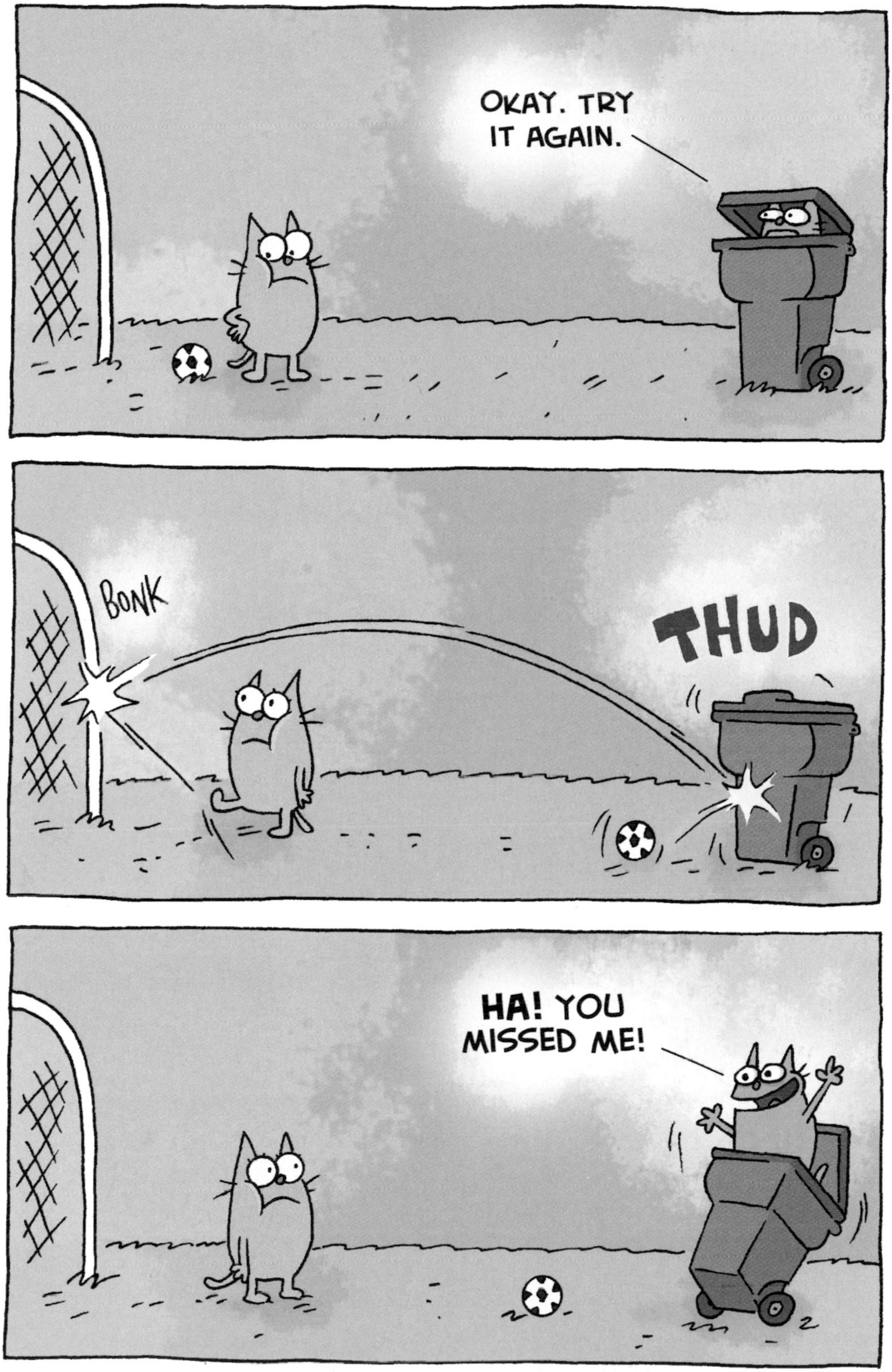
OKAY. TRY IT AGAIN.
BONK
THUD
HA! YOU MISSED ME!

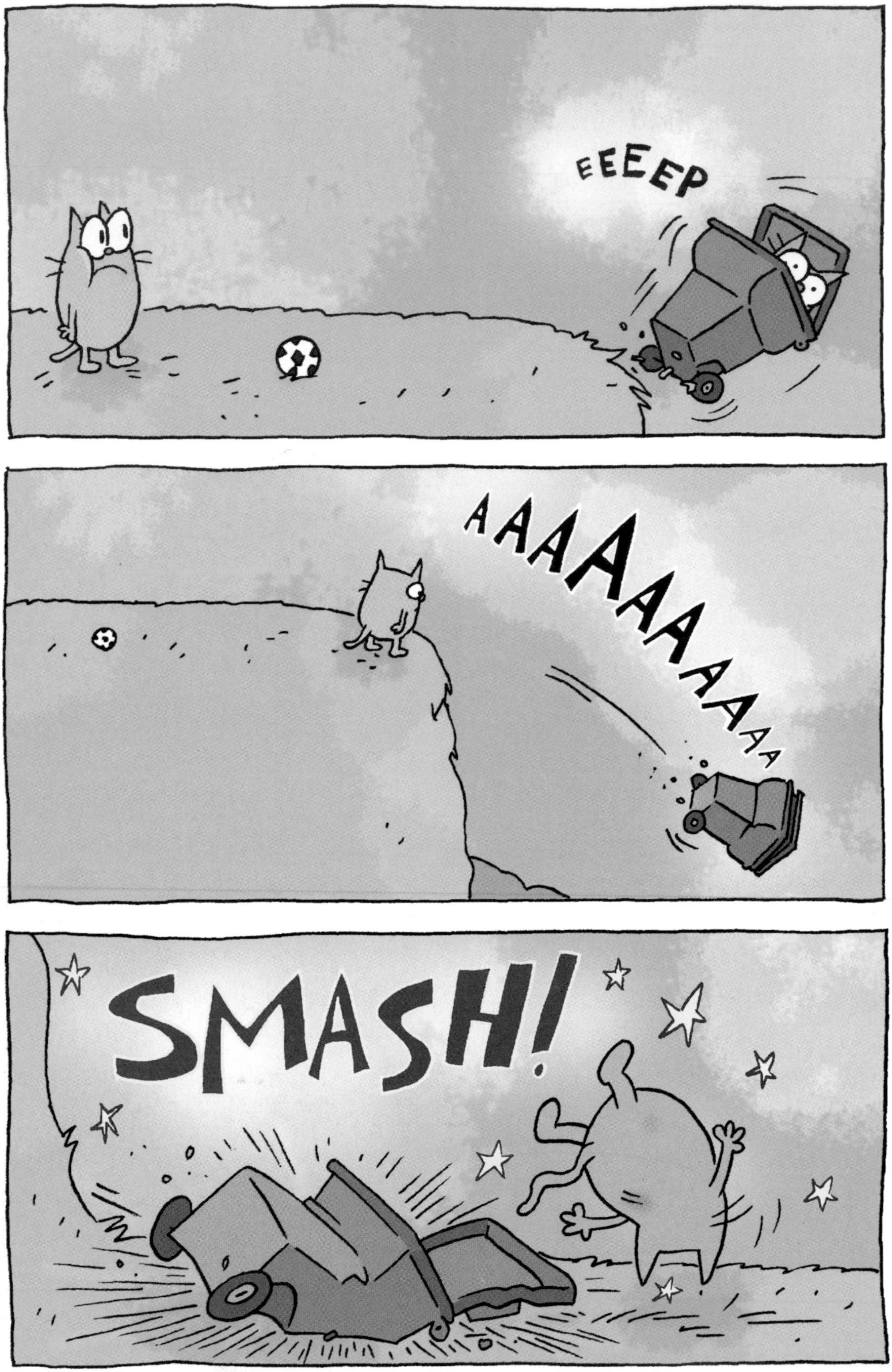
EEEEP
AAAAAAAAAAA
SMASH!

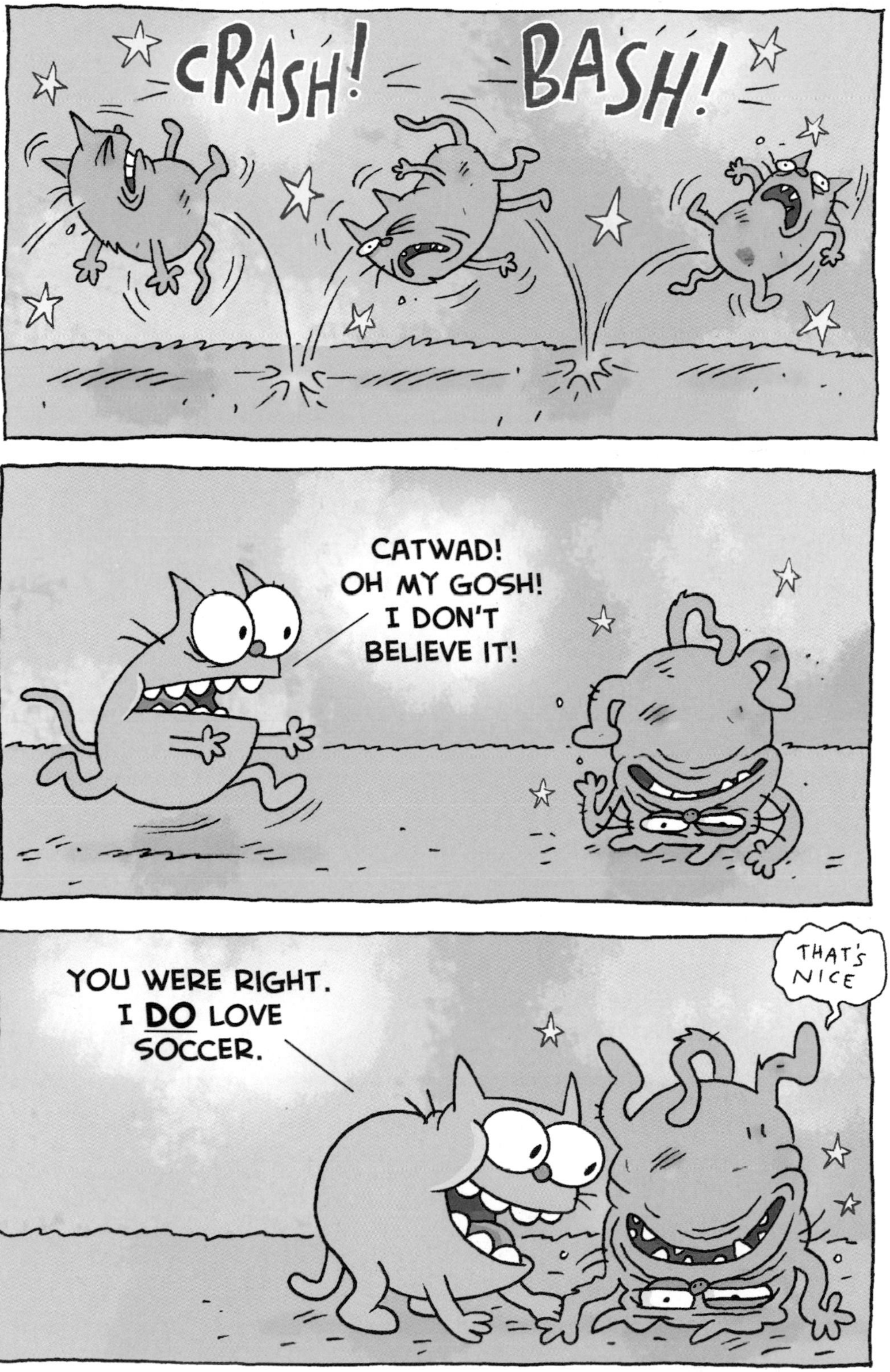
CRASH!
BASH!
CATWAD! OH MY GOSH! I DON'T BELIEVE IT!
YOU WERE RIGHT. I DO LOVE SOCCER.
THAT'S NICE

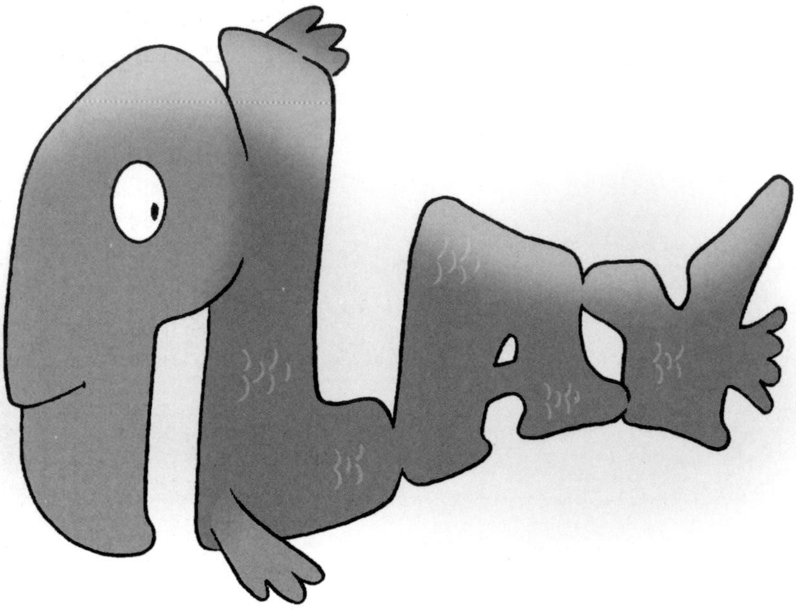
PLAY

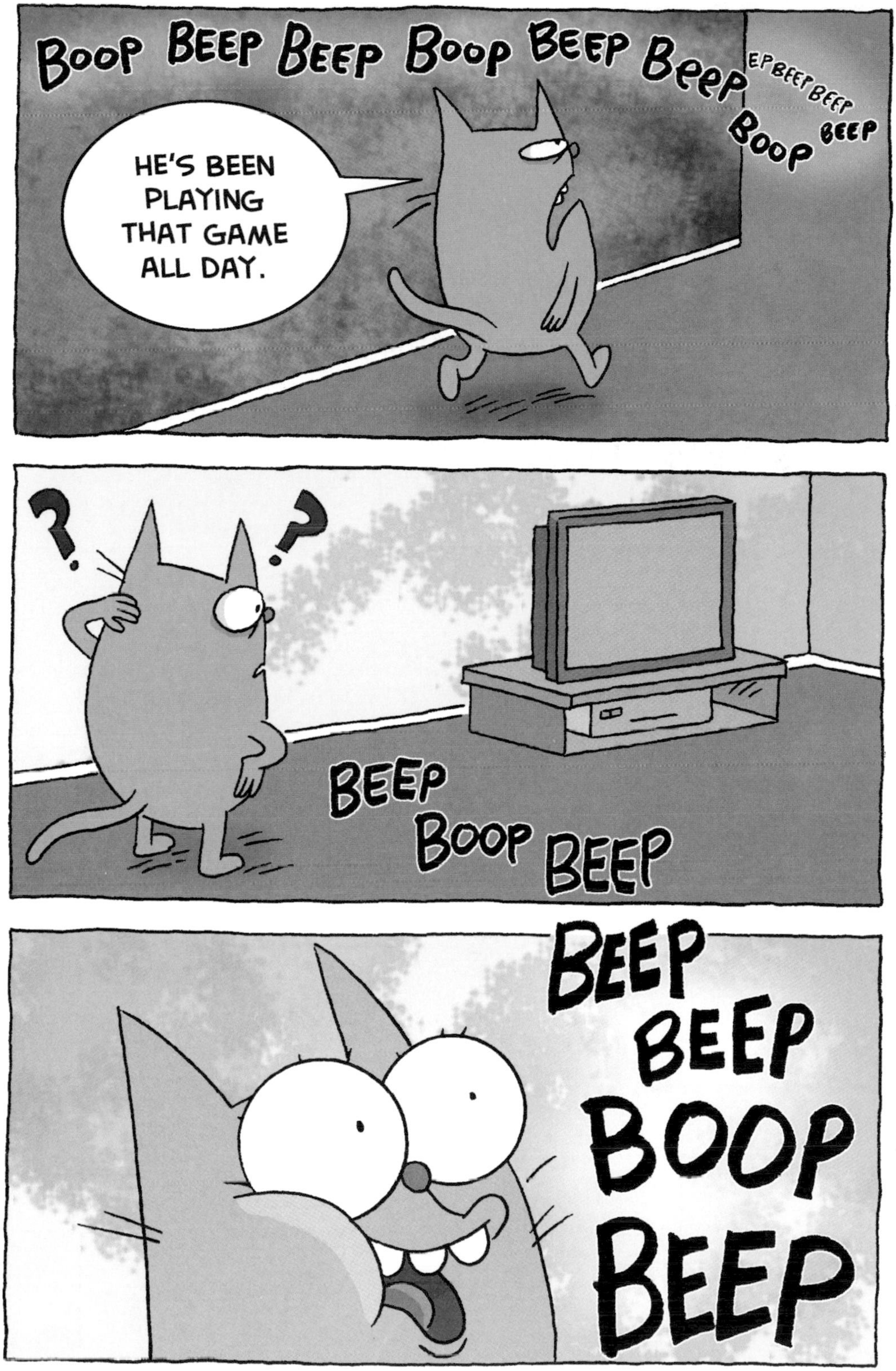

BOOP BEEP BEEP BOOP BEEP BEEP
EP BEEP BEEP BEEP
BOOP BEEP
HE'S BEEN PLAYING THAT GAME ALL DAY.
?
?
BEEP BOOP BEEP
BEEP BEEP BEEP BOOP BEEP

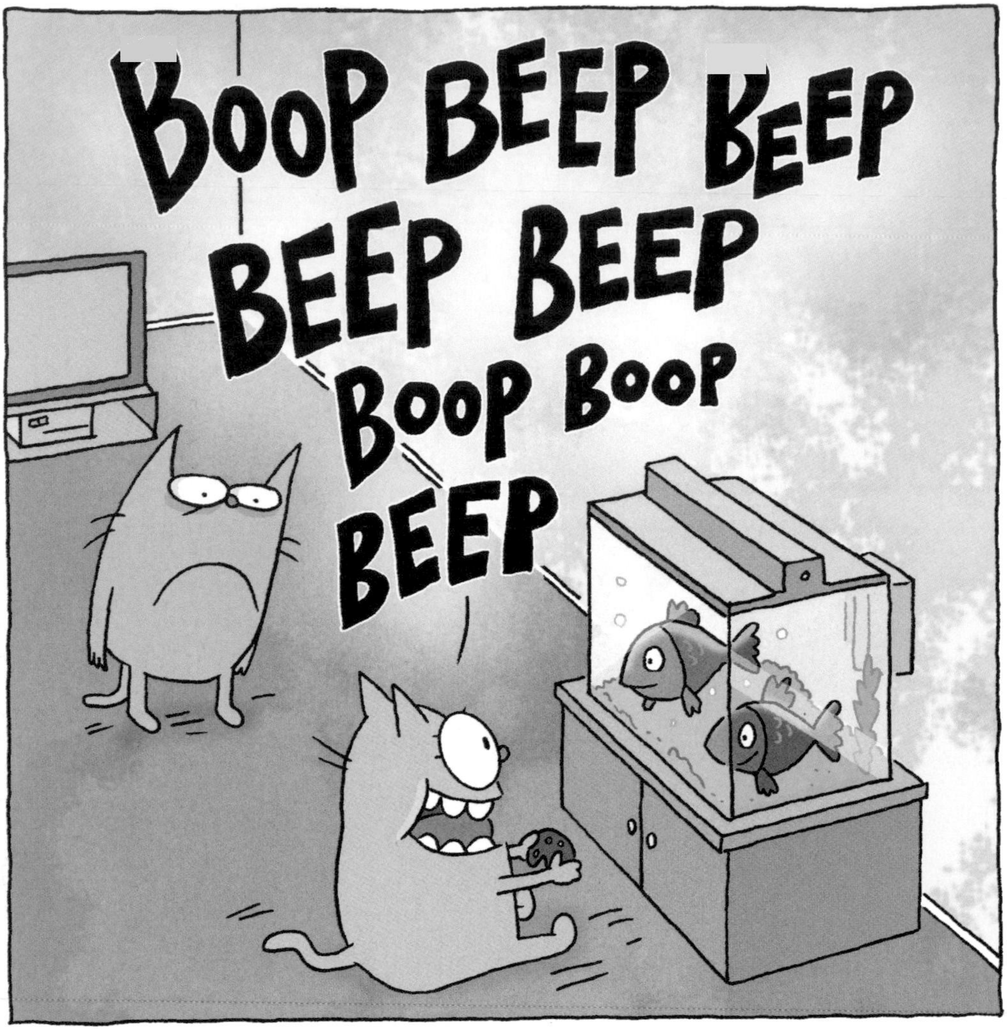
BOOP BEEP BEEP
BEEP BEEP
BOOP BOOP
BEEP

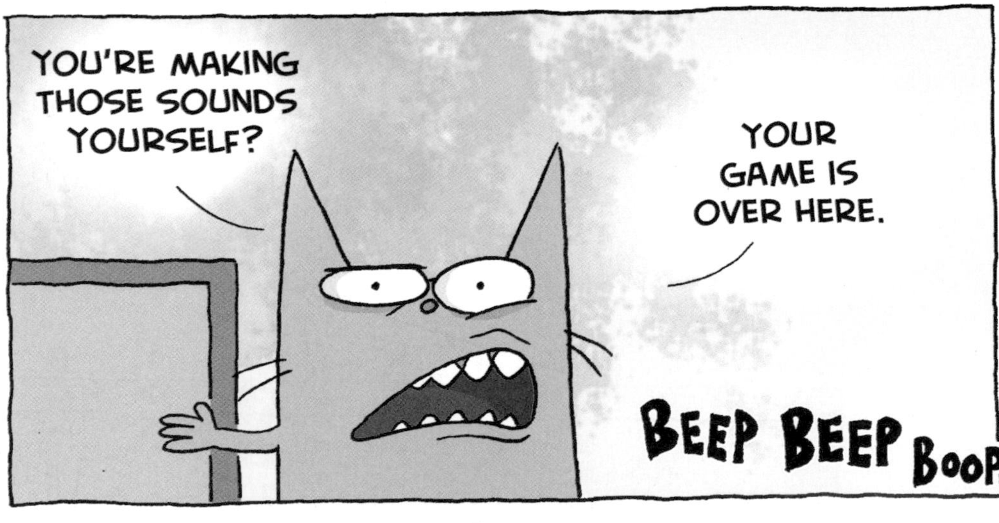
YOU'RE MAKING THOSE SOUNDS YOURSELF?
YOUR GAME IS OVER HERE.
BEEP BEEP BOOP

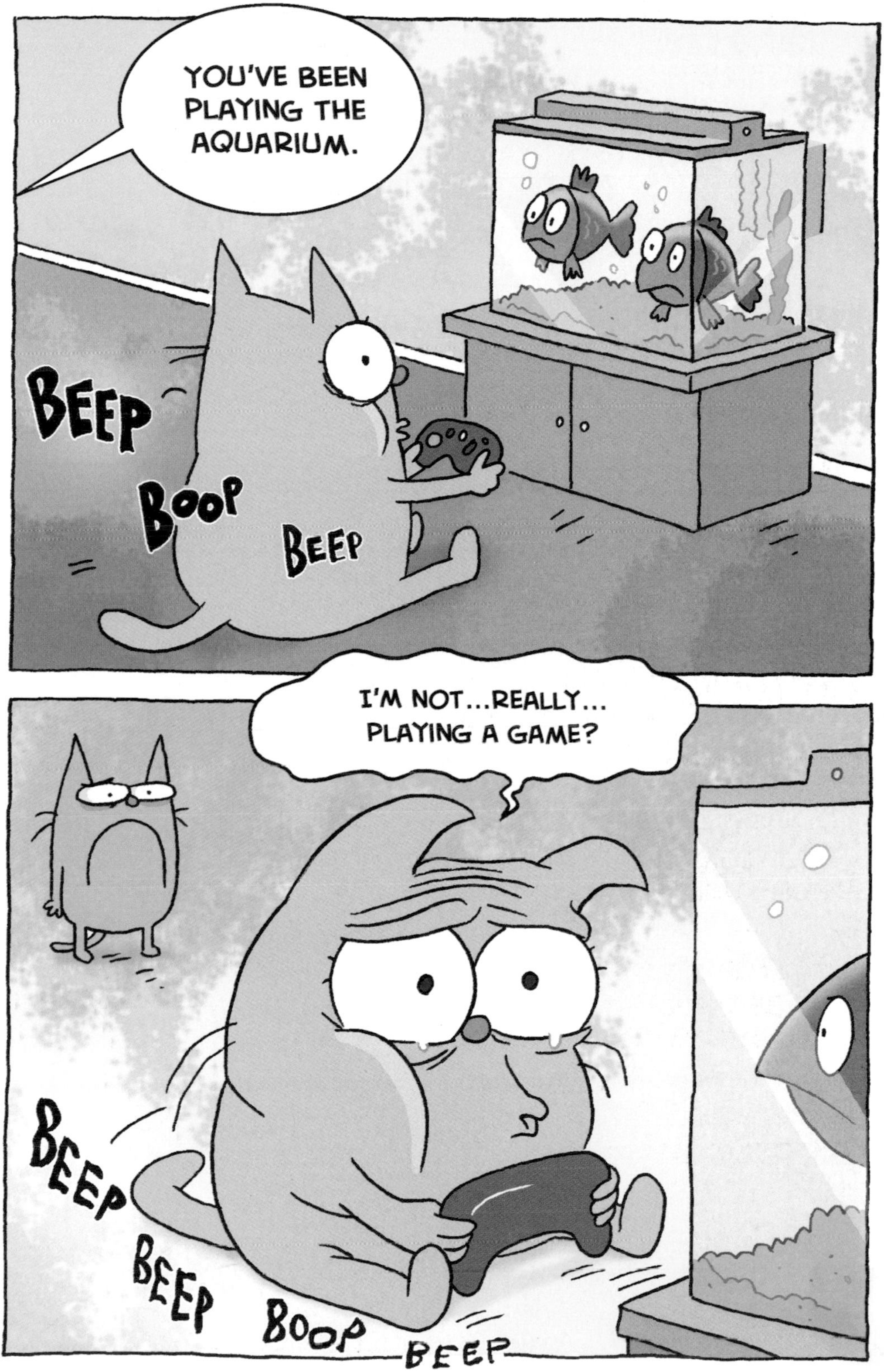
YOU'VE BEEN PLAYING THE AQUARIUM.
BEEP
BOOP
BEEP
I'M NOT...REALLY... PLAYING A GAME?
BEEP
BEEP
BOOP
BEEP

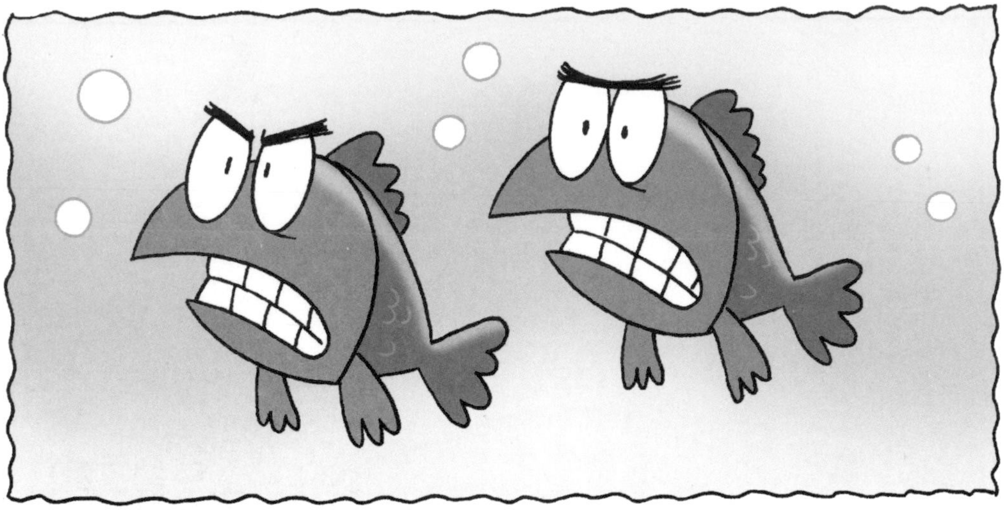

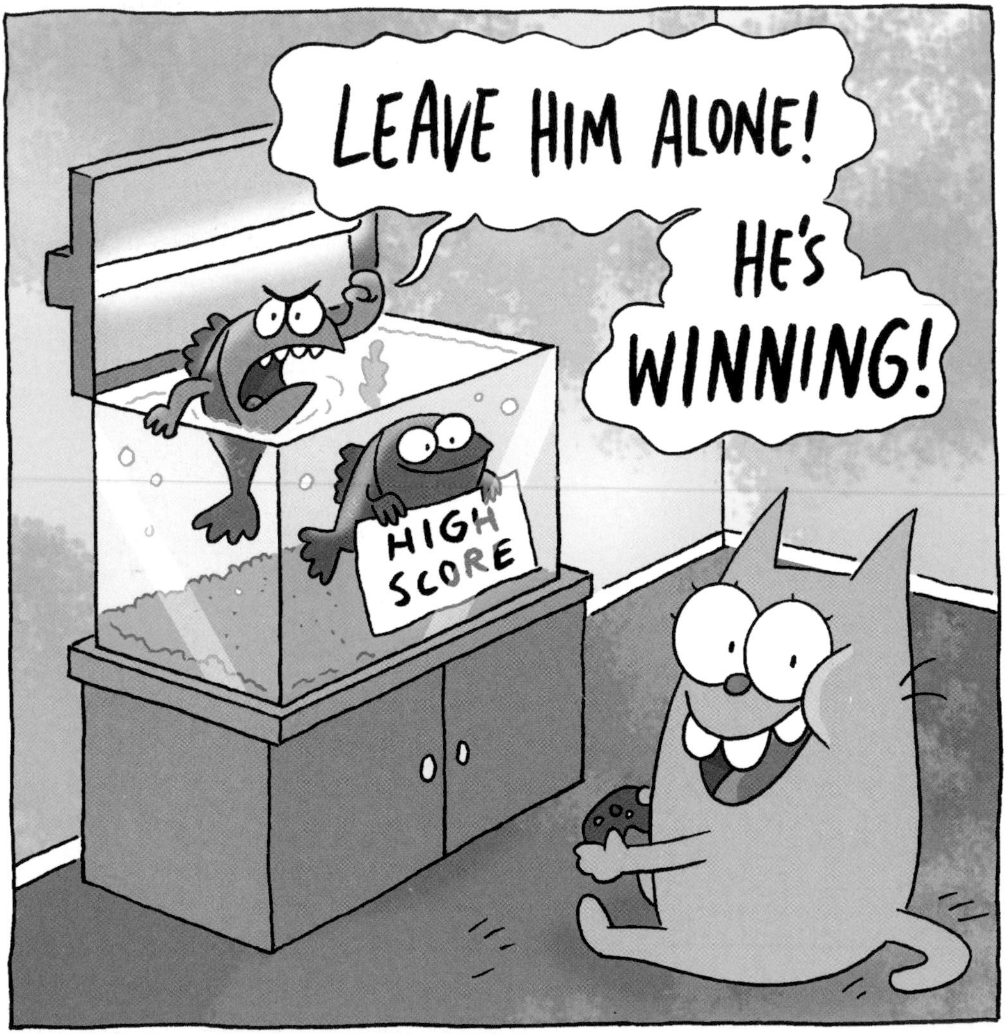
LEAVE HIM ALONE!
HE'S WINNING!
HIGH SCORE

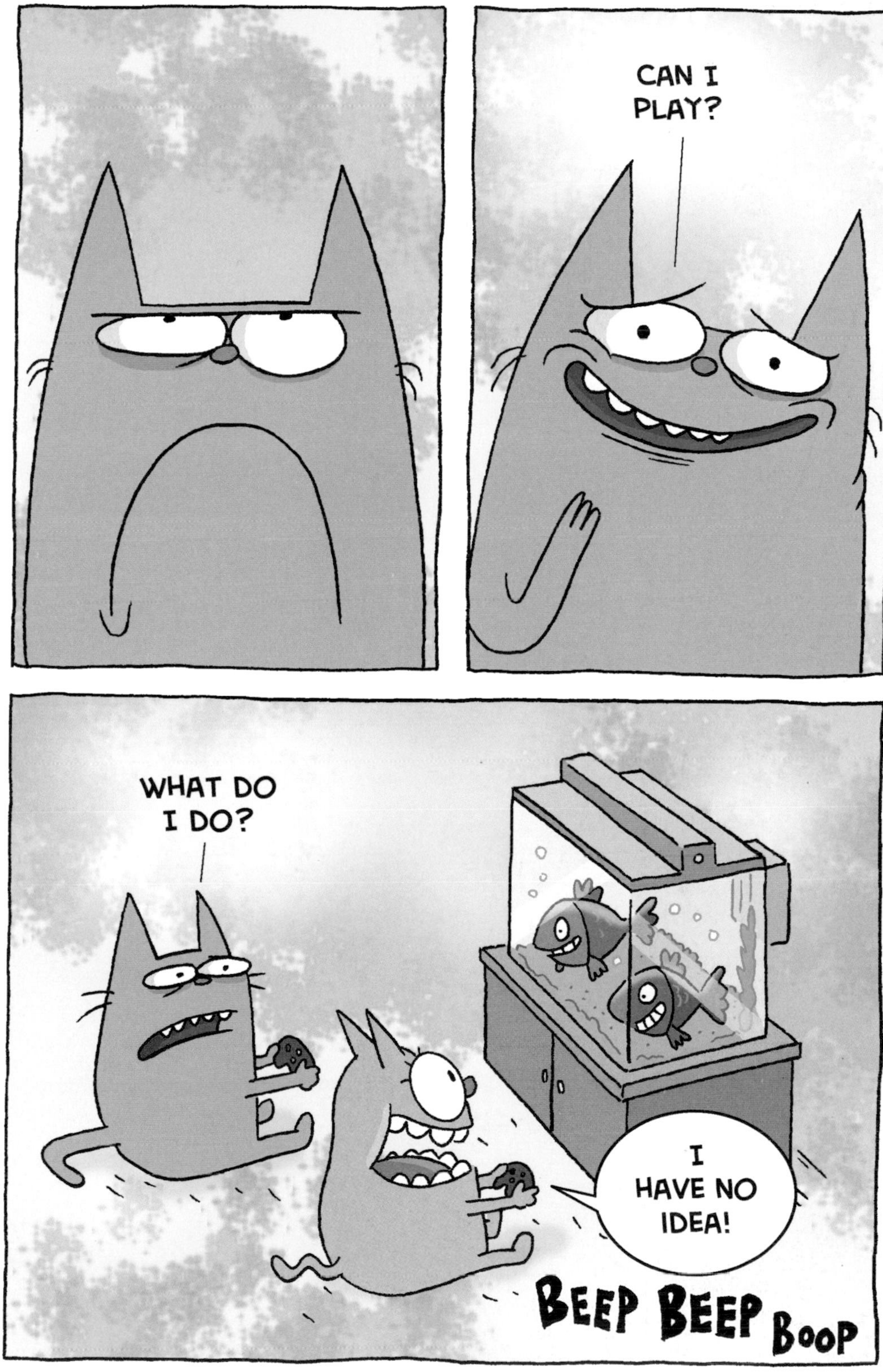
CAN I PLAY?
WHAT DO I DO?
I HAVE NO IDEA!
BEEP BEEP BOOP

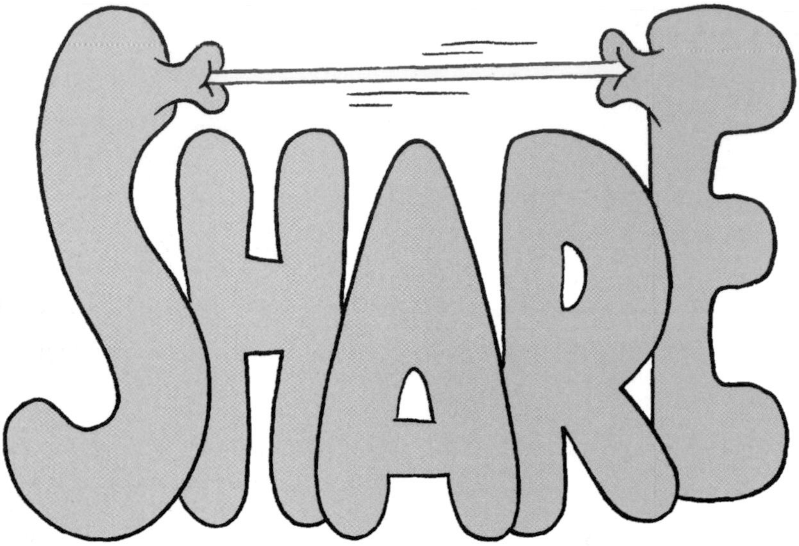
SHARE

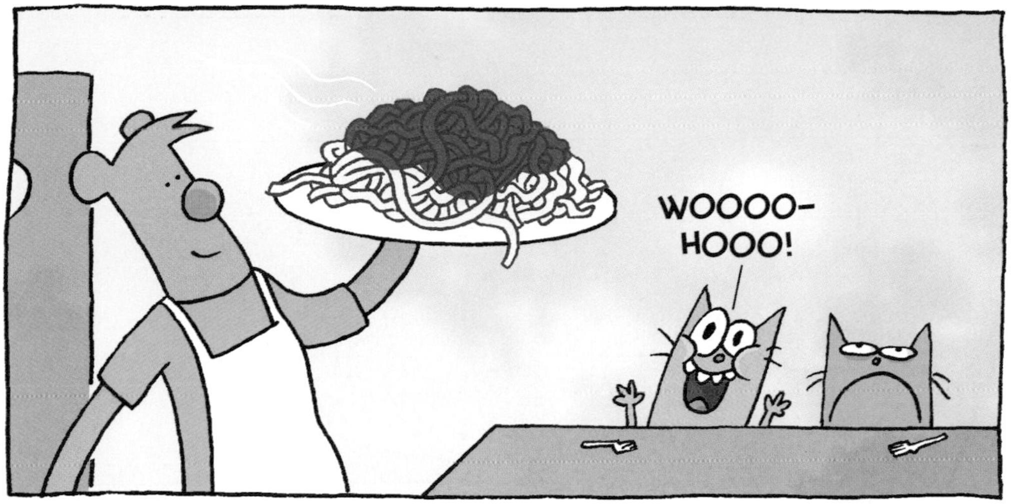
WOOOO-
HOOO!

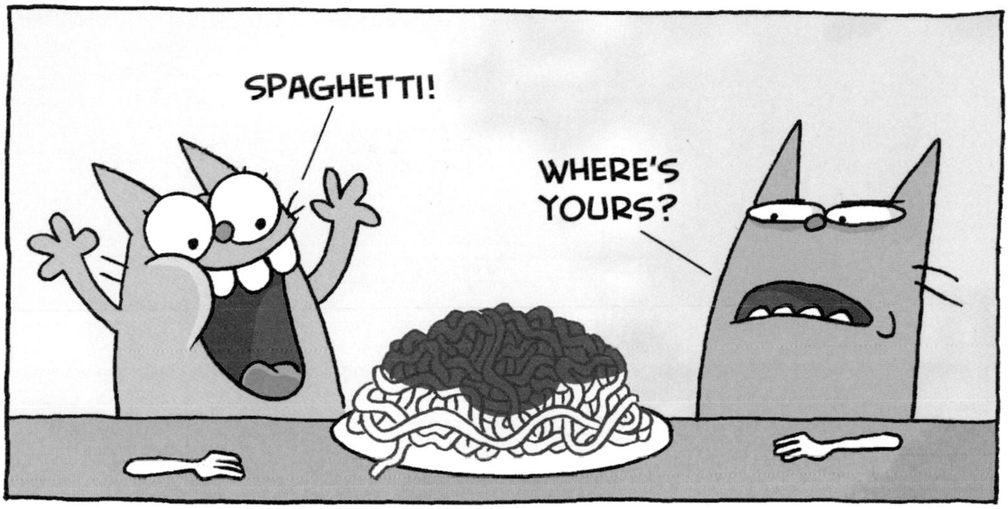
SPAGHETTI!
WHERE'S YOURS?

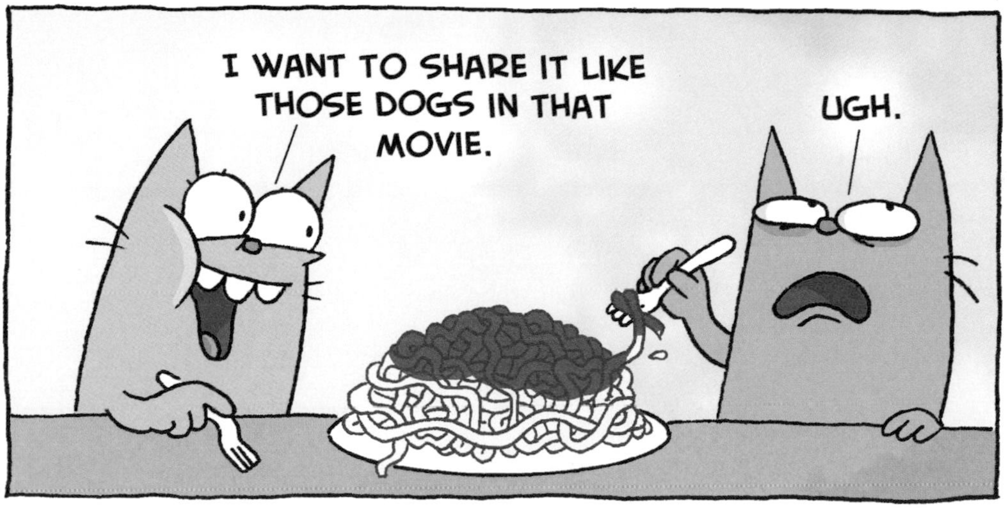
I WANT TO SHARE IT LIKE THOSE DOGS IN THAT MOVIE.
UGH.

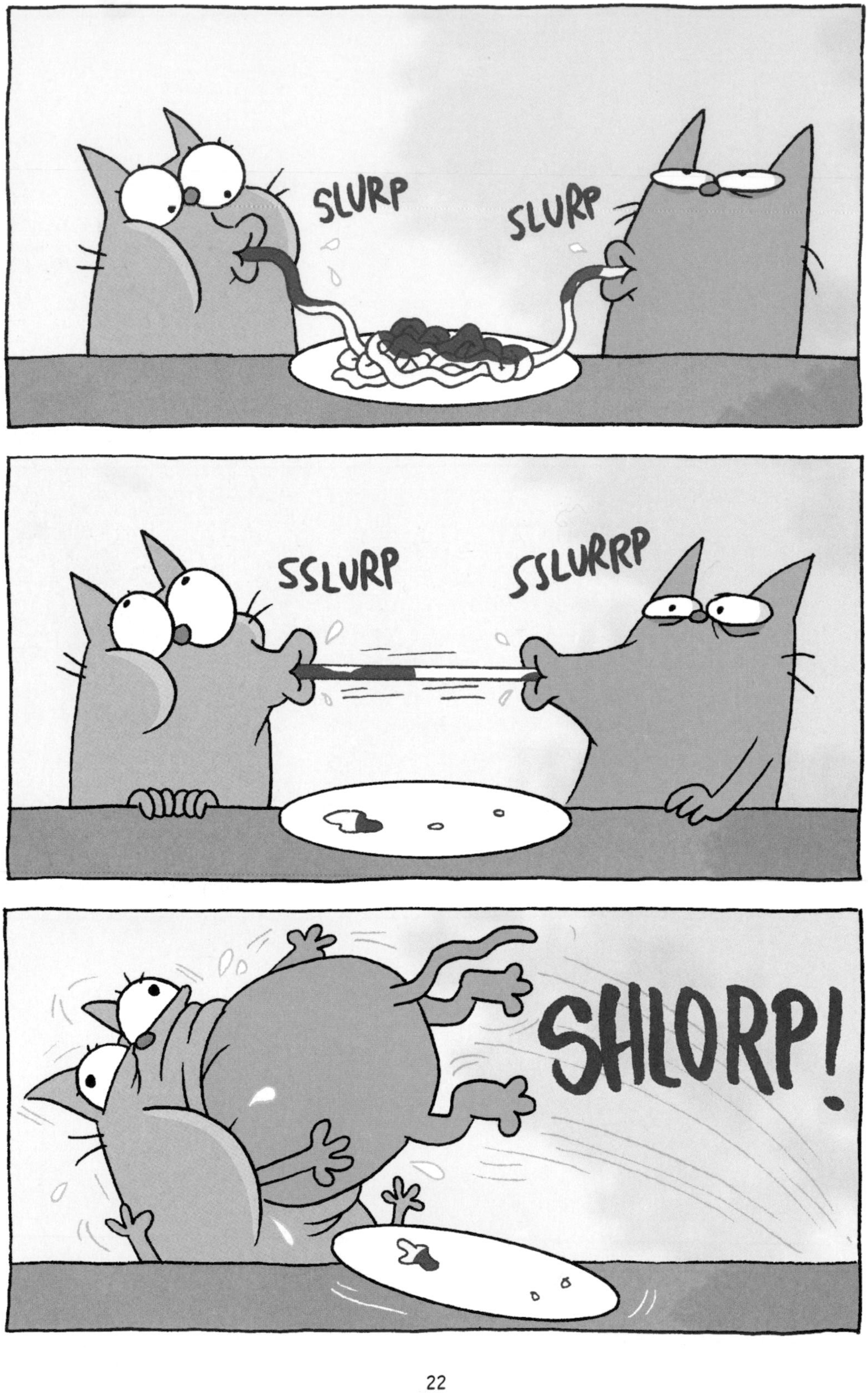
SLURP
SLURP
SSLURP
SSLURRP
SHLORP!

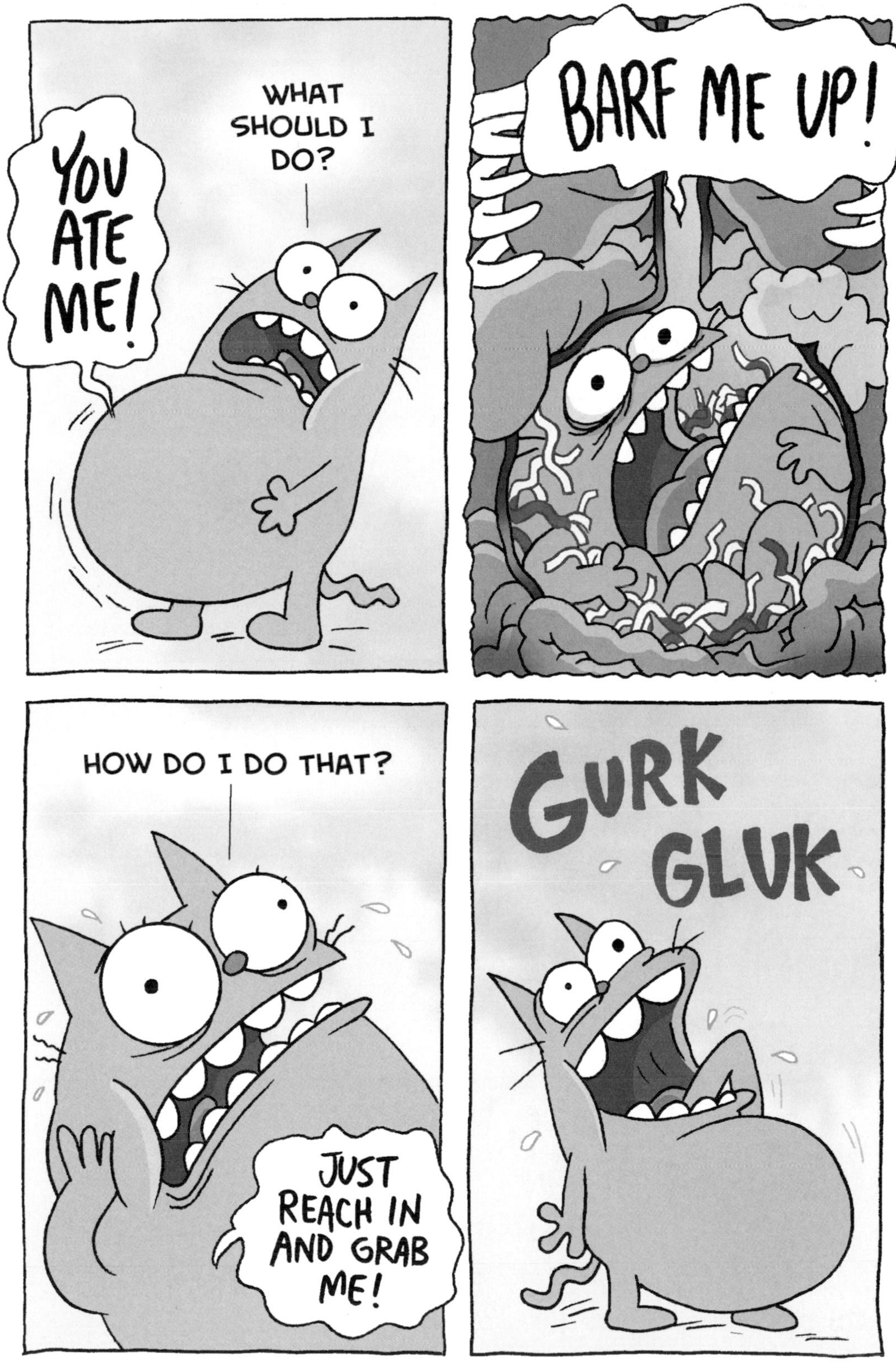
WHAT SHOULD I DO?
YOU ATE ME!
BARF ME UP!
HOW DO I DO THAT?
JUST REACH IN AND GRAB ME!
GURK
GLUK

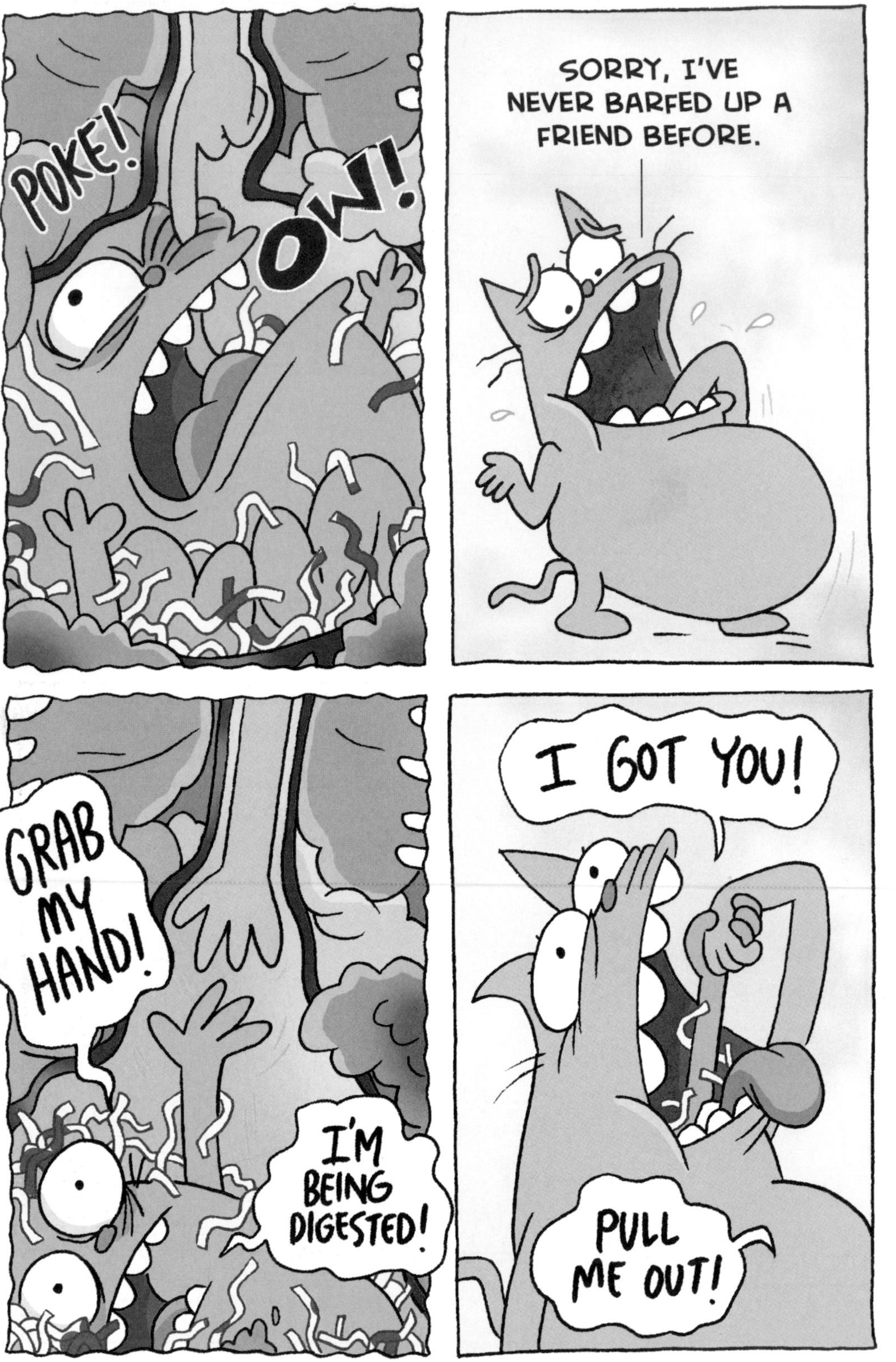
POKE!
OW!
SORRY, I'VE NEVER BARFED UP A FRIEND BEFORE.
GRAB MY HAND!
I'M BEING DIGESTED!
I GOT YOU!
PULL ME OUT!

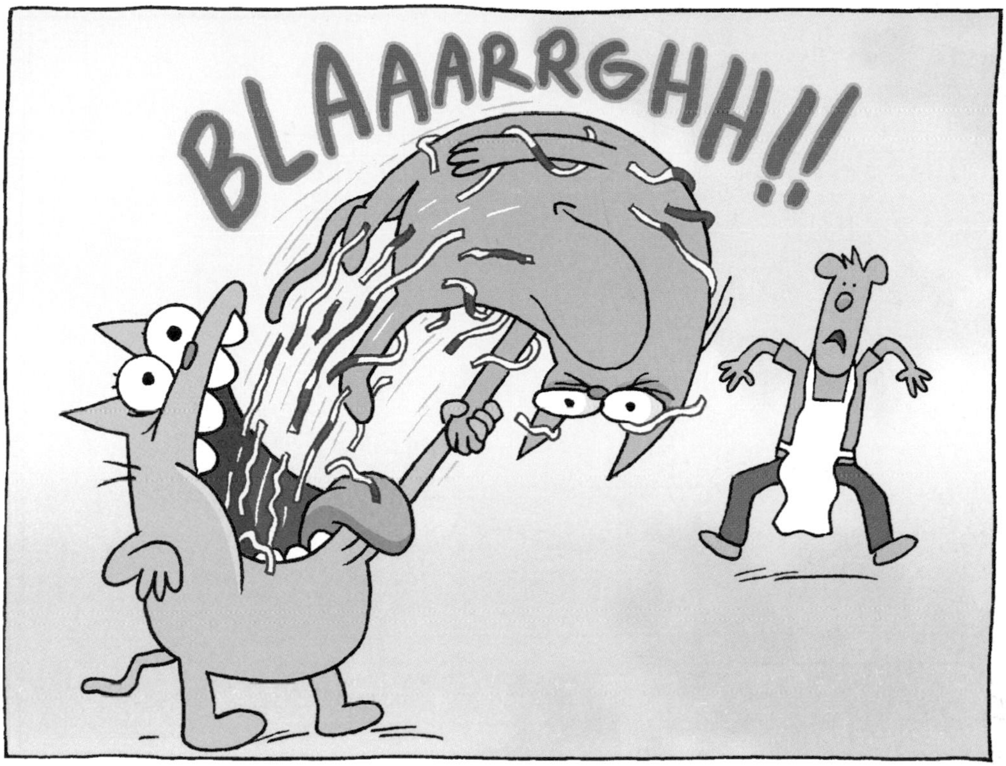
BLAAARRGHH!!

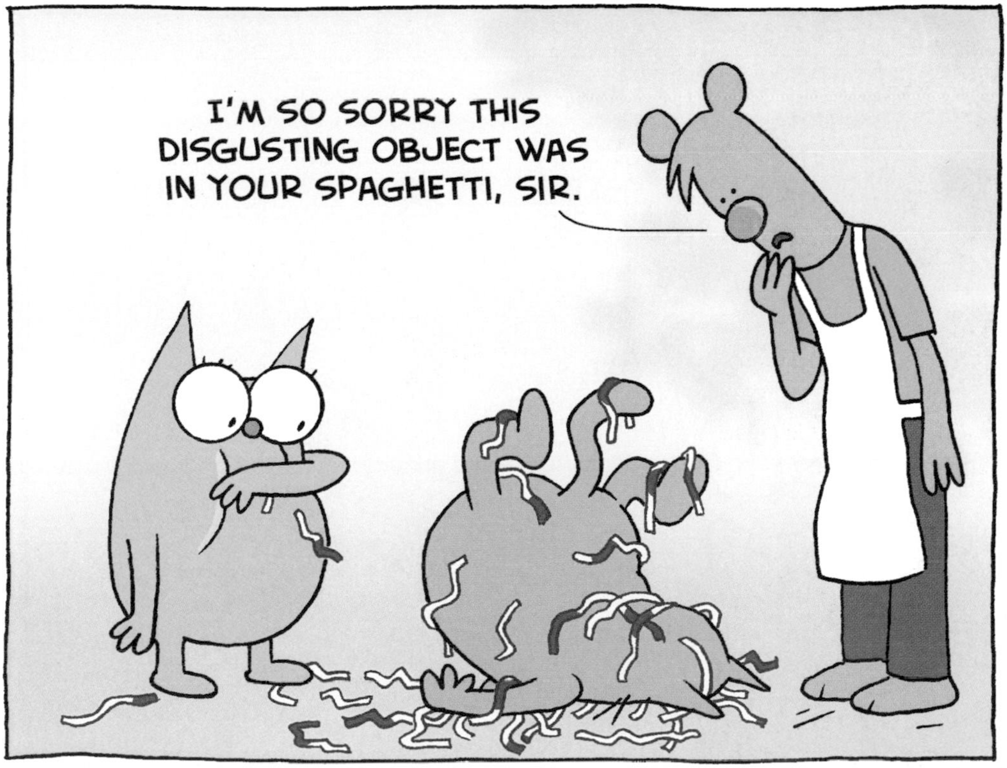
I'M SO SORRY THIS DISGUSTING OBJECT WAS IN YOUR SPAGHETTI, SIR.

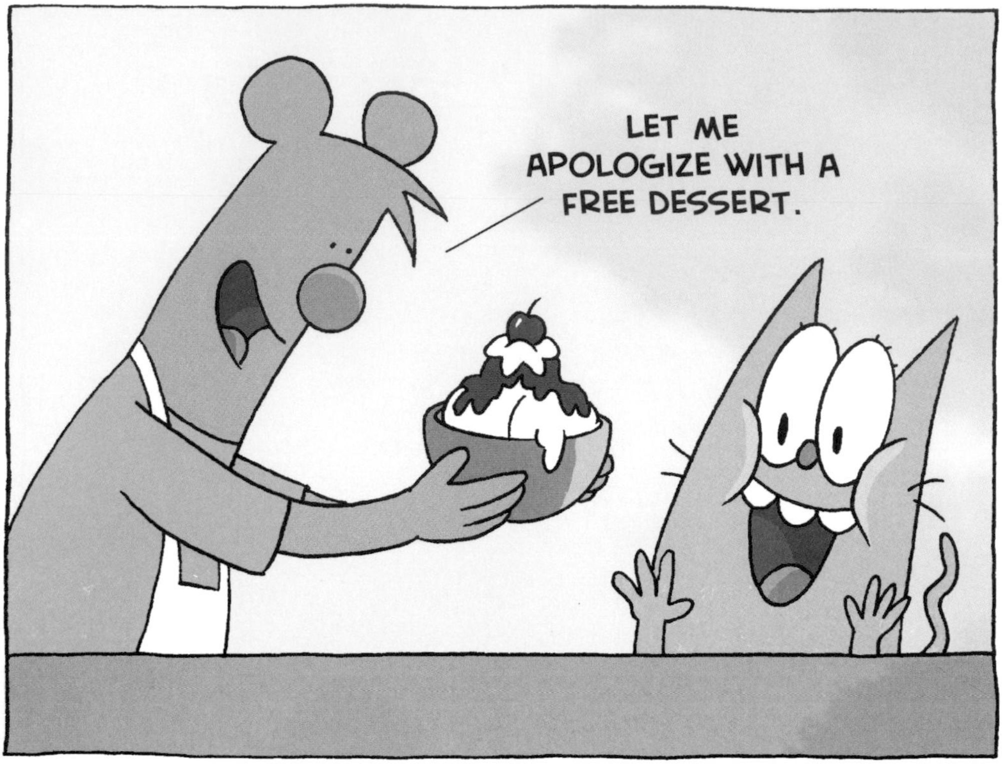
LET ME APOLOGIZE WITH A FREE DESSERT.

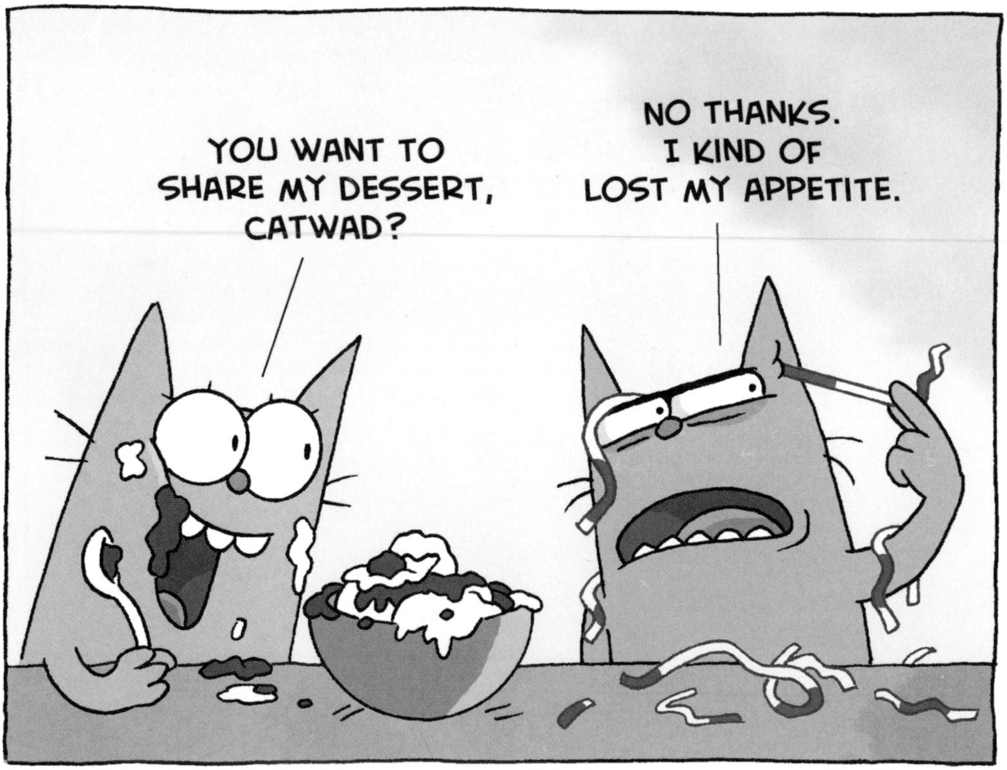
YOU WANT TO SHARE MY DESSERT, CATWAD?
NO THANKS. I KIND OF LOST MY APPETITE.

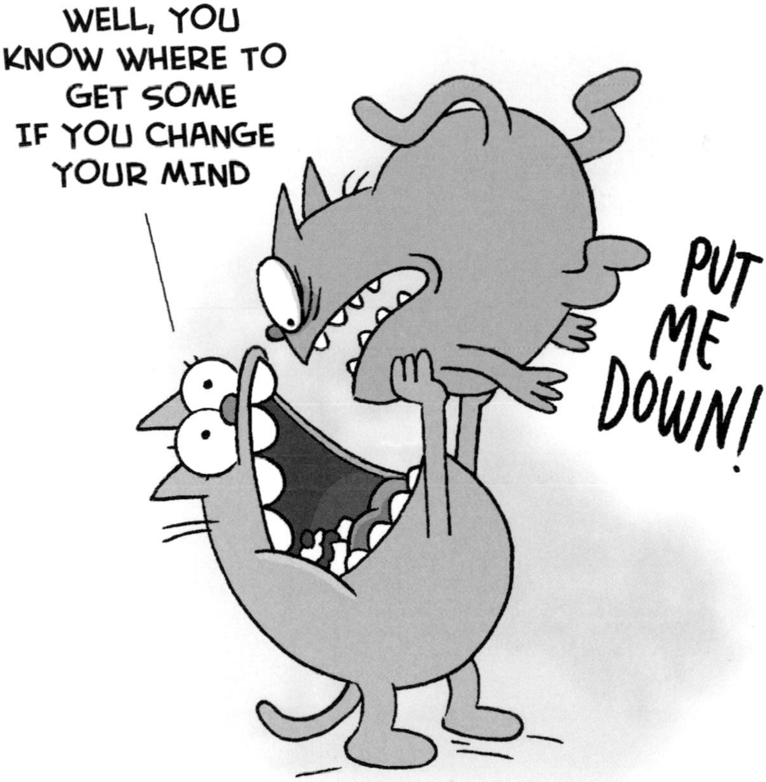
WELL, YOU KNOW WHERE TO GET SOME IF YOU CHANGE YOUR MIND
PUT ME DOWN!

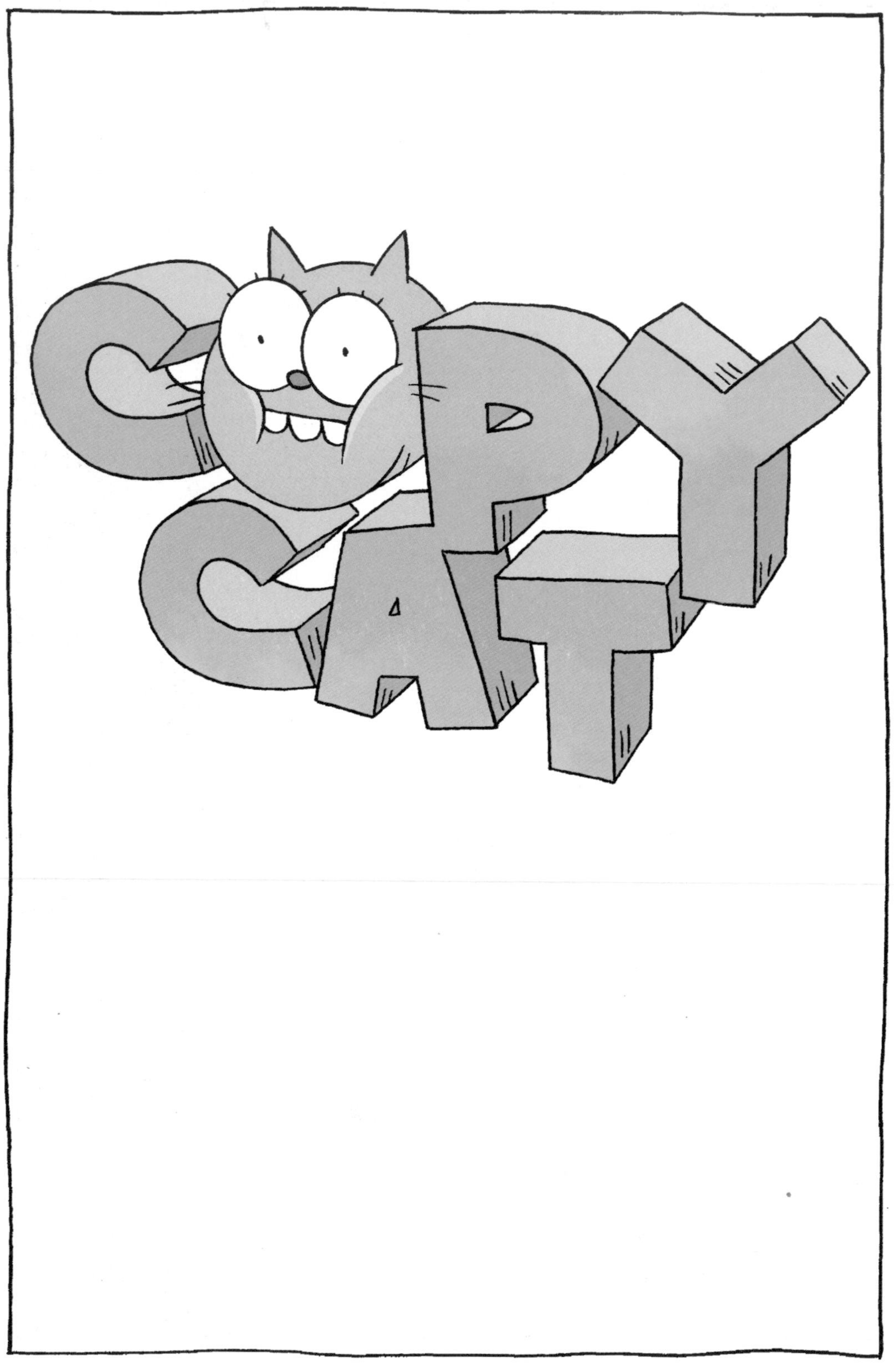
COPY
CAT

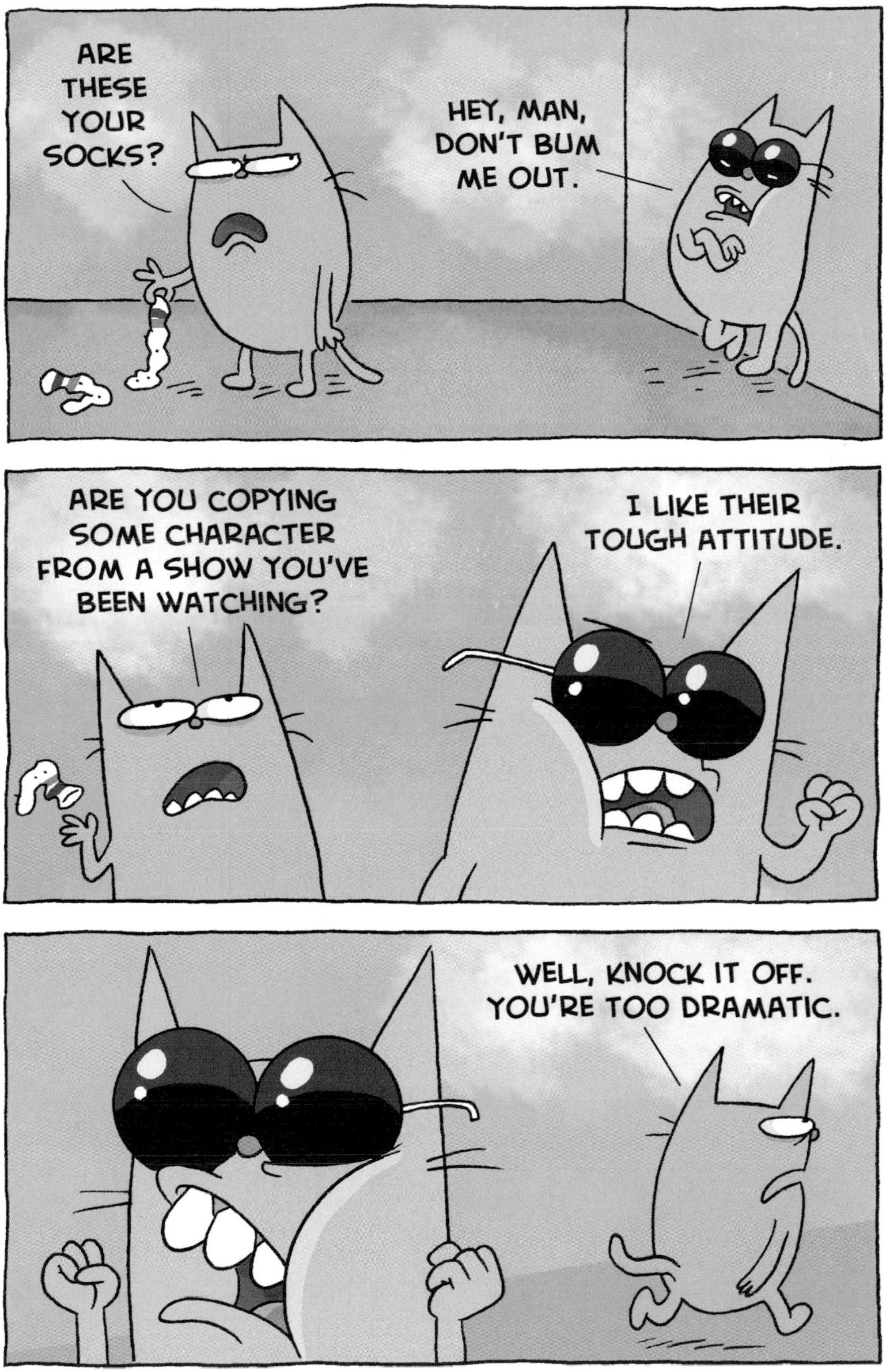
ARE THESE YOUR SOCKS?
HEY, MAN, DON'T BUM ME OUT.
ARE YOU COPYING SOME CHARACTER FROM A SHOW YOU'VE BEEN WATCHING?
I LIKE THEIR TOUGH ATTITUDE.
WELL, KNOCK IT OFF. YOU'RE TOO DRAMATIC.

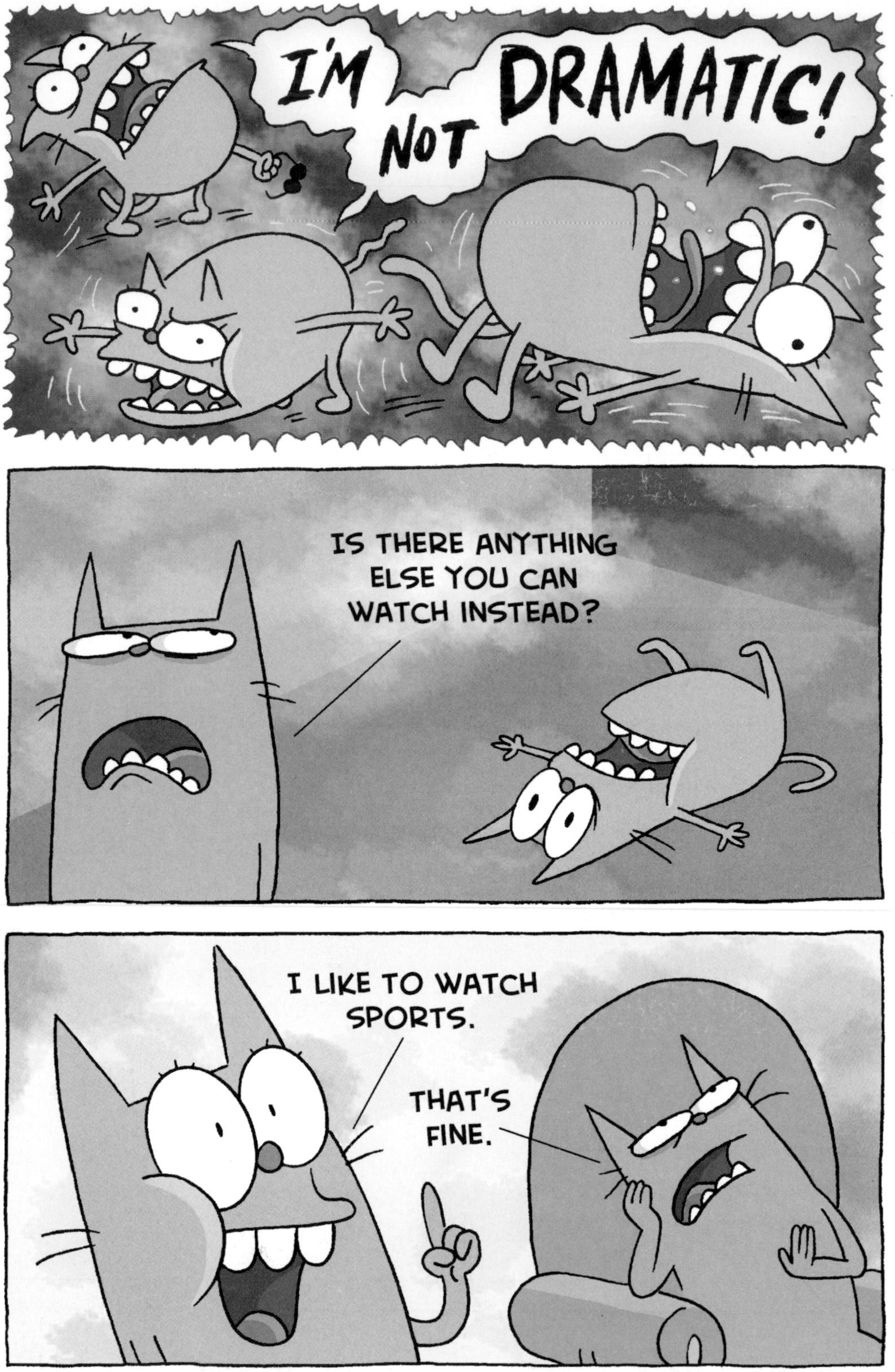
I'M NOT DRAMATIC!
IS THERE ANYTHING ELSE YOU CAN WATCH INSTEAD?
I LIKE TO WATCH SPORTS.
THAT'S FINE.

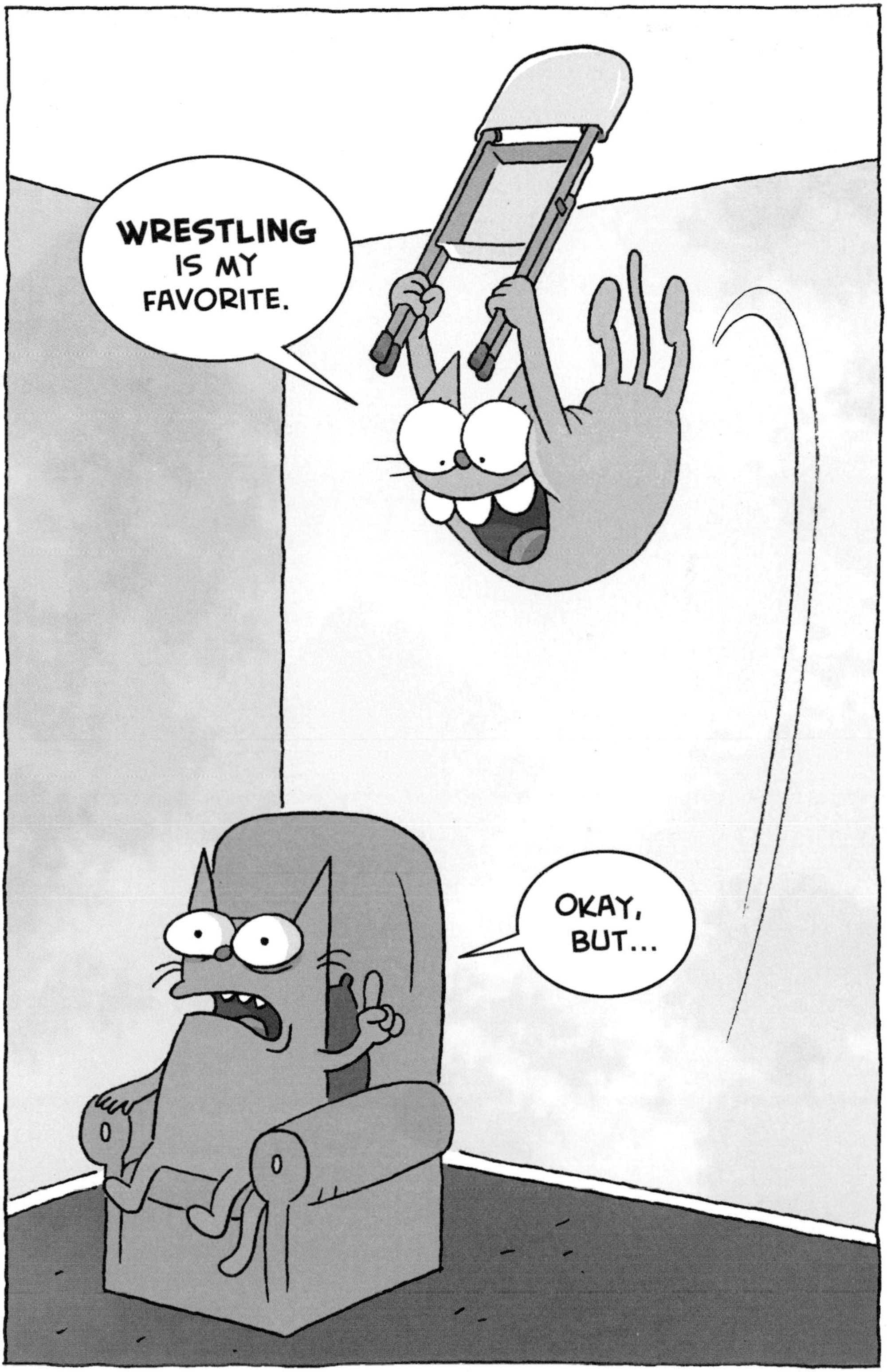
WRESTLING IS MY FAVORITE.
OKAY, BUT...

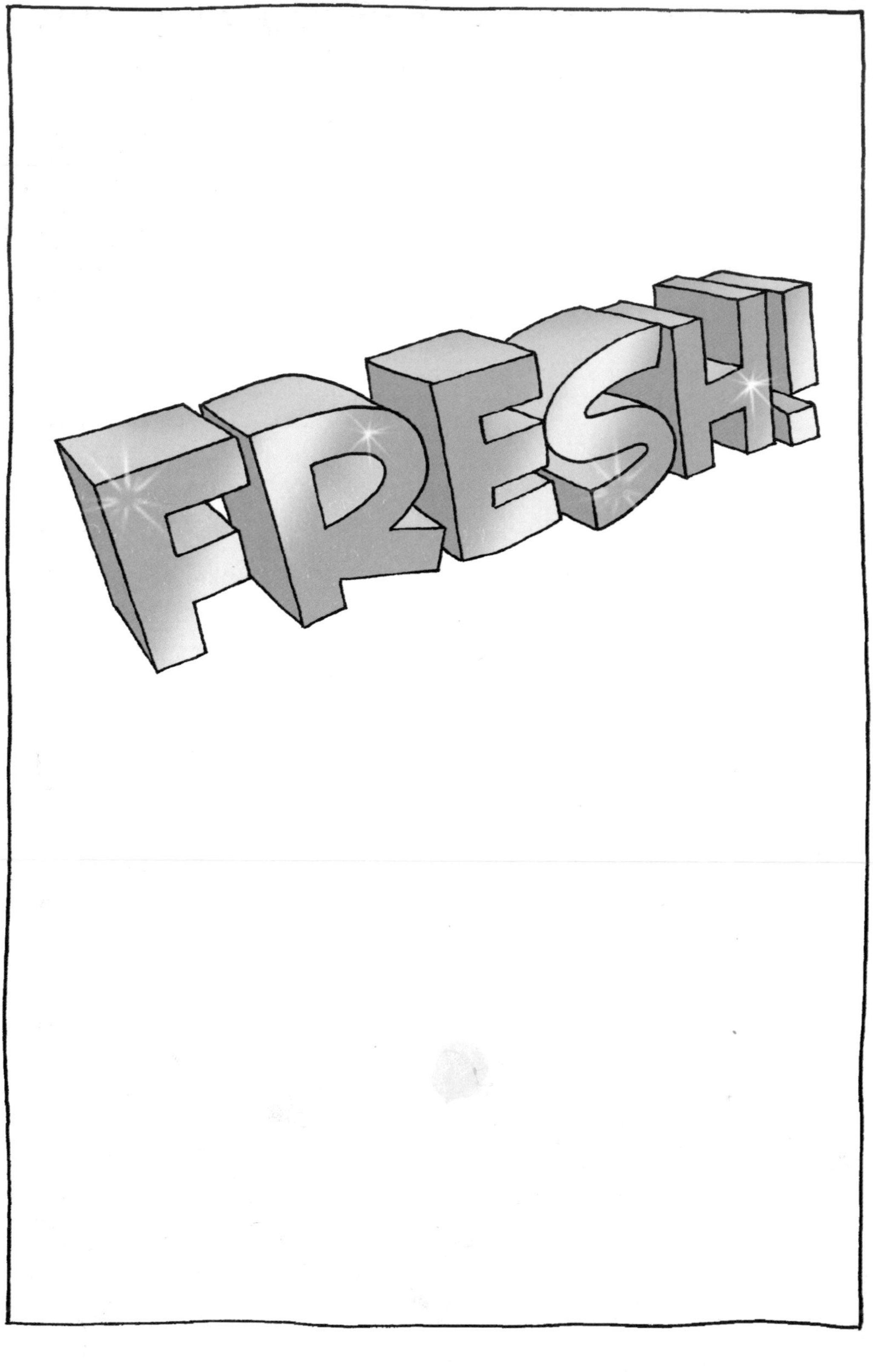
FRESH!!

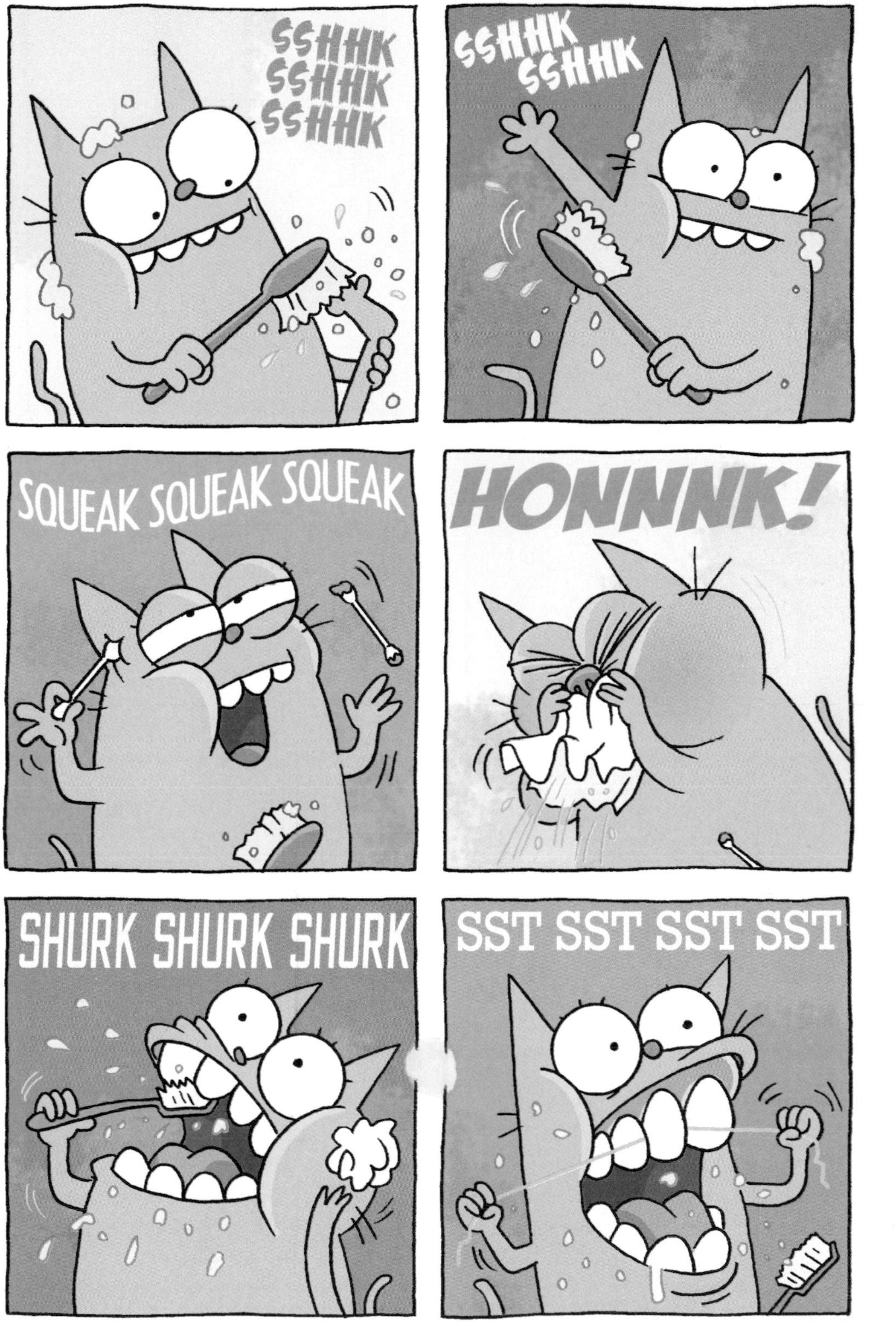
SSHHK
SSHHK
SSHHK
SSHHK
SSHHK
SQUEAK SQUEAK SQUEAK
HONNNK!
SHURK SHURK SHURK
SST SST SST SST

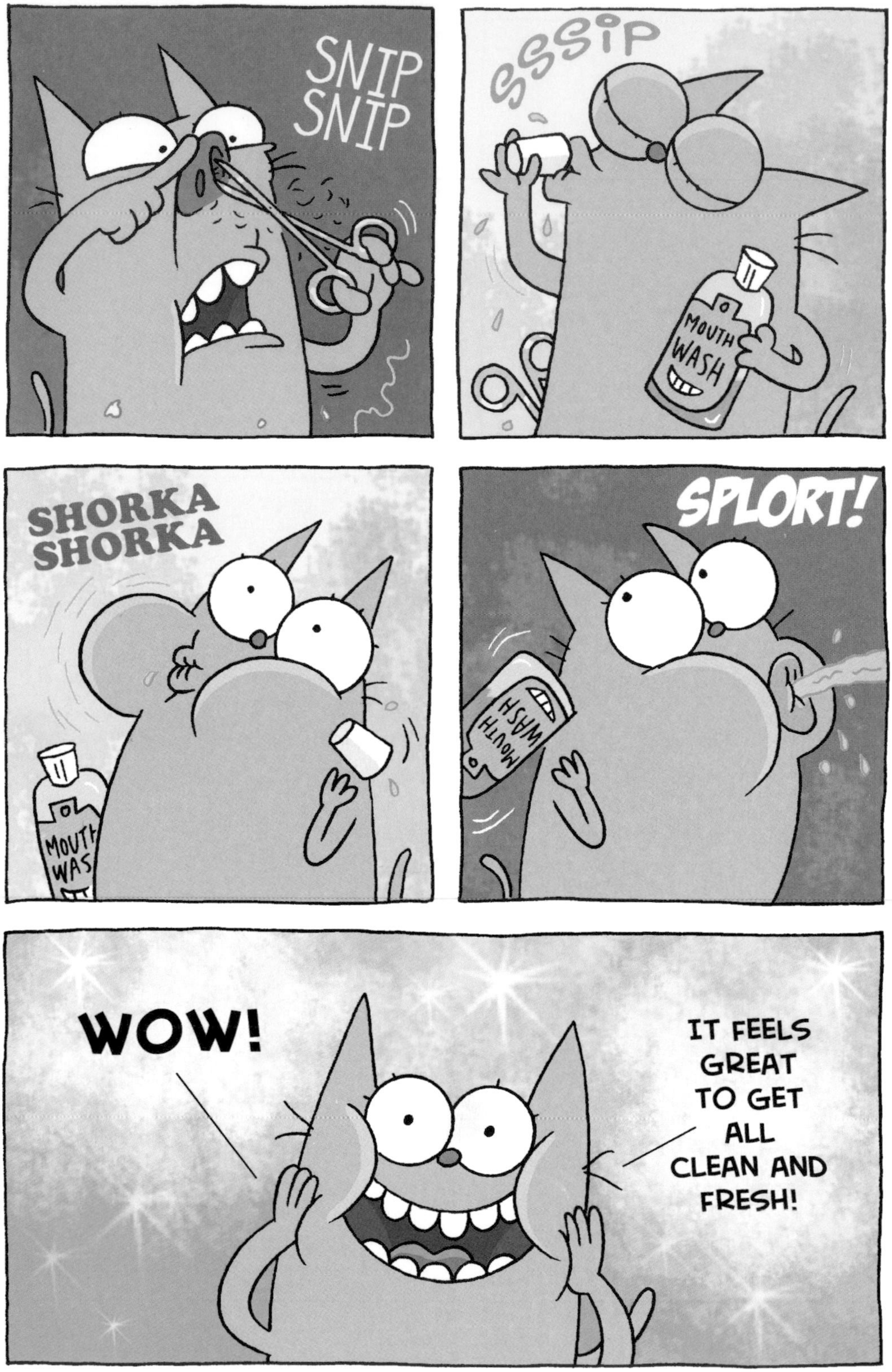
SNIP
SNIP
SSSIP
MOUTH WASH
SHORKA
SHORKA
MOUTH WAS
SPLORT!
MOUTH WASH
WOW!
IT FEELS GREAT TO GET ALL CLEAN AND FRESH!

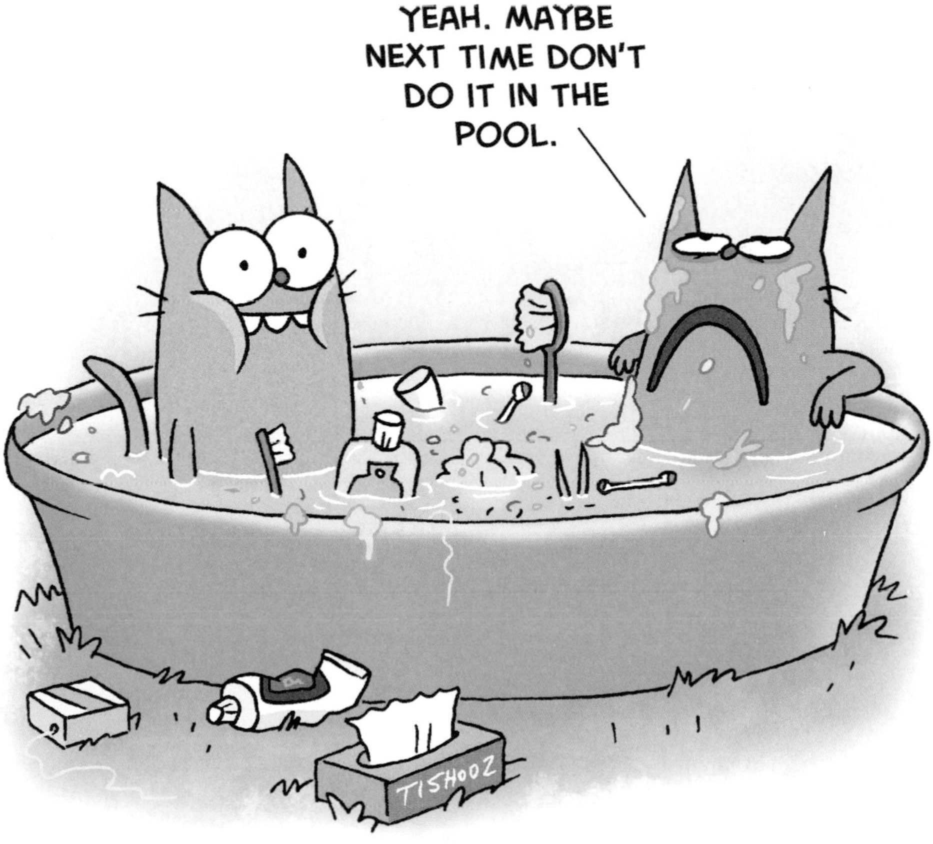
YEAH. MAYBE NEXT TIME DON'T DO IT IN THE POOL.
TISHOOZ

MIRROR

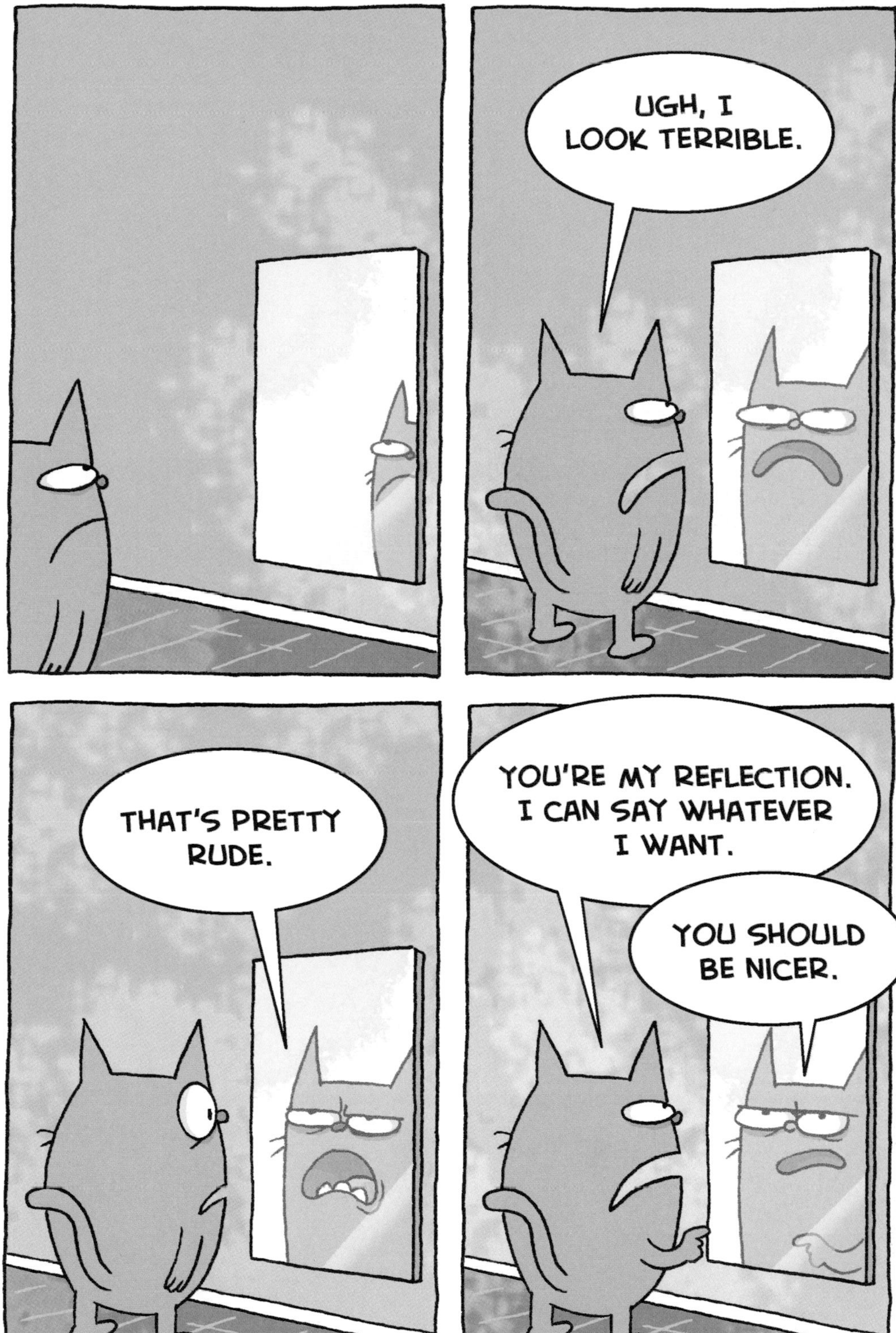
UGH, I LOOK TERRIBLE.
THAT'S PRETTY RUDE.
YOU'RE MY REFLECTION. I CAN SAY WHATEVER I WANT.
YOU SHOULD BE NICER.

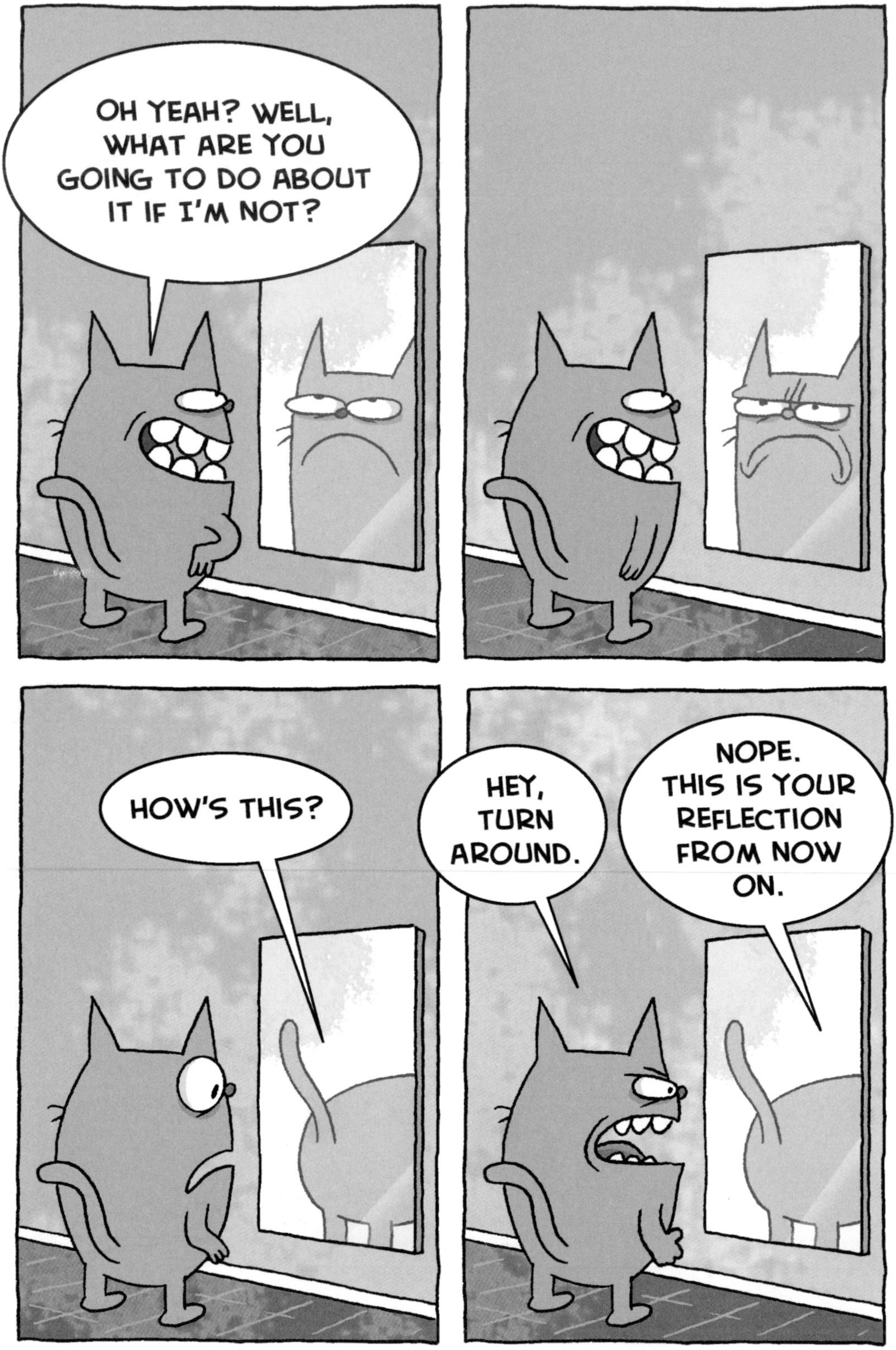
OH YEAH? WELL, WHAT ARE YOU GOING TO DO ABOUT IT IF I'M NOT?
HOW'S THIS?
HEY, TURN AROUND.
NOPE. THIS IS YOUR REFLECTION FROM NOW ON.

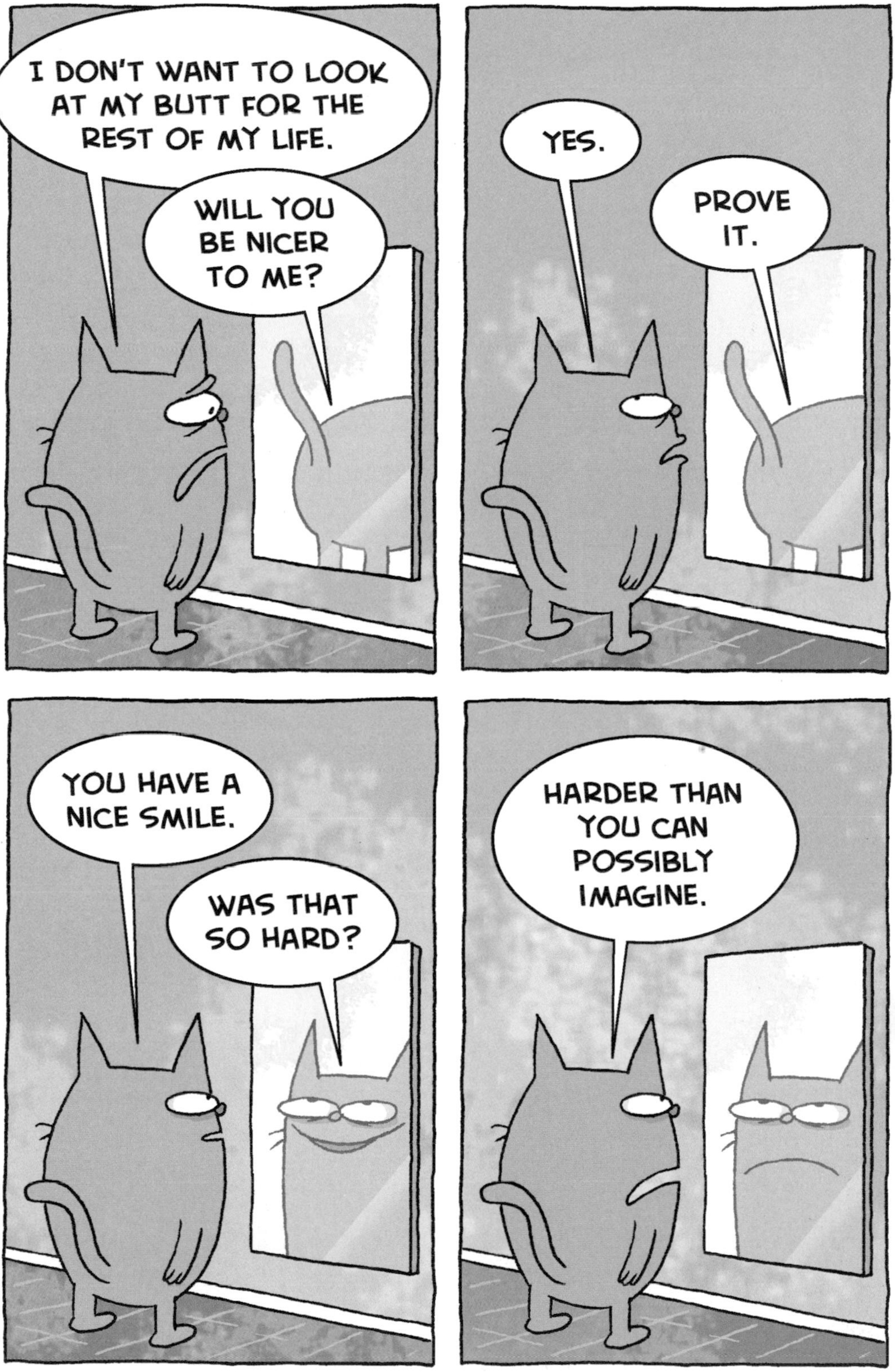
I DON'T WANT TO LOOK AT MY BUTT FOR THE REST OF MY LIFE.
WILL YOU BE NICER TO ME?
YES.
PROVE IT.
YOU HAVE A NICE SMILE.
WAS THAT SO HARD?
HARDER THAN YOU CAN POSSIBLY IMAGINE.

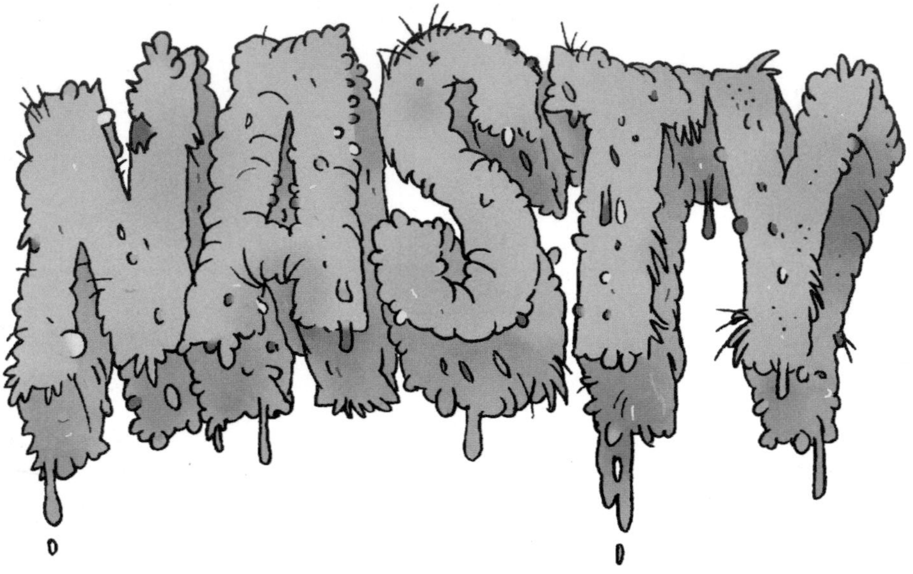
NASTY

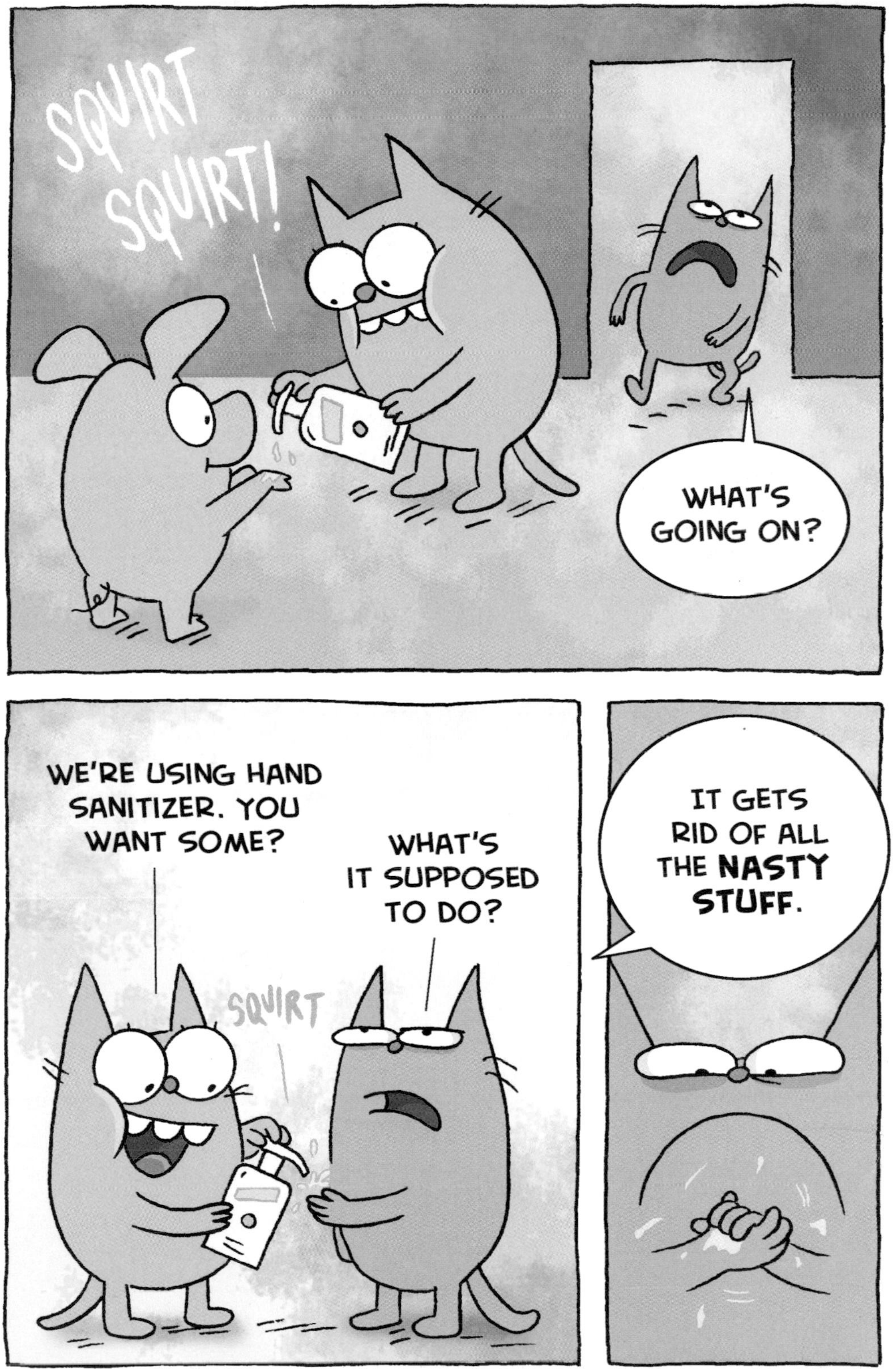
SQUIRT
SQUIRT!
WHAT'S GOING ON?
WE'RE USING HAND SANITIZER. YOU WANT SOME?
SQUIRT
WHAT'S IT SUPPOSED TO DO?
IT GETS RID OF ALL THE **NASTY STUFF**.

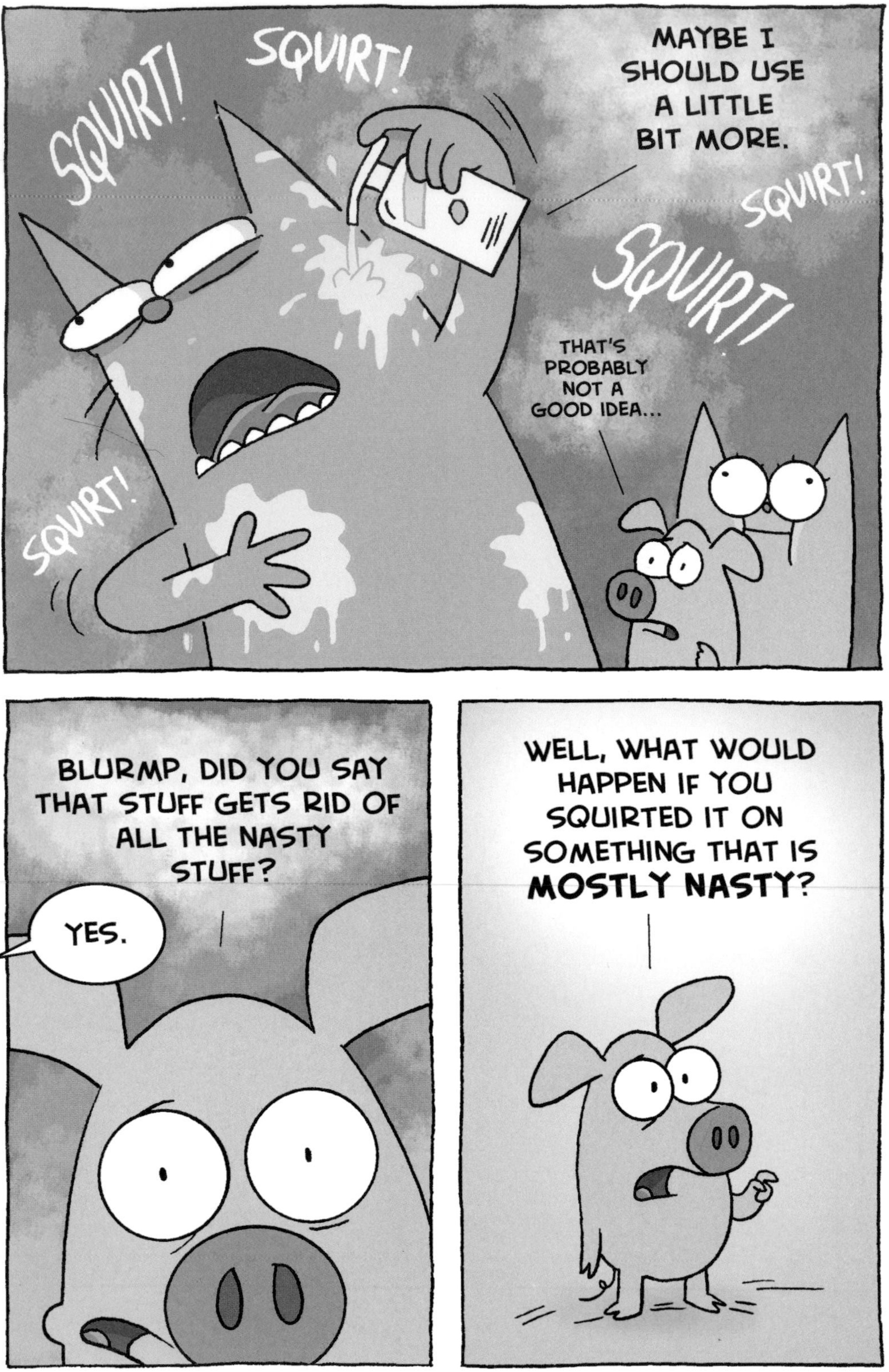

SQUIRT!
SQUIRT!
MAYBE I SHOULD USE A LITTLE BIT MORE.
SQUIRT!
SQUIRT!
SQUIRT!
THAT'S PROBABLY NOT A GOOD IDEA...
SQUIRT!
BLURMP, DID YOU SAY THAT STUFF GETS RID OF ALL THE NASTY STUFF?
YES.
WELL, WHAT WOULD HAPPEN IF YOU SQUIRTED IT ON SOMETHING THAT IS MOSTLY NASTY?

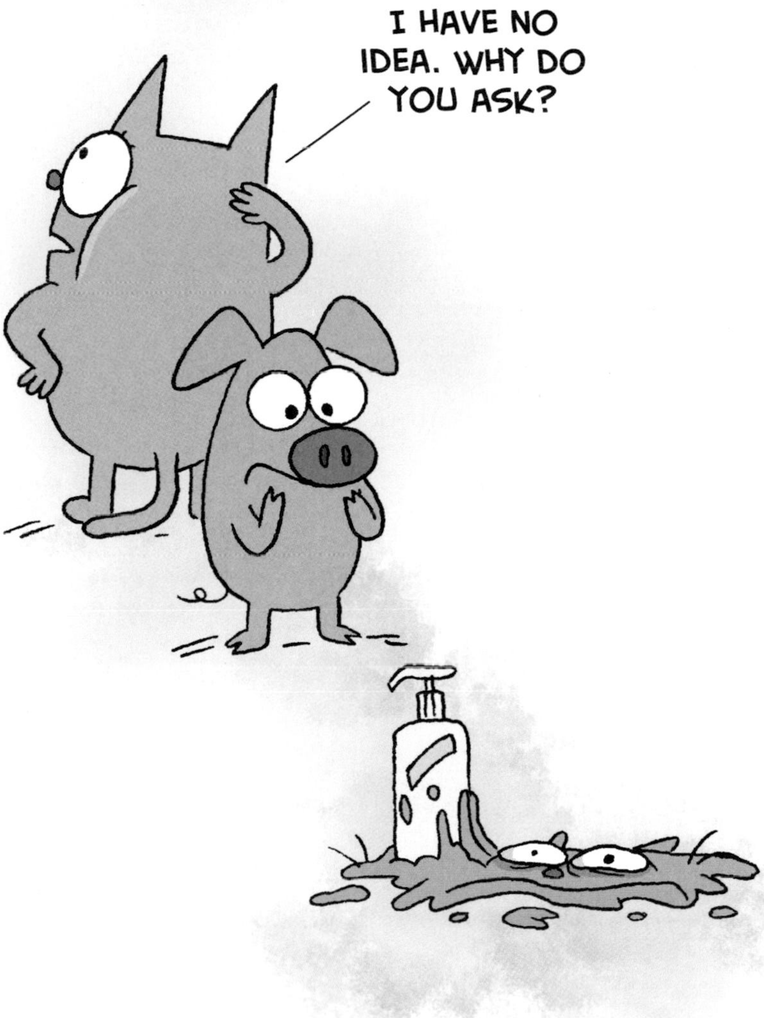
I HAVE NO IDEA. WHY DO YOU ASK?

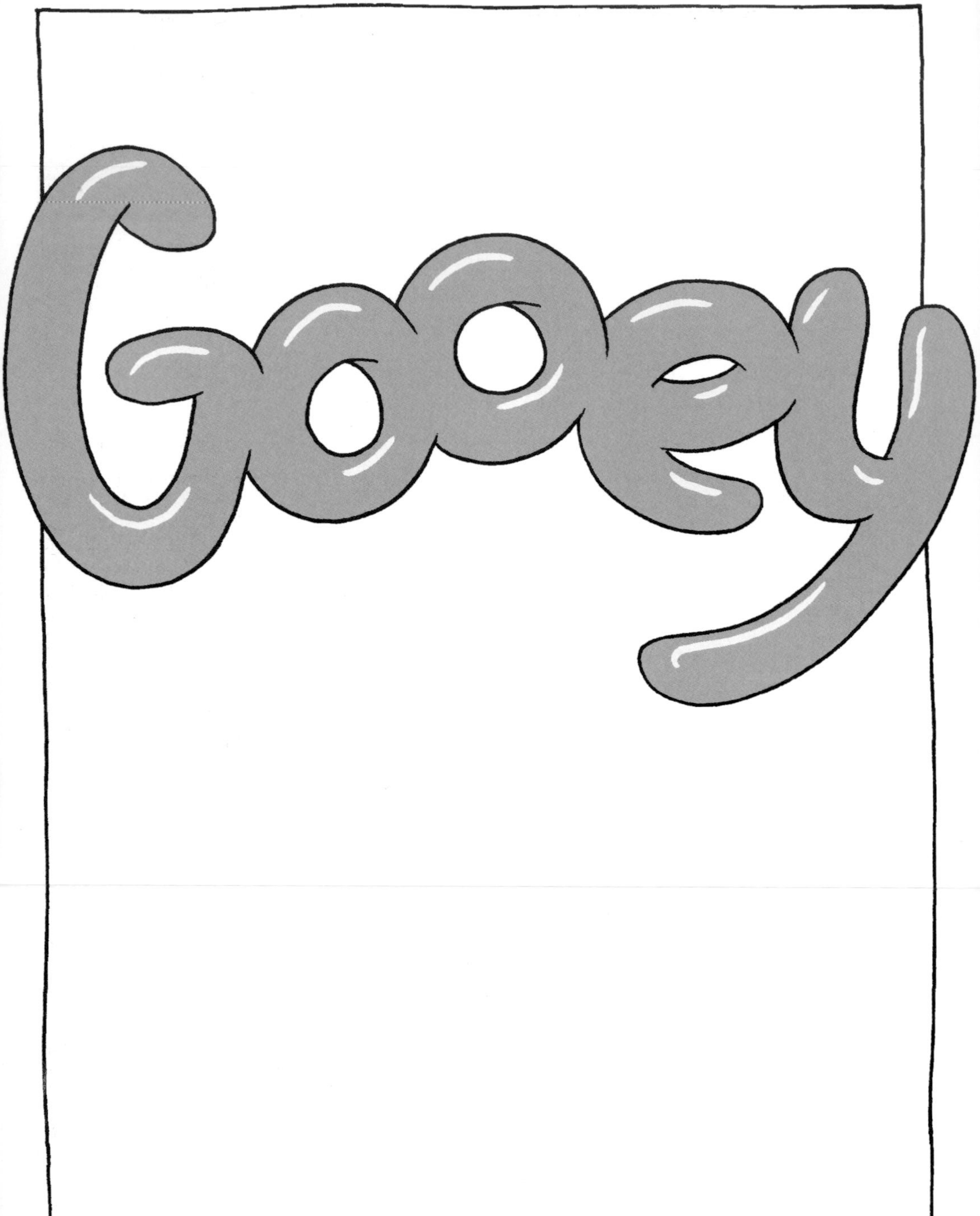
Gooey

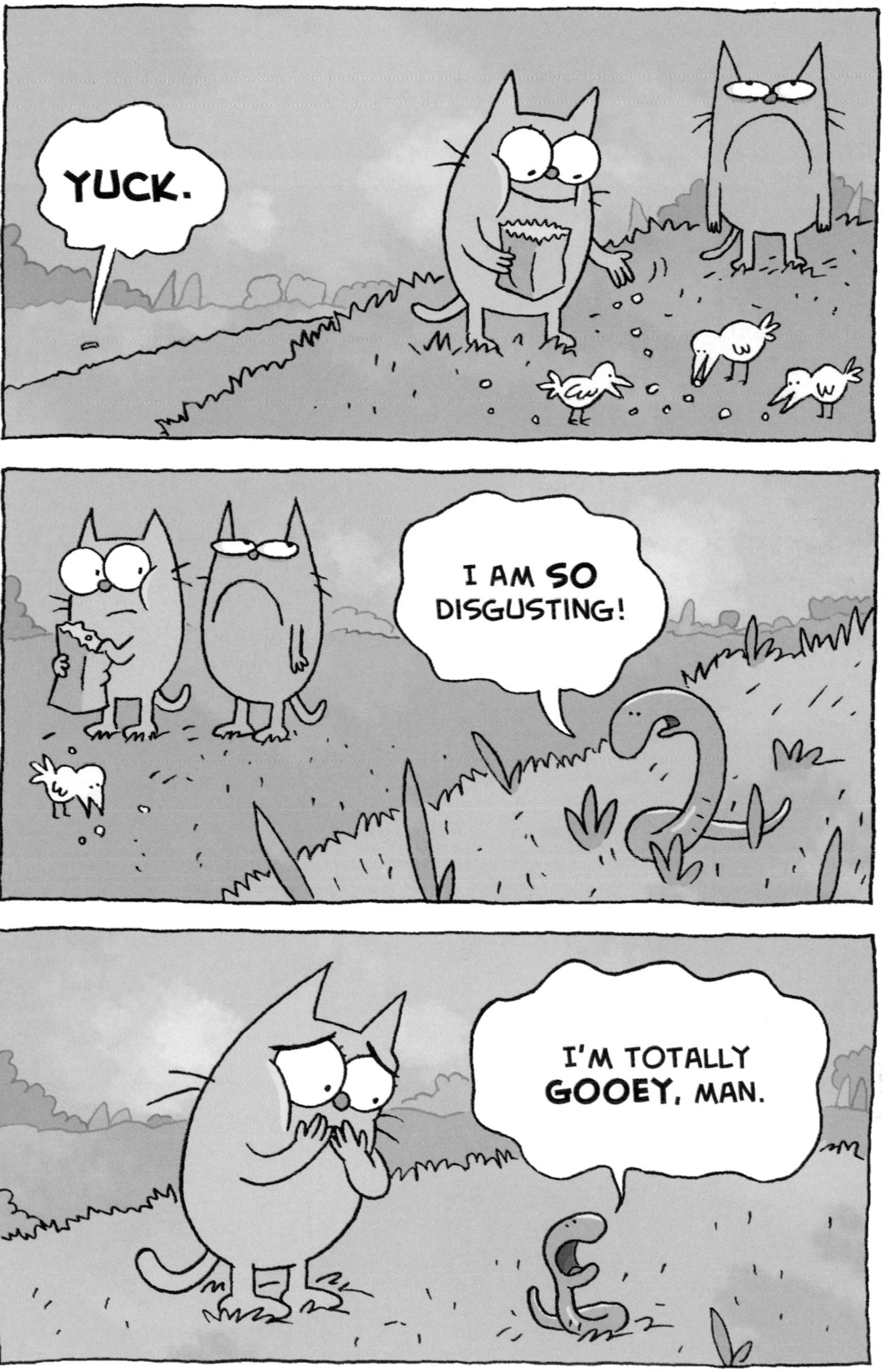
YUCK.
I AM SO DISGUSTING!
I'M TOTALLY GOOEY, MAN.

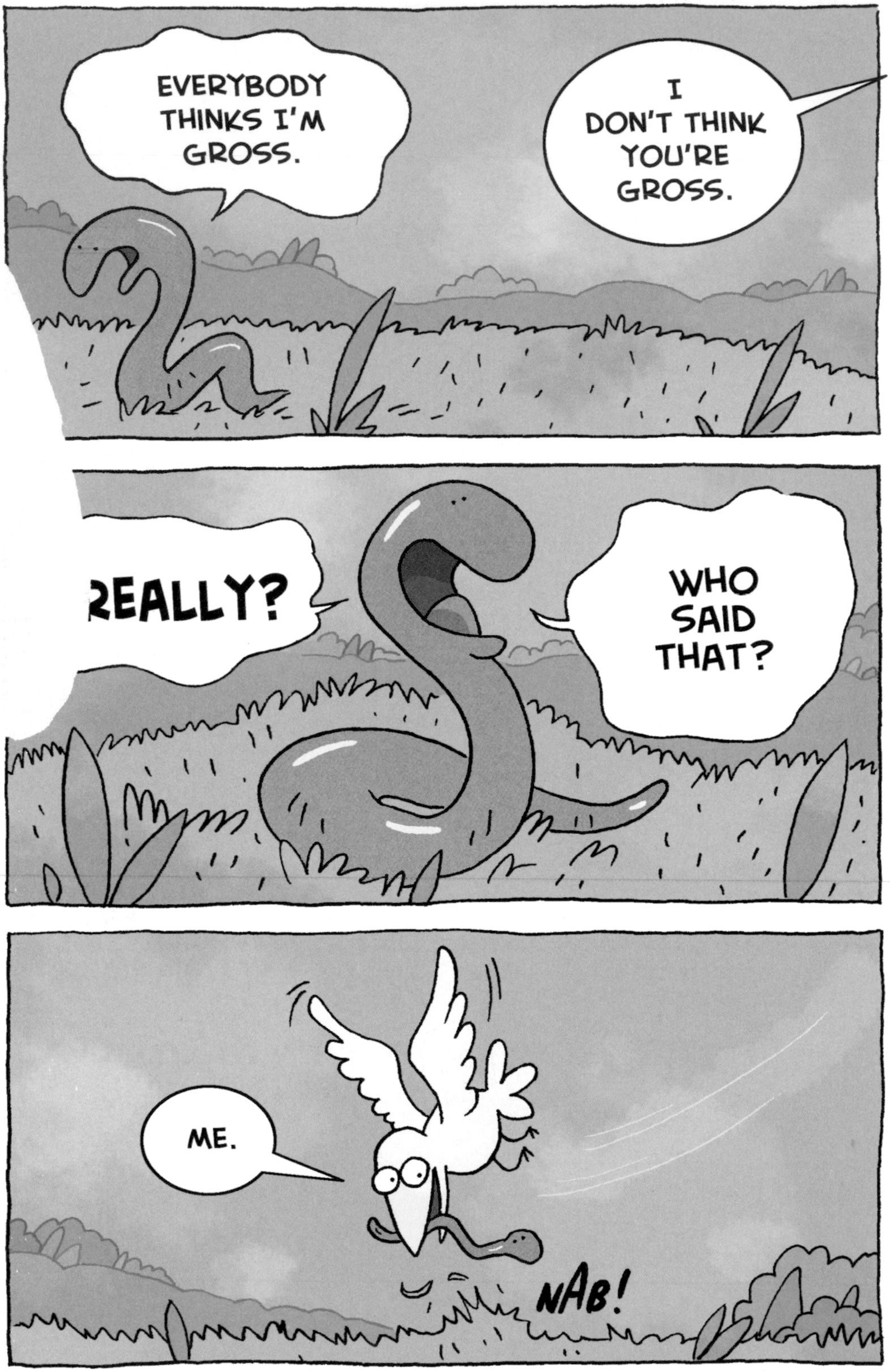
EVERYBODY THINKS I'M GROSS.
I DON'T THINK YOU'RE GROSS.
REALLY?
WHO SAID THAT?
ME.
NAB!

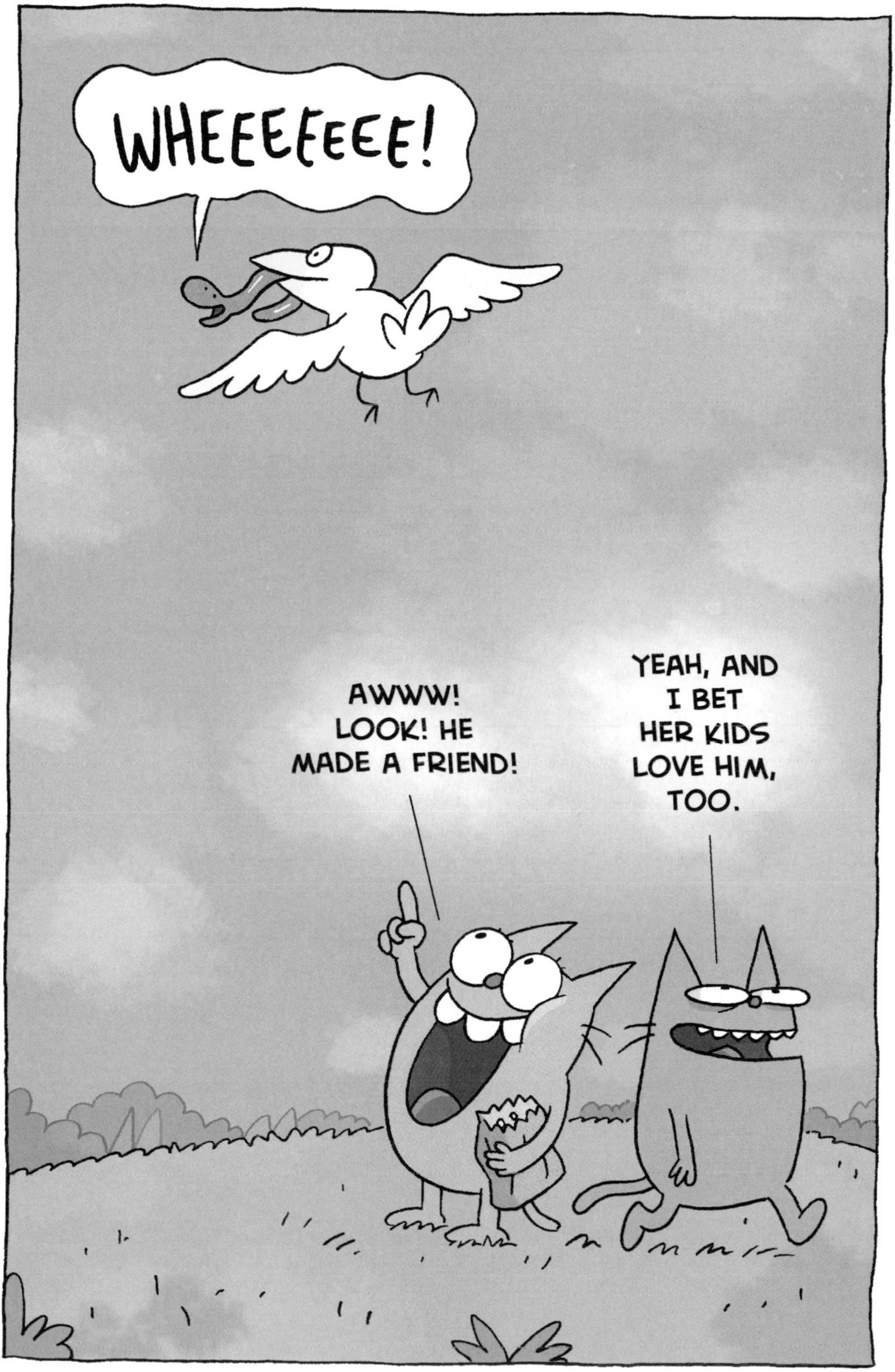
WHEEEEEEE!
AWWW! LOOK! HE MADE A FRIEND!
YEAH, AND I BET HER KIDS LOVE HIM, TOO.

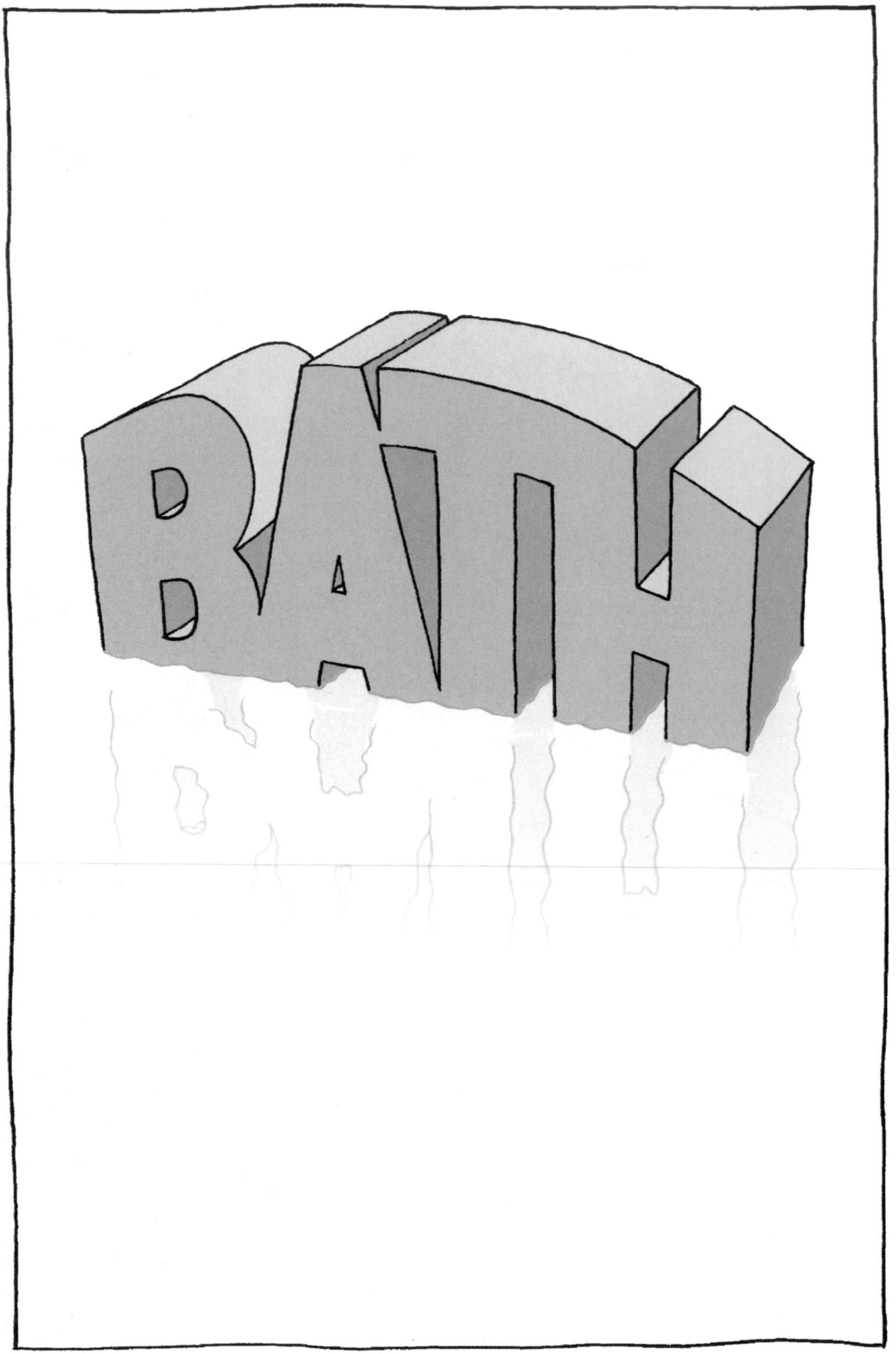
BATH

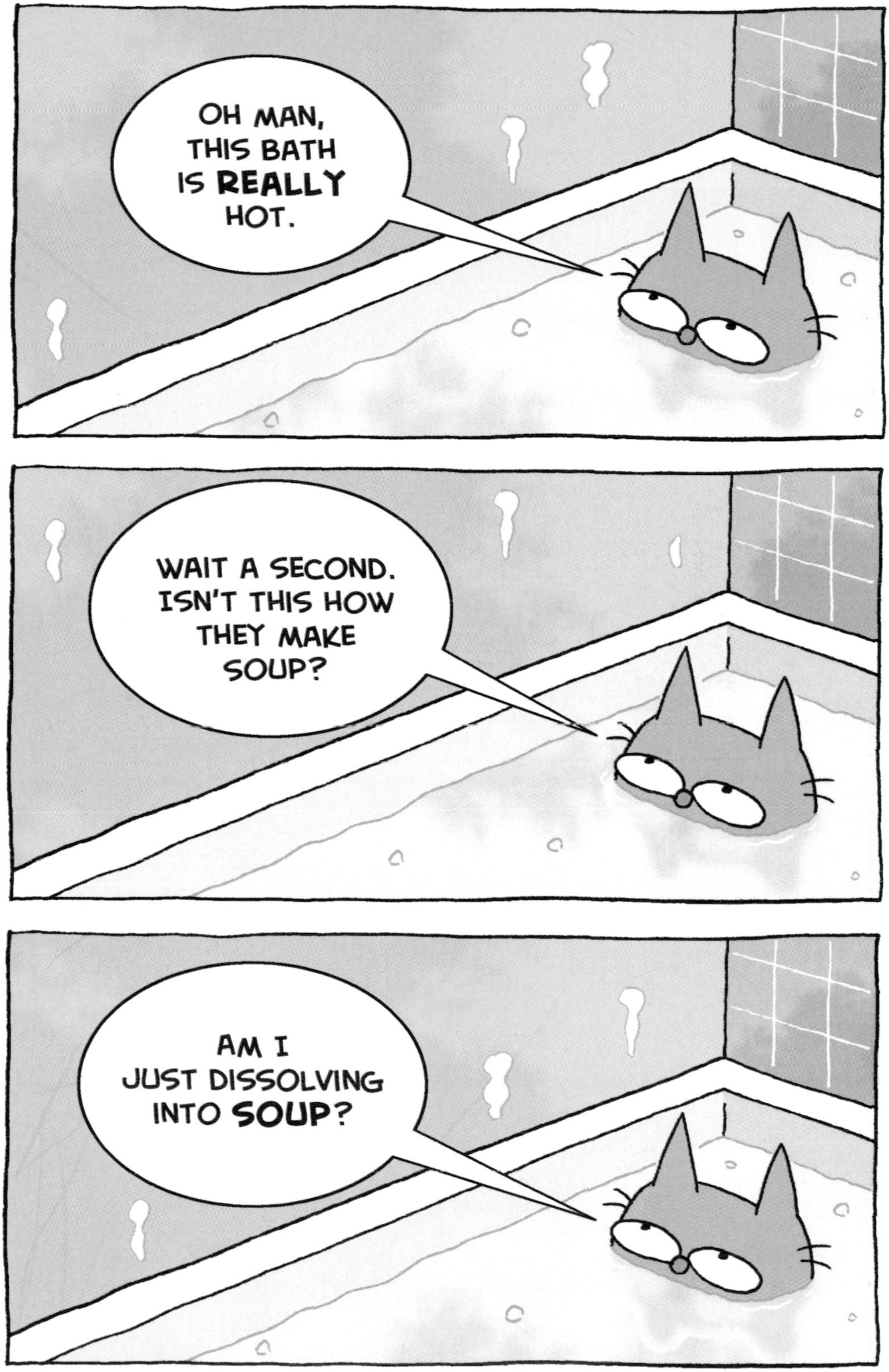
OH MAN, THIS BATH IS **REALLY** HOT.
WAIT A SECOND. ISN'T THIS HOW THEY MAKE SOUP?
AM I JUST DISSOLVING INTO **SOUP**?

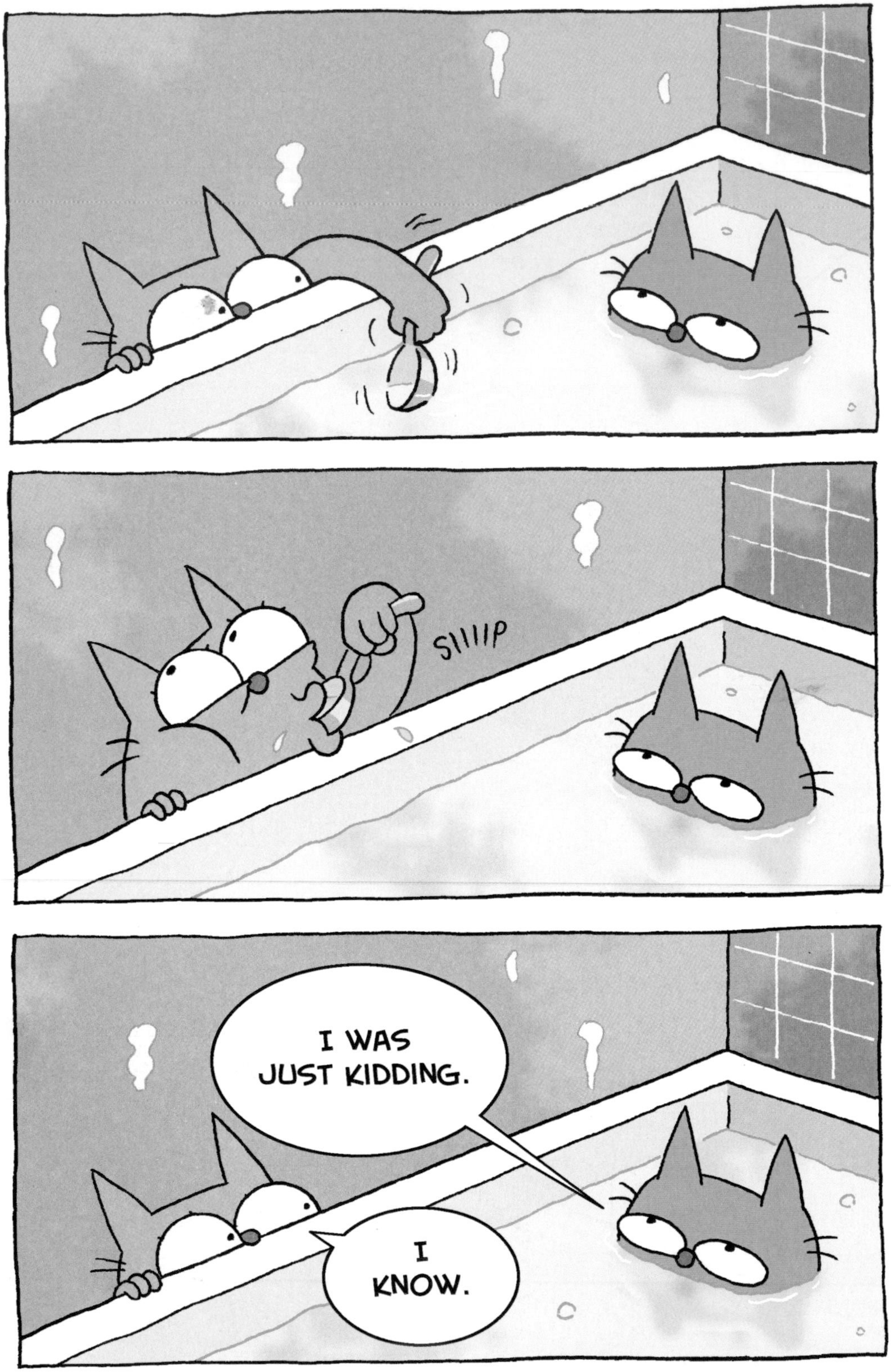
SIIIIP
I WAS JUST KIDDING.
I KNOW.

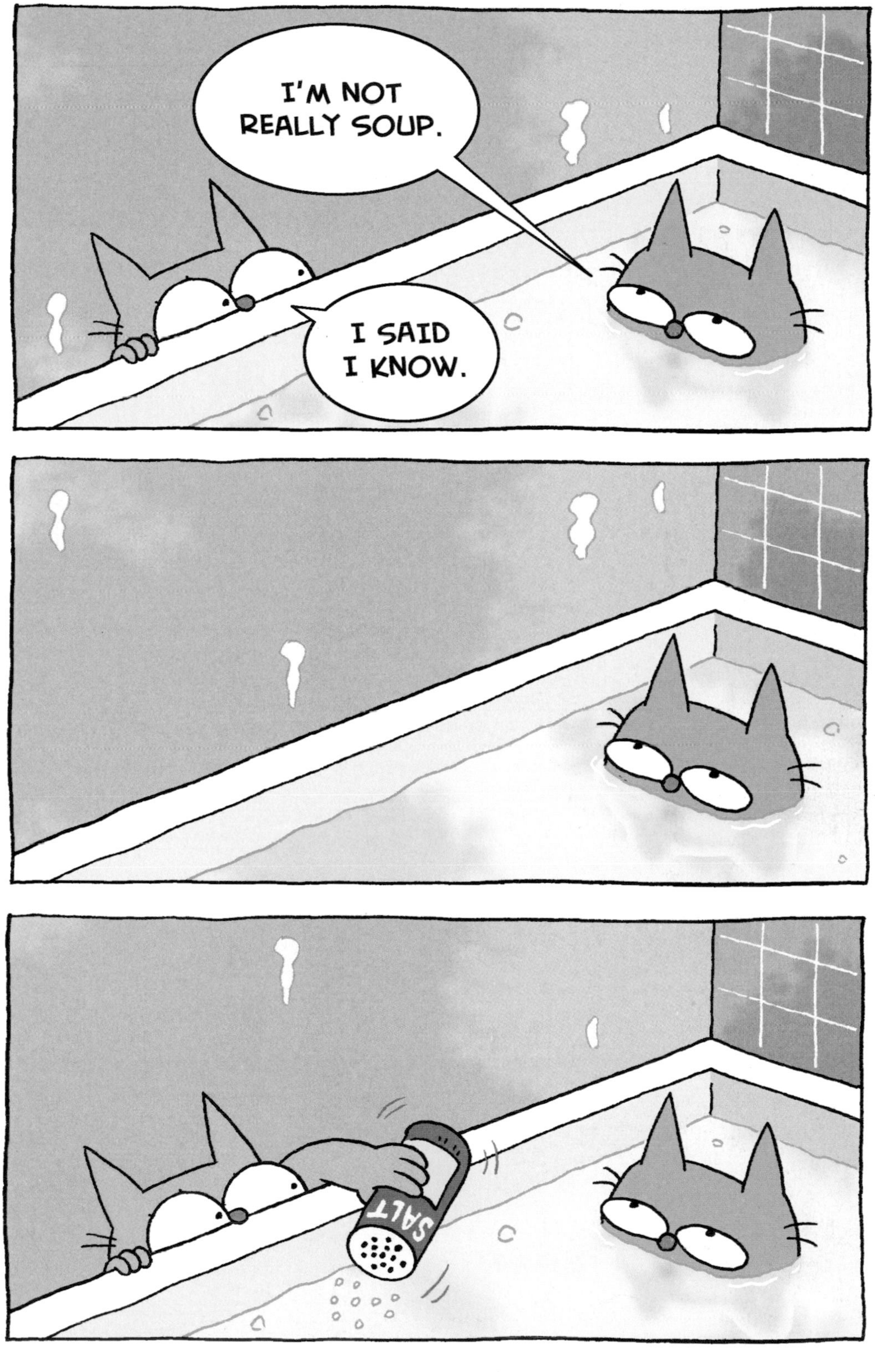
I'M NOT
REALLY SOUP.
I SAID
I KNOW.
SALT

SKELETON

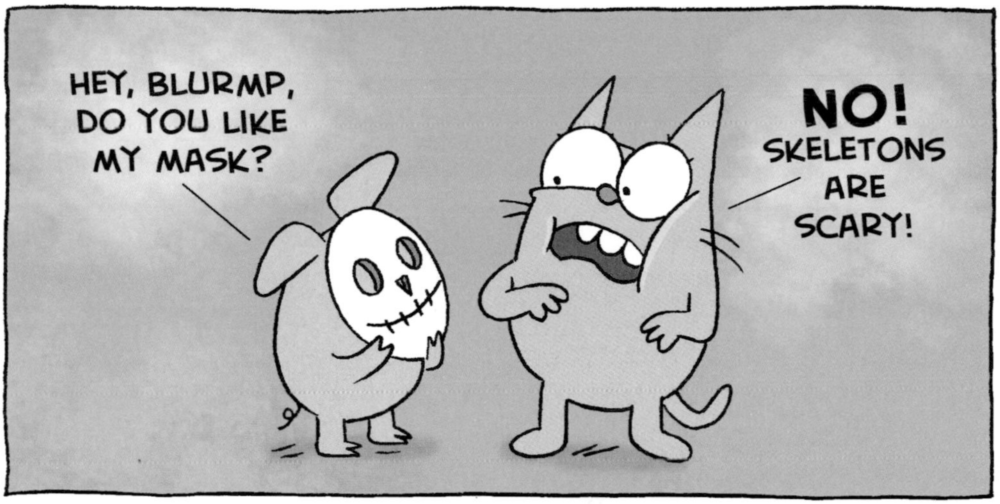
HEY, BLURMP, DO YOU LIKE MY MASK?
NO! SKELETONS ARE SCARY!

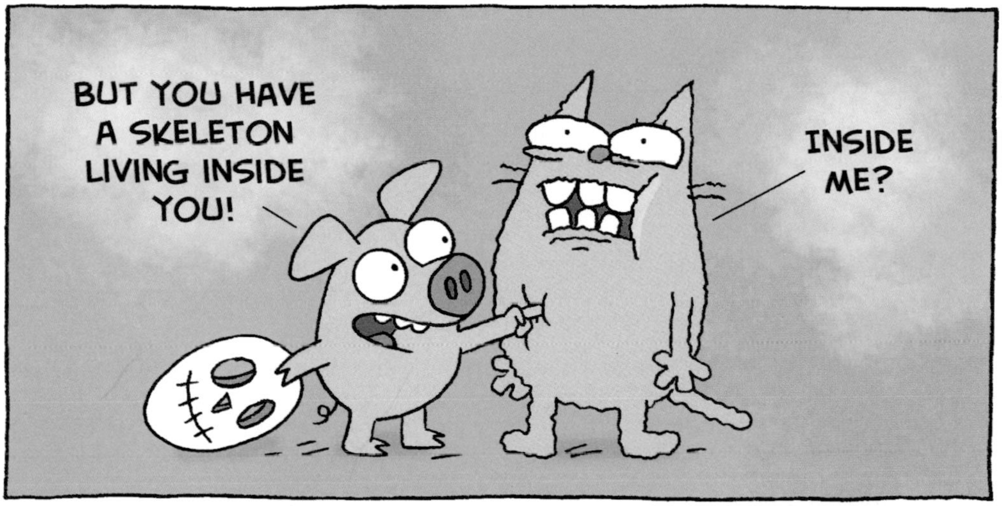
BUT YOU HAVE A SKELETON LIVING INSIDE YOU!
INSIDE ME?

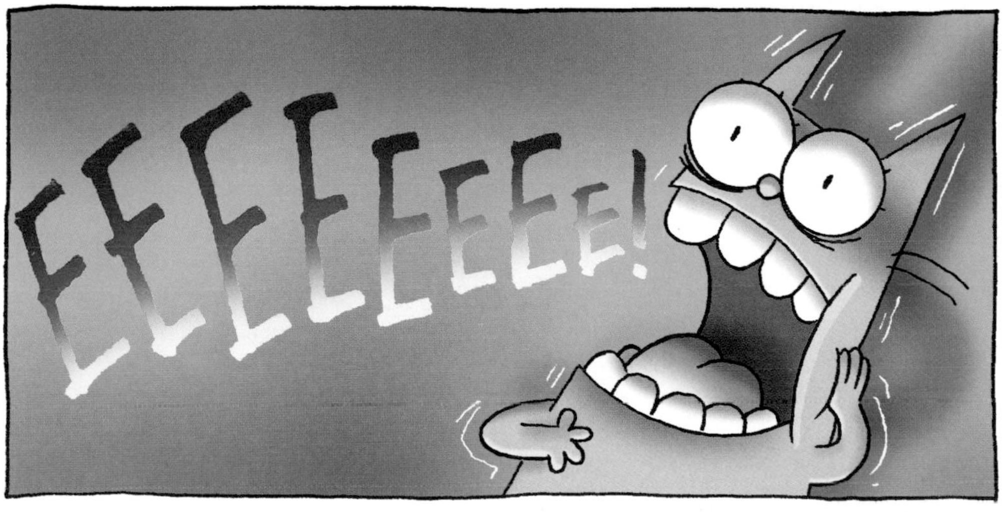
EEEEEEEE!

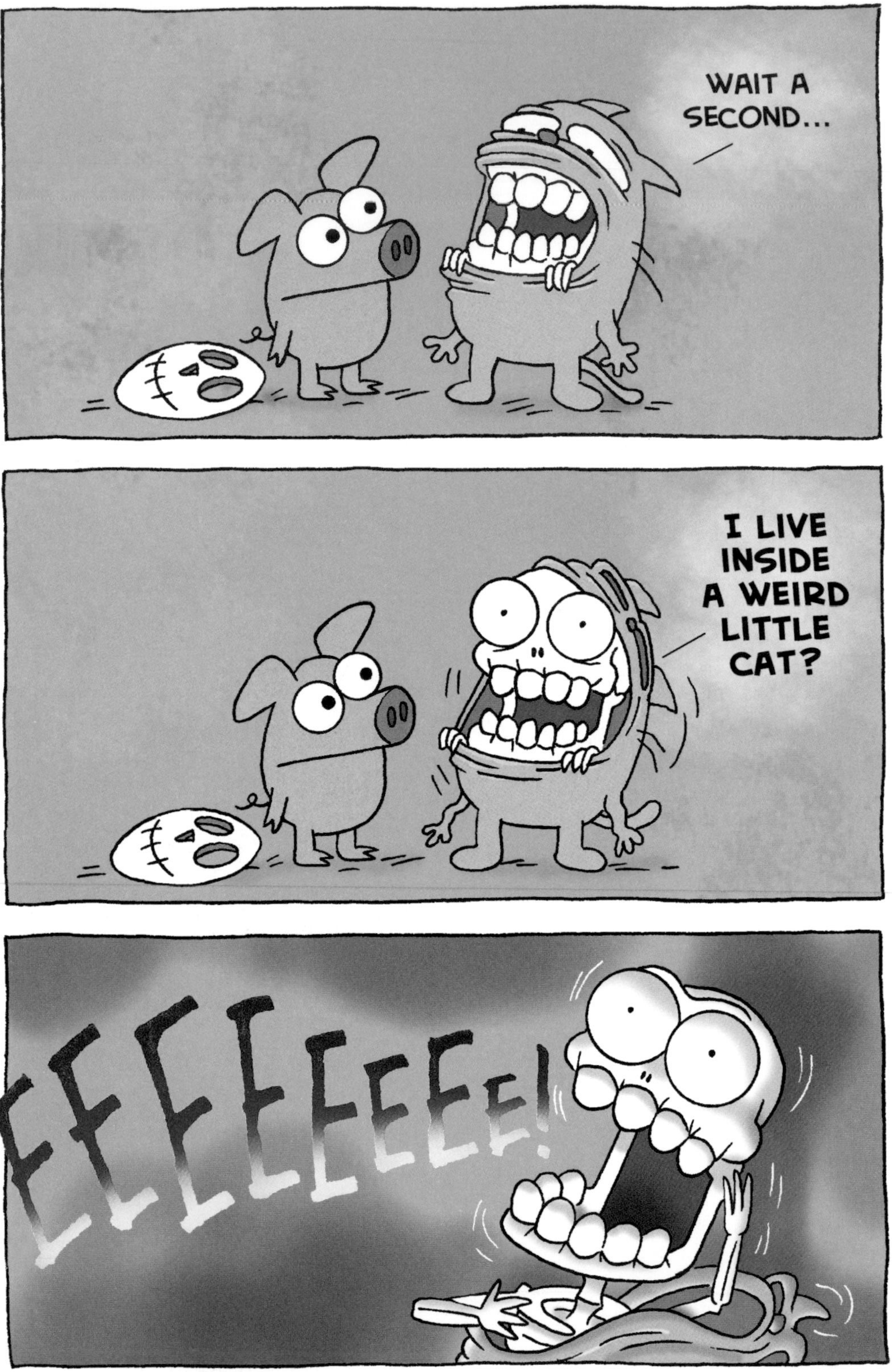
WAIT A SECOND...
I LIVE INSIDE A WEIRD LITTLE CAT?
EEEEEEEEE!

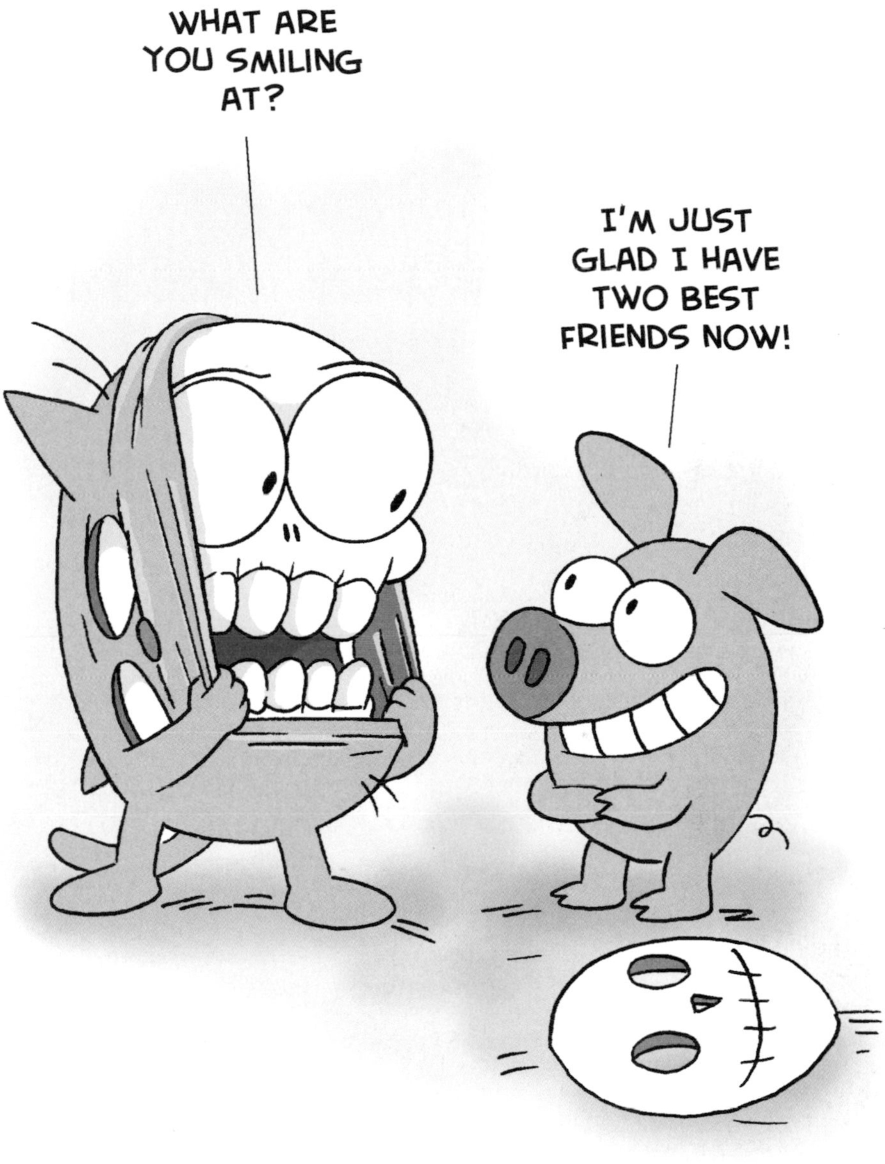
WHAT ARE YOU SMILING AT?
I'M JUST GLAD I HAVE TWO BEST FRIENDS NOW!

POLITE

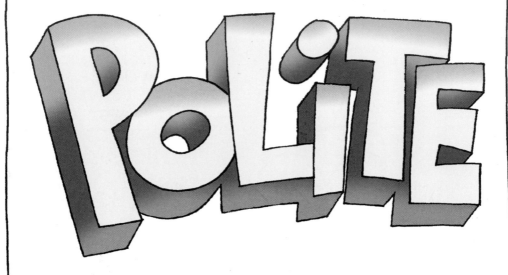

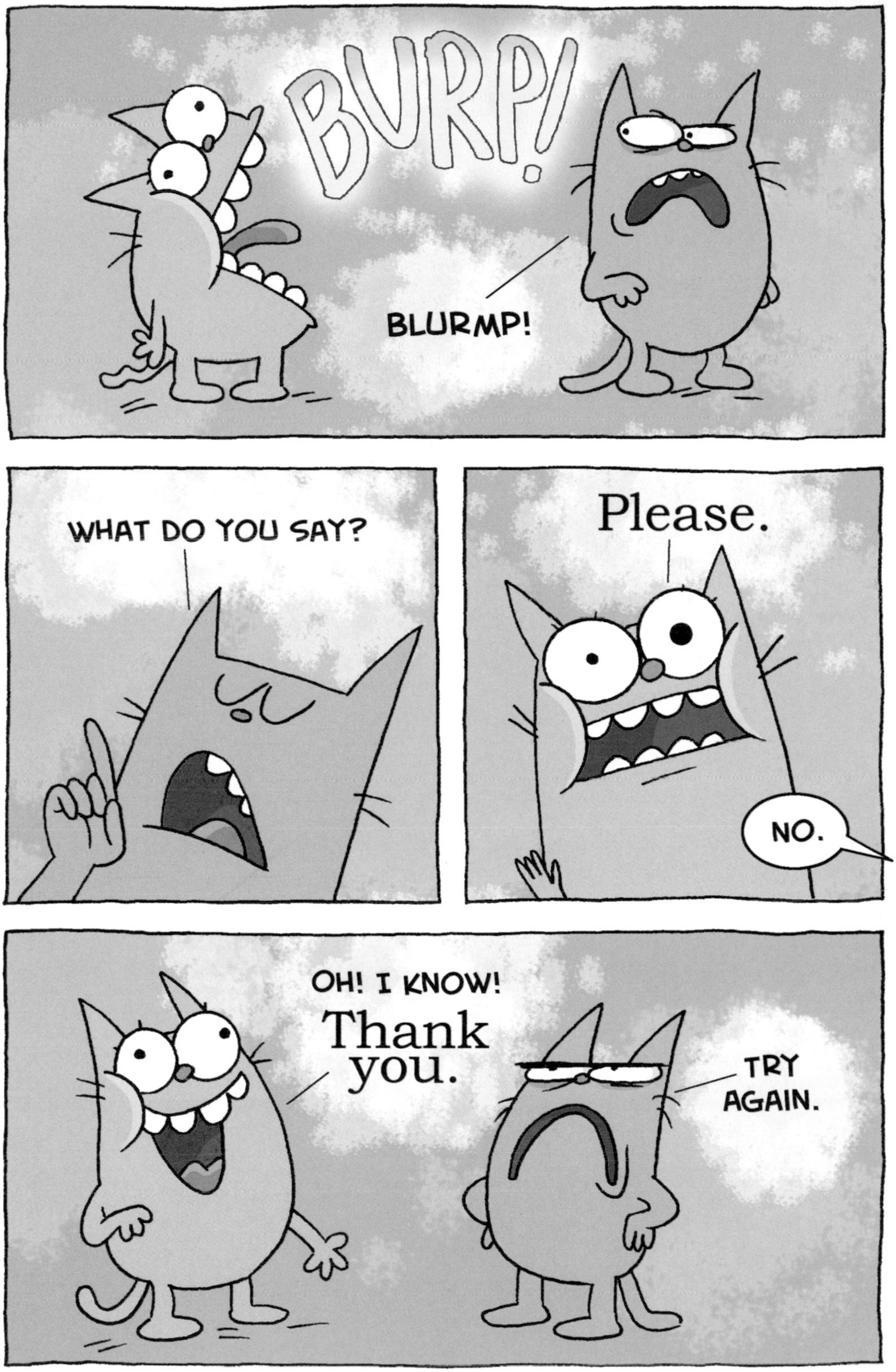
BURP!
BLURMP!
WHAT DO YOU SAY?
Please.
NO.
OH! I KNOW!
Thank you.
TRY AGAIN.

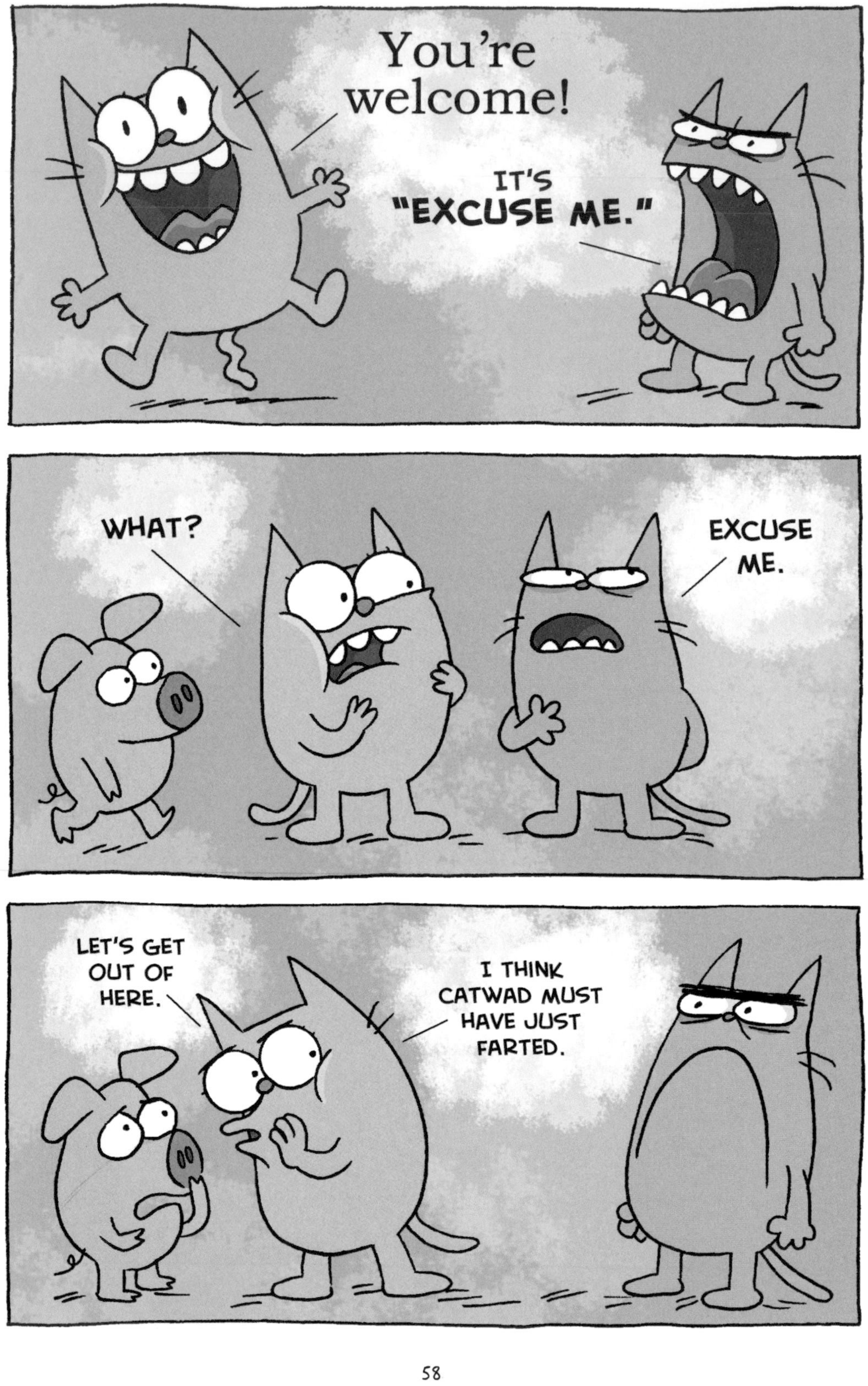
You're welcome!
IT'S "EXCUSE ME."
WHAT?
EXCUSE ME.
LET'S GET OUT OF HERE.
I THINK CATWAD MUST HAVE JUST FARTED.

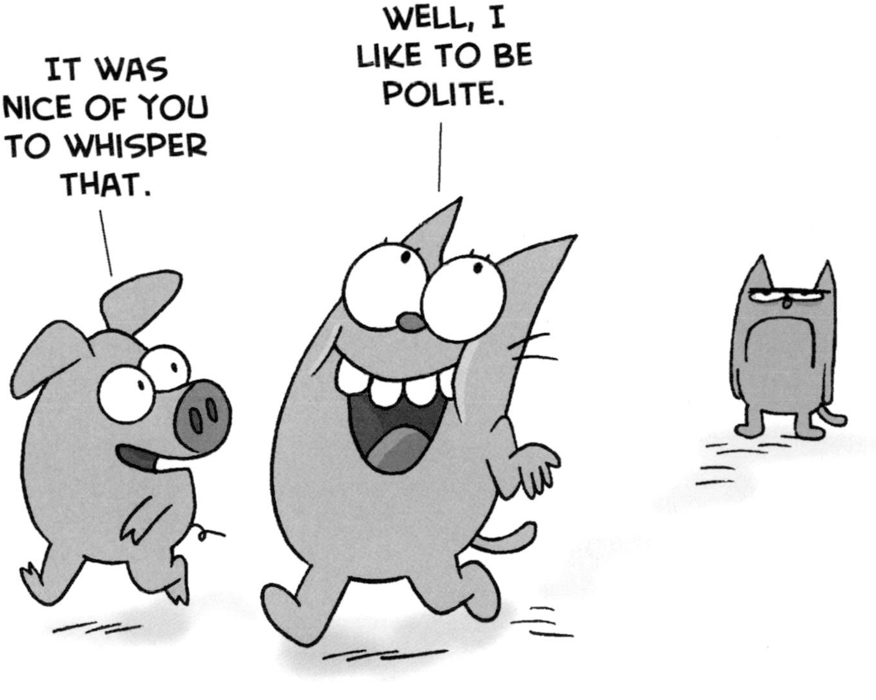
IT WAS NICE OF YOU TO WHISPER THAT.
WELL, I LIKE TO BE POLITE.

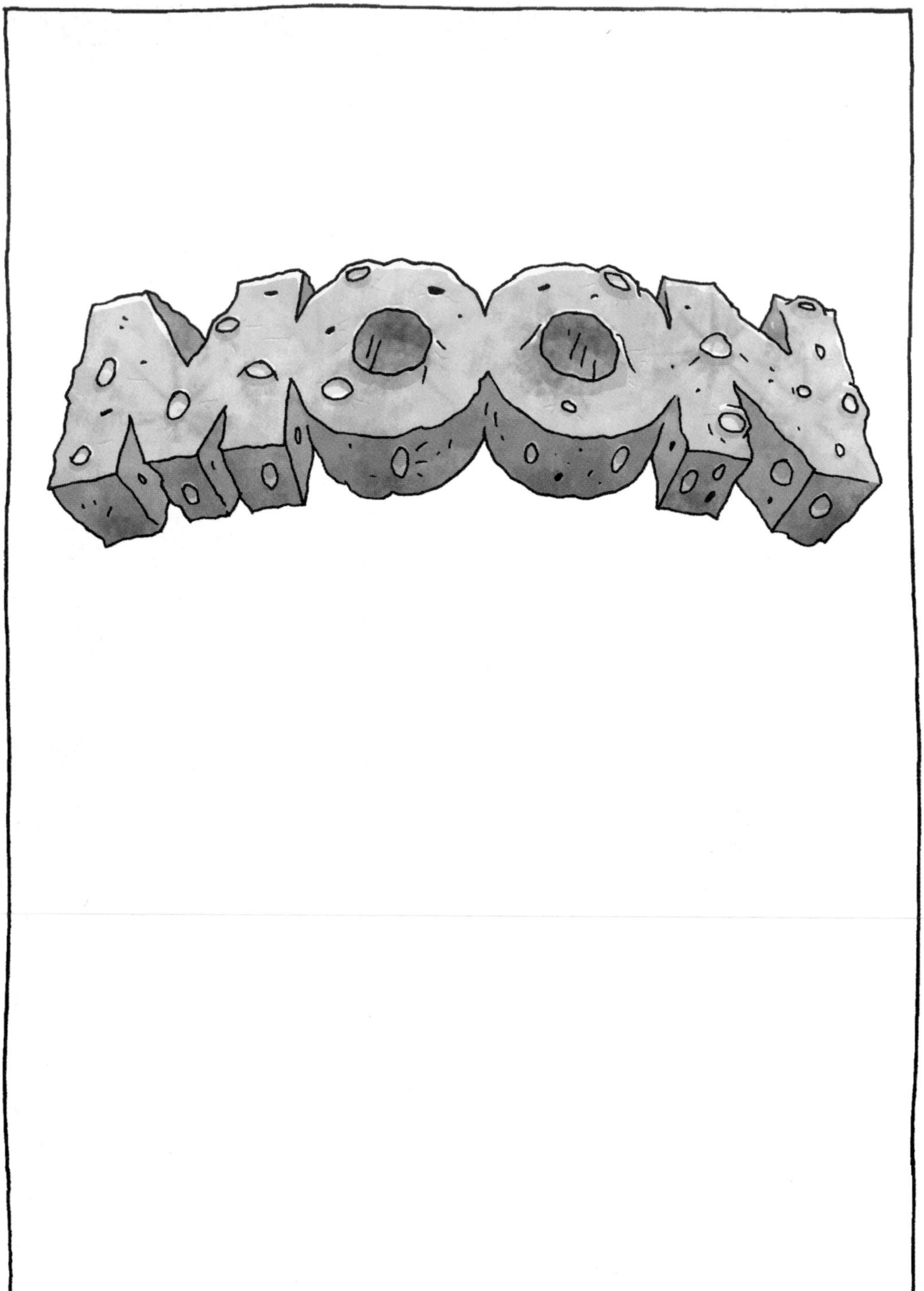
MOON

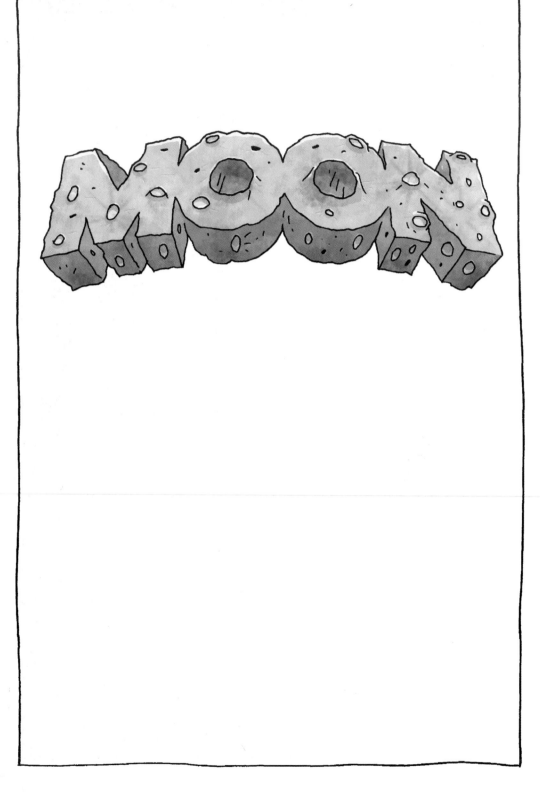

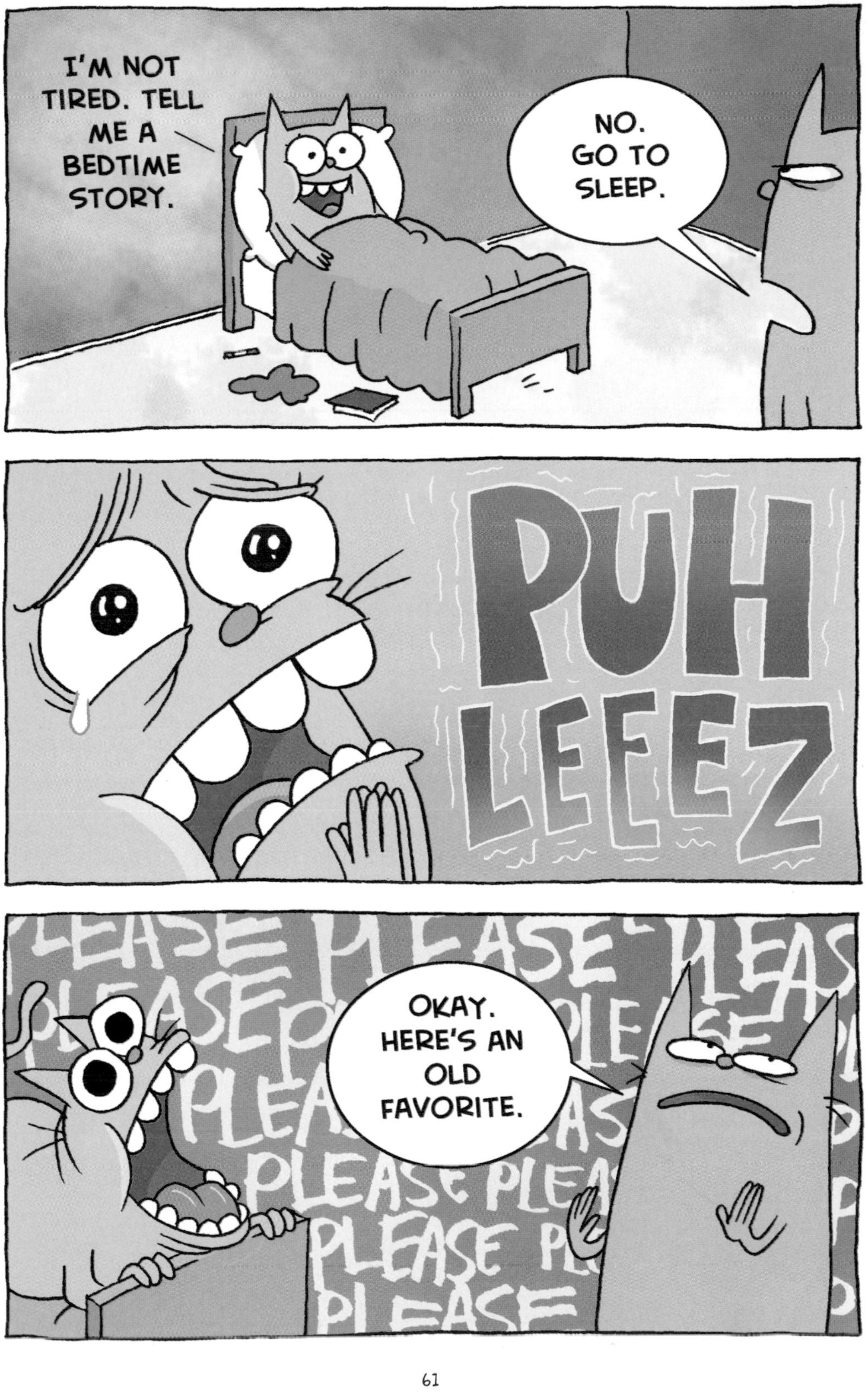
I'M NOT TIRED. TELL ME A BEDTIME STORY.
NO. GO TO SLEEP.
PUH LEEEZ
OKAY. HERE'S AN OLD FAVORITE.

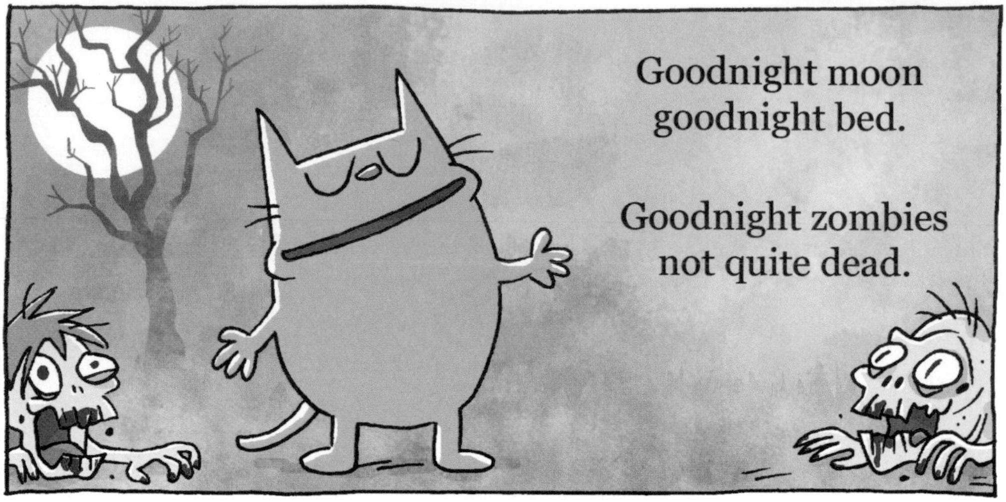
Goodnight moon
goodnight bed.
Goodnight zombies
not quite dead.

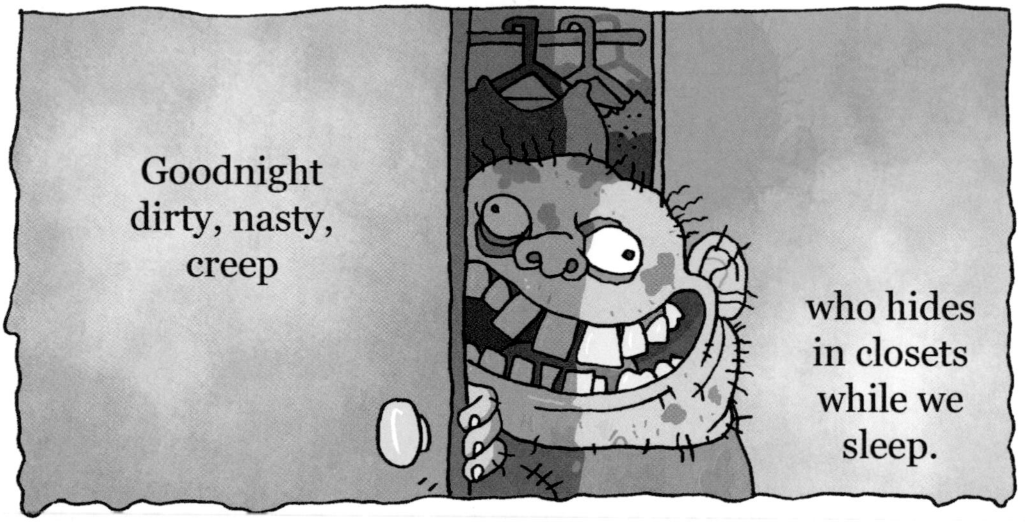
Goodnight
dirty, nasty,
creep
who hides
in closets
while we
sleep.

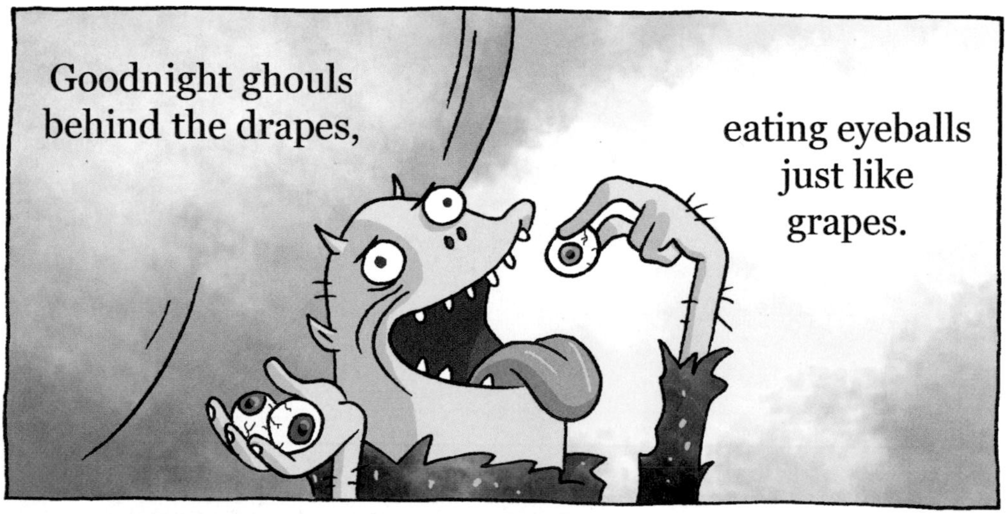
Goodnight ghouls
behind the drapes,
eating eyeballs
just like
grapes.

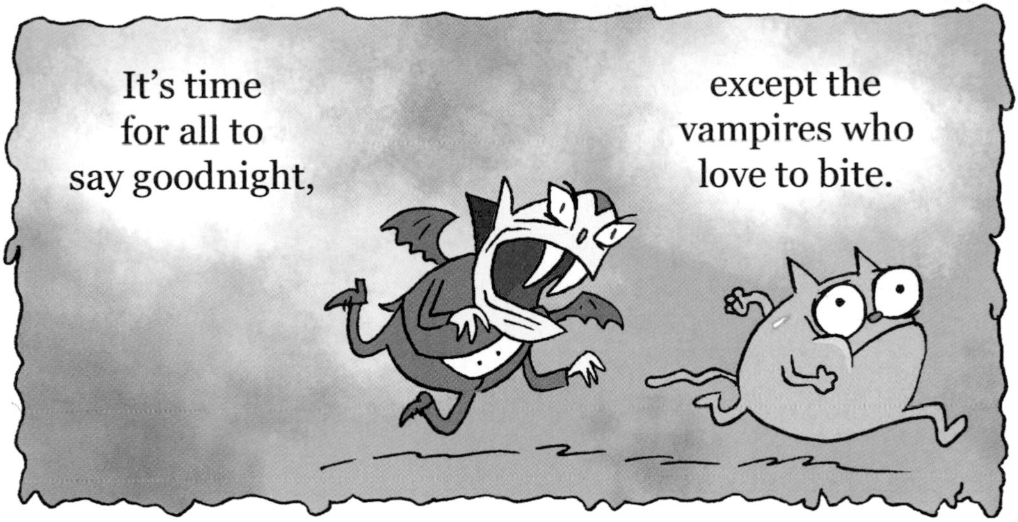
It's time
for all to
say goodnight,
except the
vampires who
love to bite.

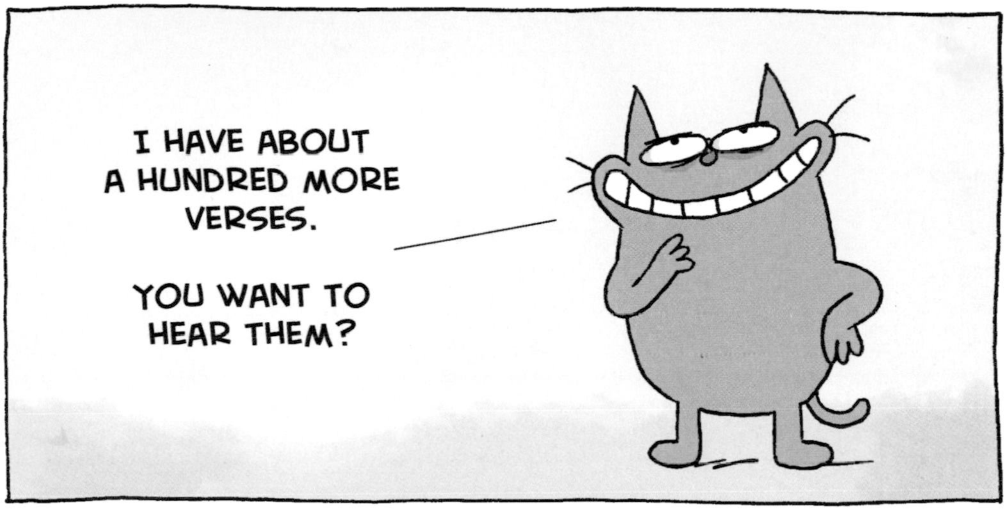
I HAVE ABOUT
A HUNDRED MORE
VERSES.
YOU WANT TO
HEAR THEM?

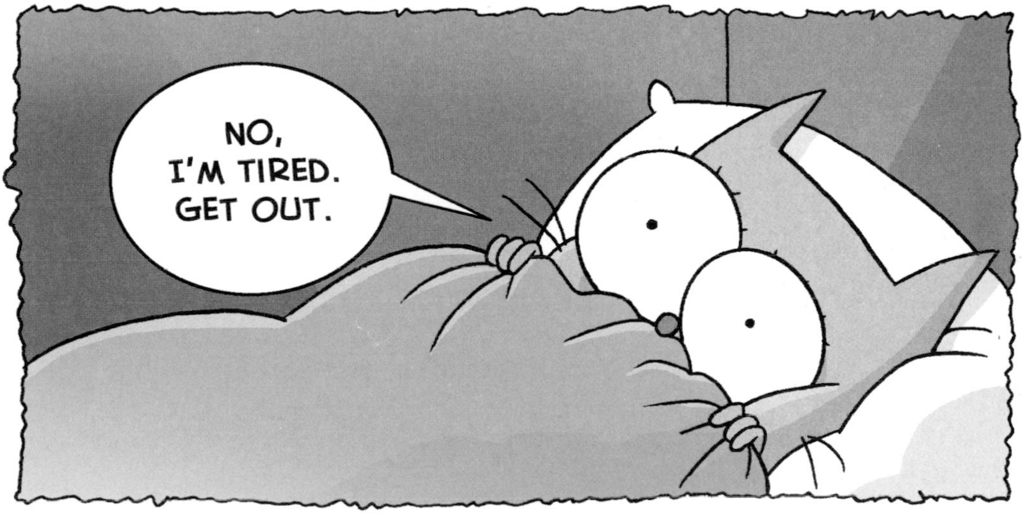
NO,
I'M TIRED.
GET OUT.

INSIDE

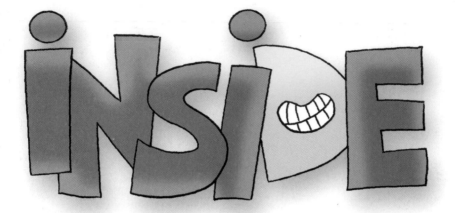

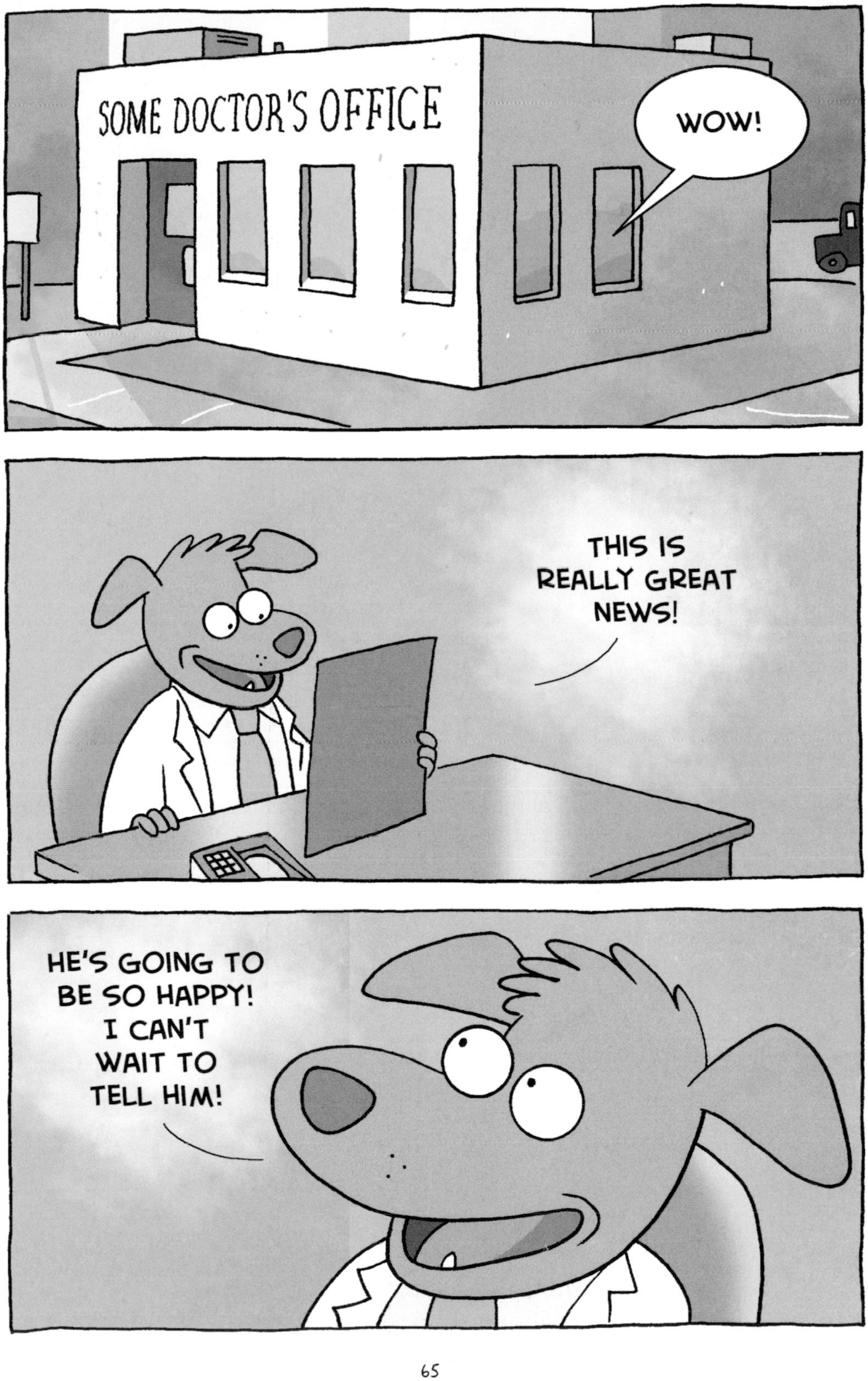
SOME DOCTOR'S OFFICE
WOW!
THIS IS REALLY GREAT NEWS!
HE'S GOING TO BE SO HAPPY! I CAN'T WAIT TO TELL HIM!

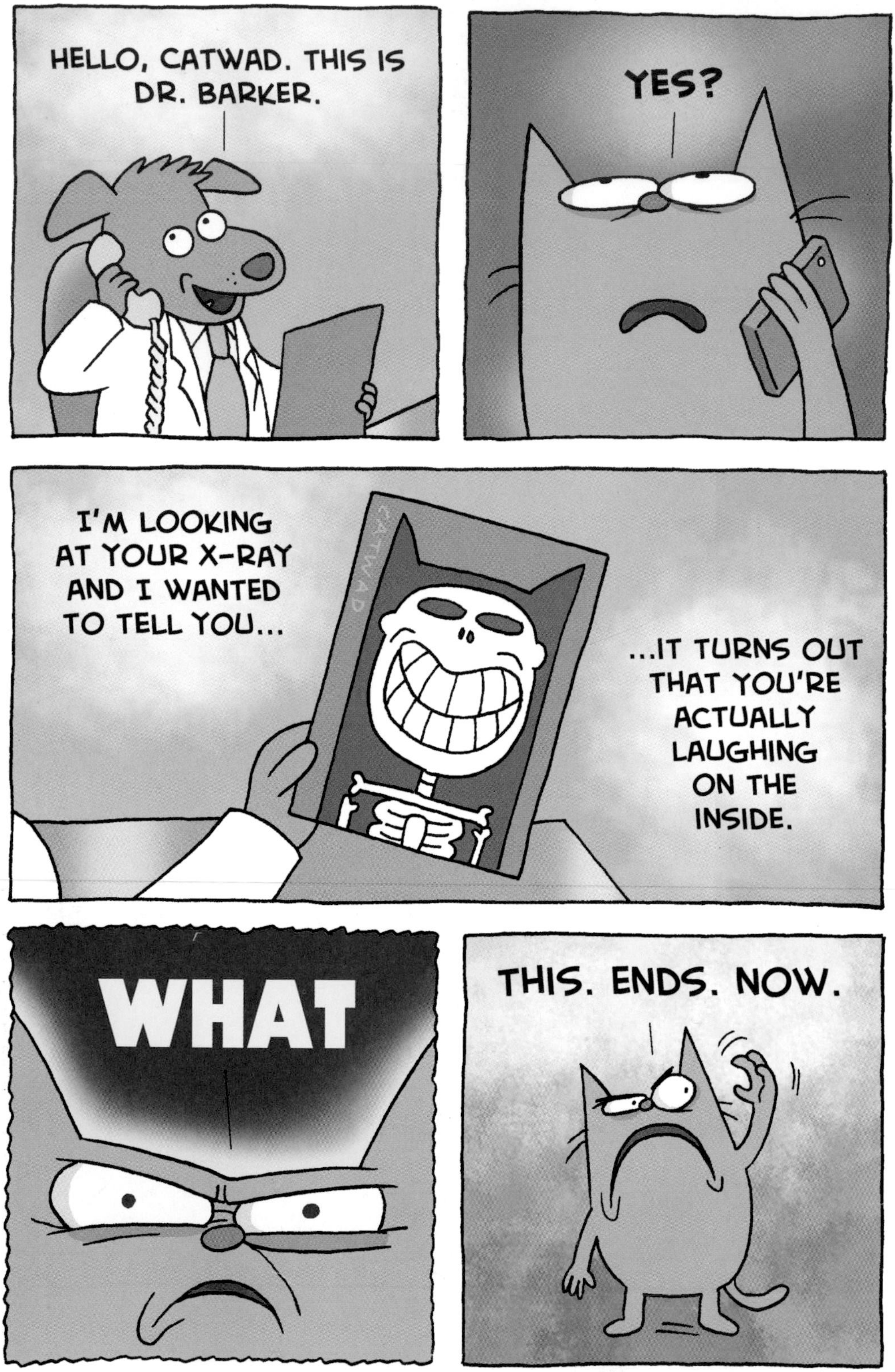
HELLO, CATWAD. THIS IS DR. BARKER.
YES?
I'M LOOKING AT YOUR X-RAY AND I WANTED TO TELL YOU...
CATWAD
...IT TURNS OUT THAT YOU'RE ACTUALLY LAUGHING ON THE INSIDE.
WHAT
THIS. ENDS. NOW.

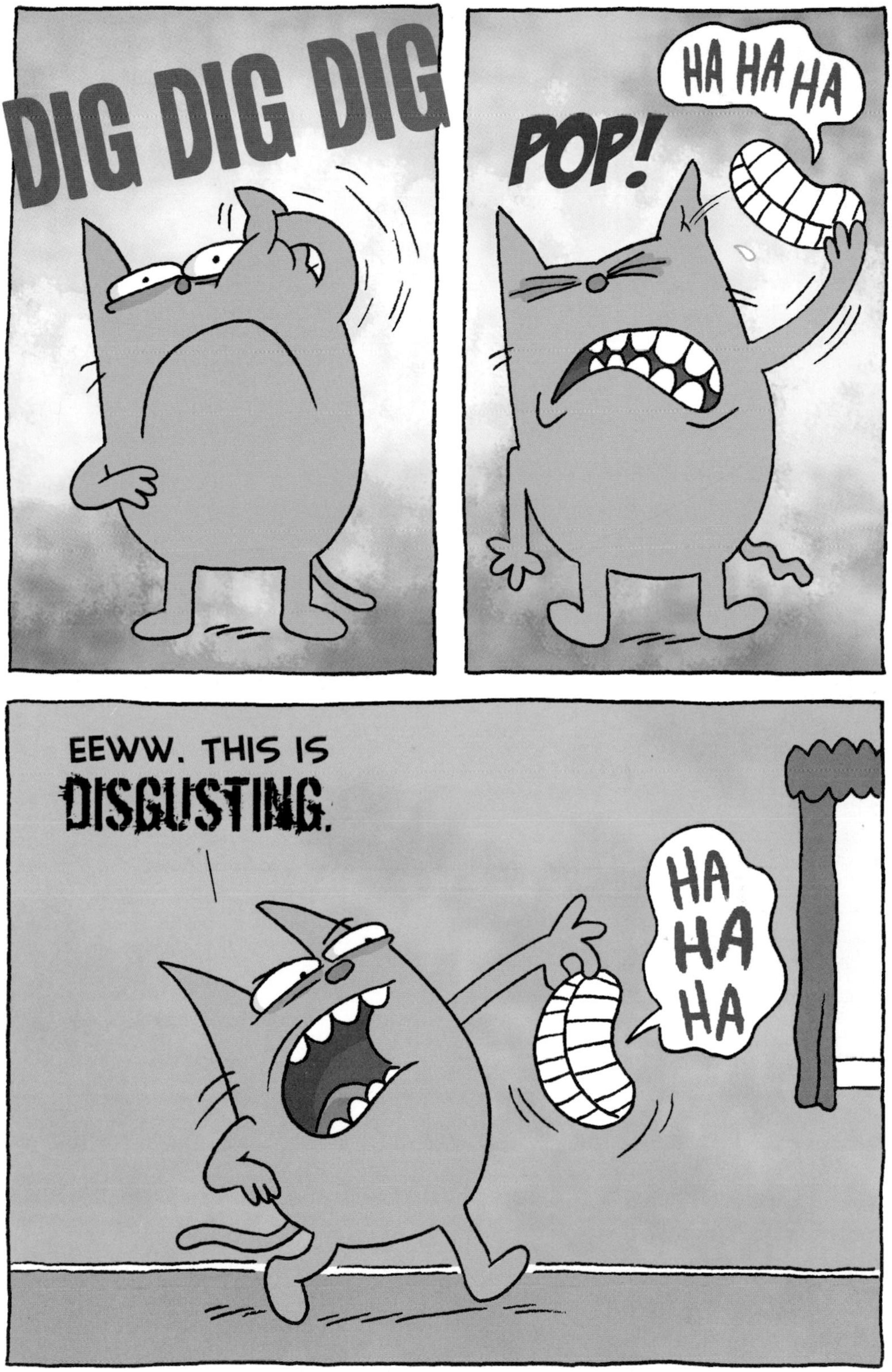
DIG DIG DIG
POP!
HA HA HA
EEWW. THIS IS DISGUSTING.
HA HA HA

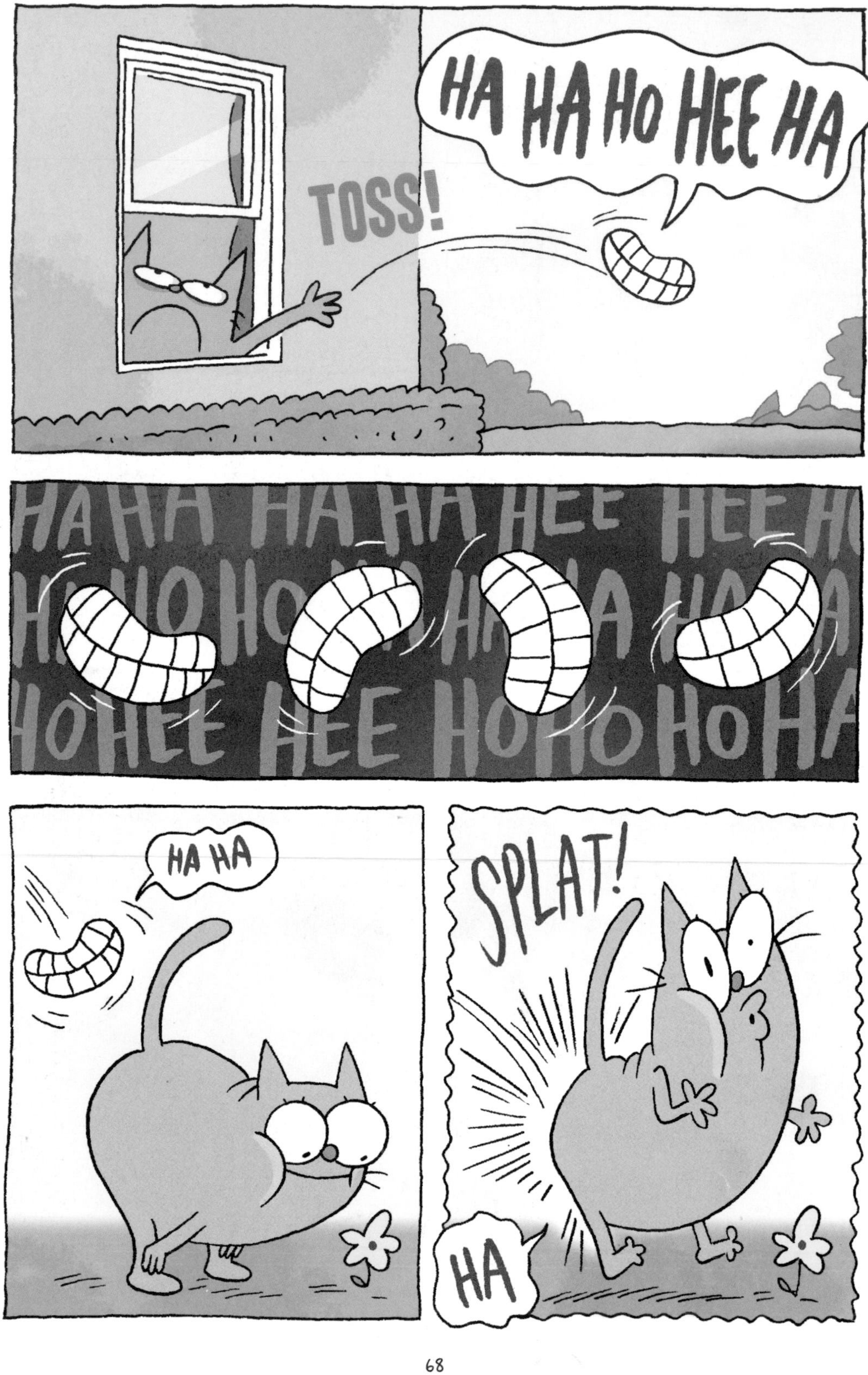
TOSS!
HA HA HO HEE HA
HA HA HA HA HA HEE HEE HO
HO HO HO HA HA HA HA
HO HEE HEE HO HO HO HA
HA HA
SPLAT!
HA

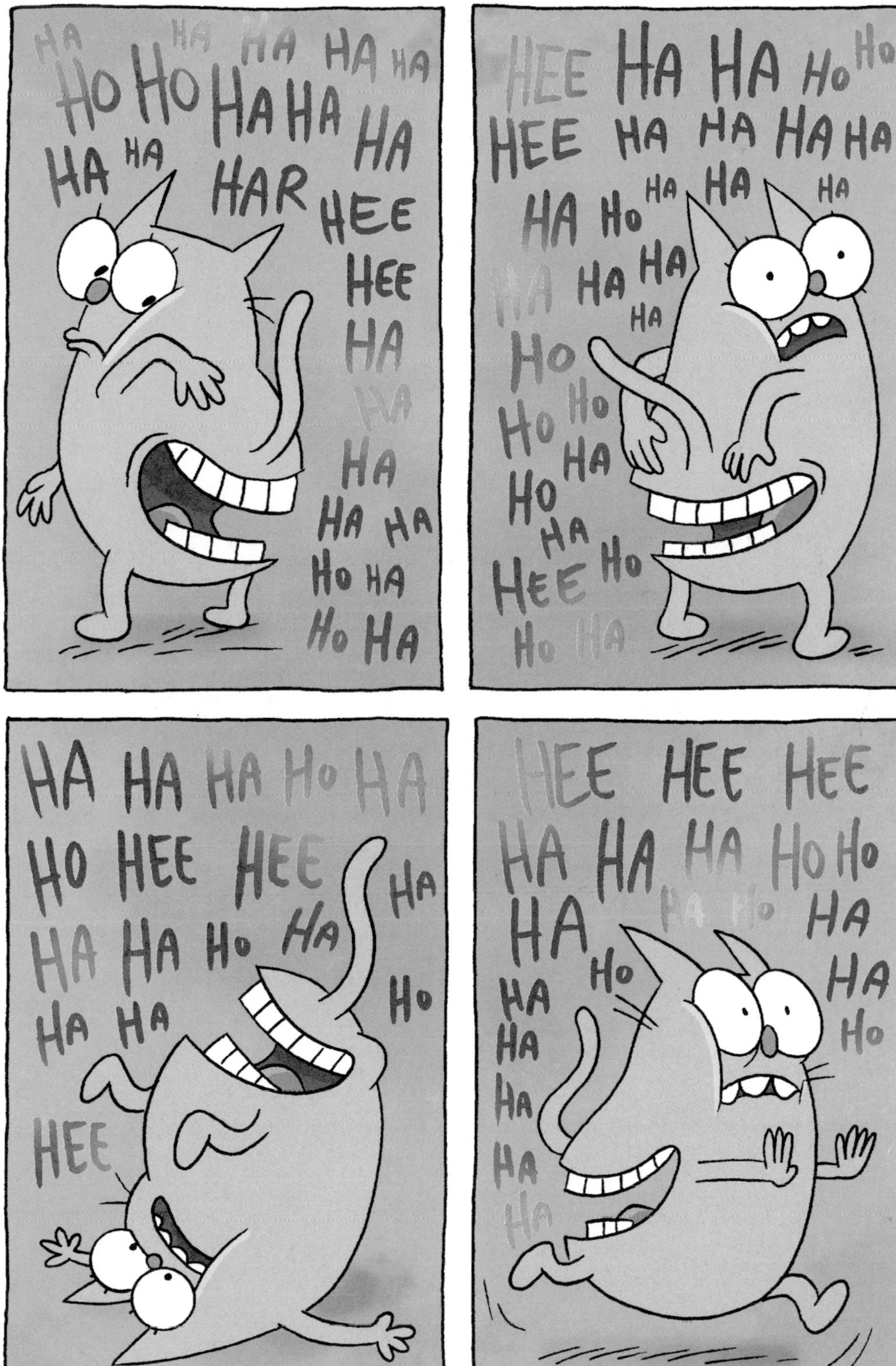
HA HA HA HA HA
HO HO HA HA HA
HA HA HAR HEE
HEE HA HA HA
HA HA HA HO HA HO HA
HEE HA HA HO HO
HEE HA HA HA HA
HA HO HA HA HA
HA HA HA HA
HO HO HO HA HO HA
HEE HO HO HA
HA HA HA HO HA
HO HEE HEE HA
HA HA HO HA
HA HA HO
HEE
HEE HEE HEE
HA HA HA HO HO
HA HA HO HA
HA HO HA
HA HO
HA HA HA HA

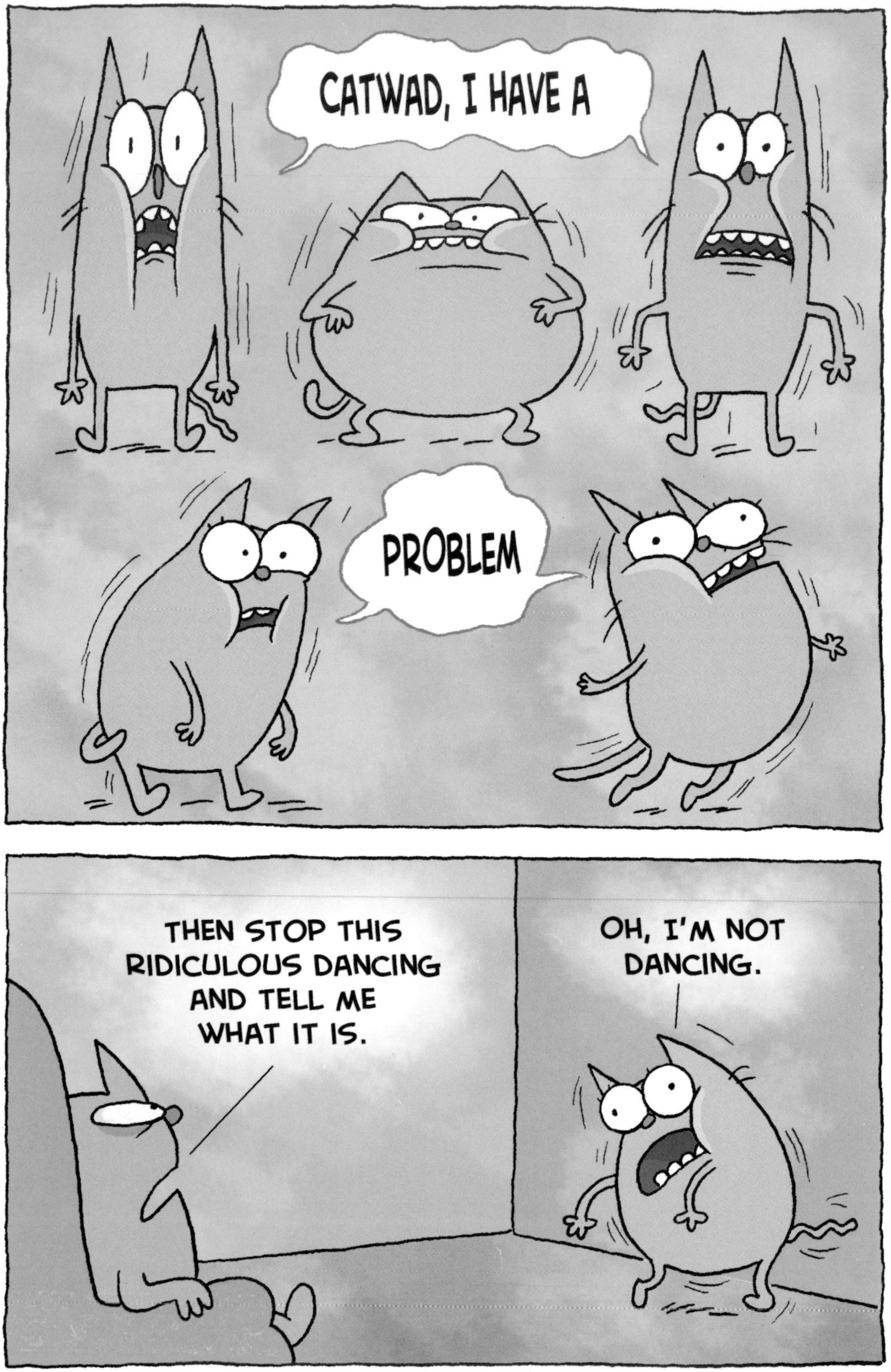
CATWAD, I HAVE A
PROBLEM
THEN STOP THIS RIDICULOUS DANCING AND TELL ME WHAT IT IS.
OH, I'M NOT DANCING.

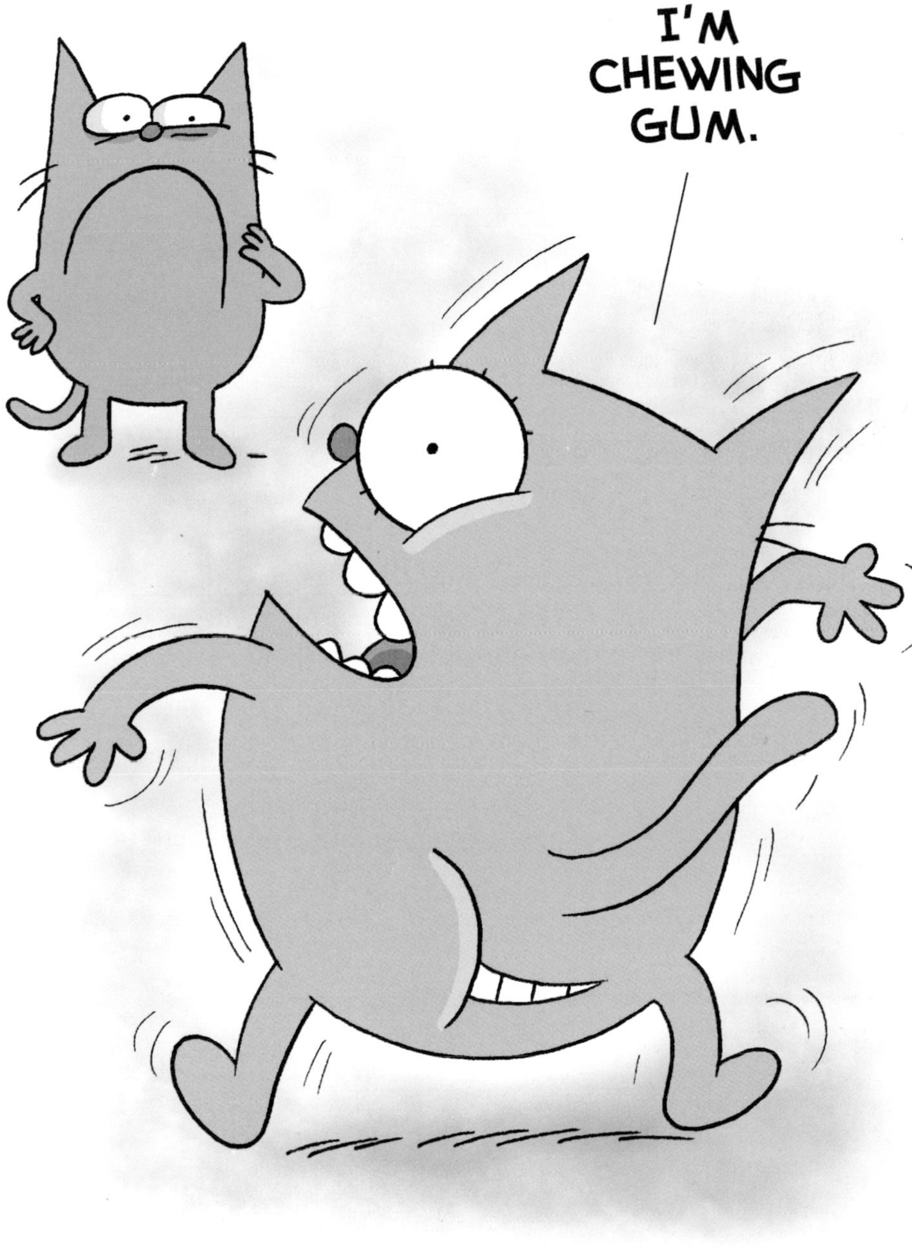
I'M CHEWING GUM.

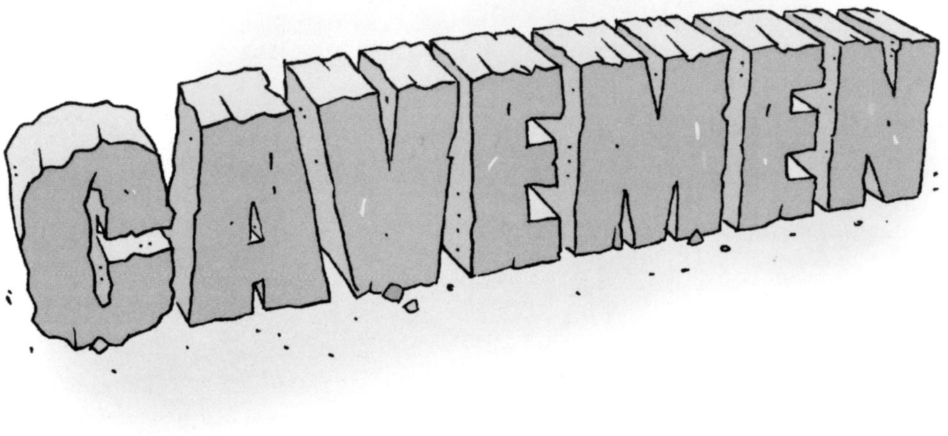
CAVEMEN

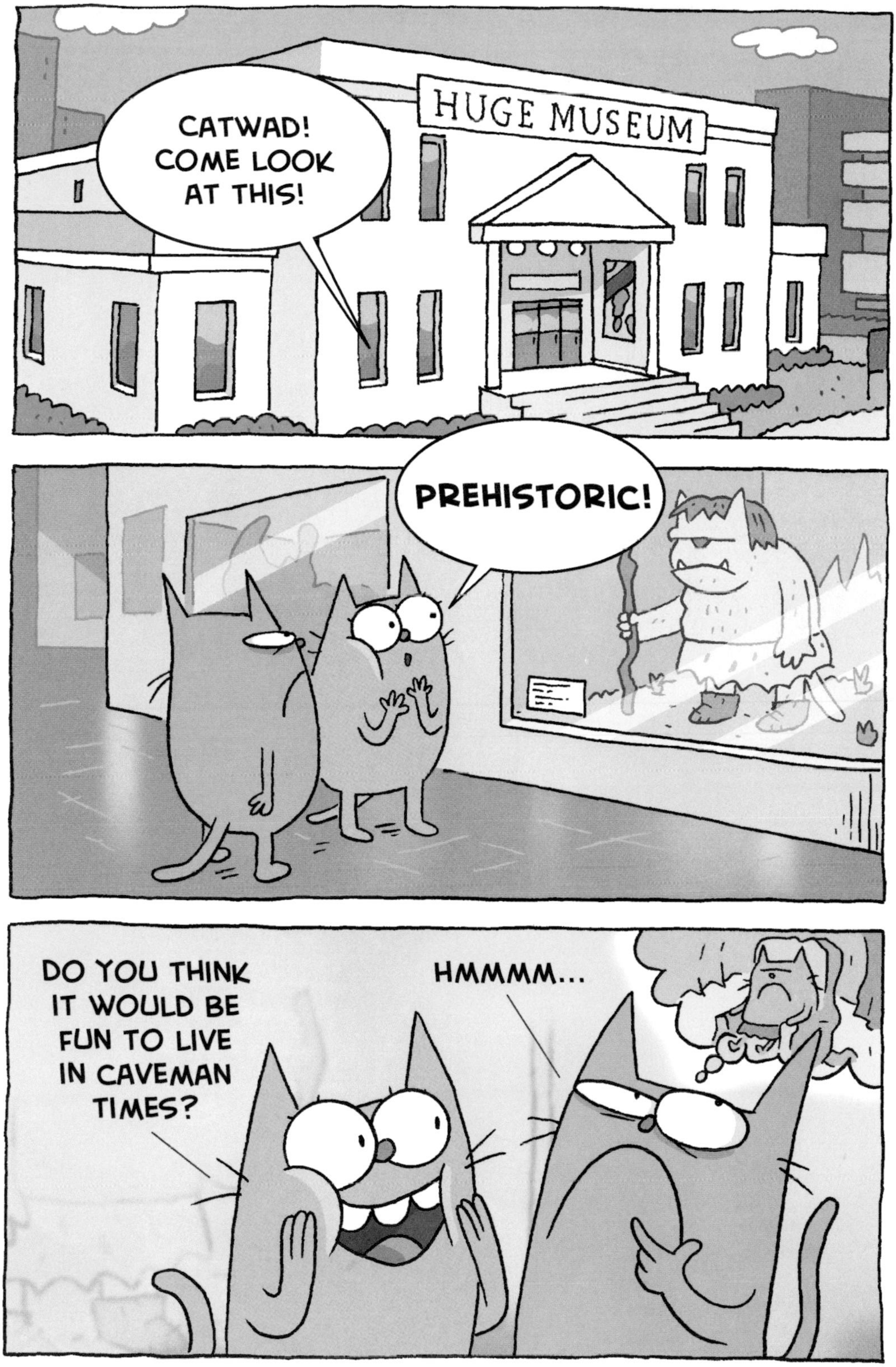
HUGE MUSEUM
CATWAD! COME LOOK AT THIS!
PREHISTORIC!
DO YOU THINK IT WOULD BE FUN TO LIVE IN CAVEMAN TIMES?
HMMMM...

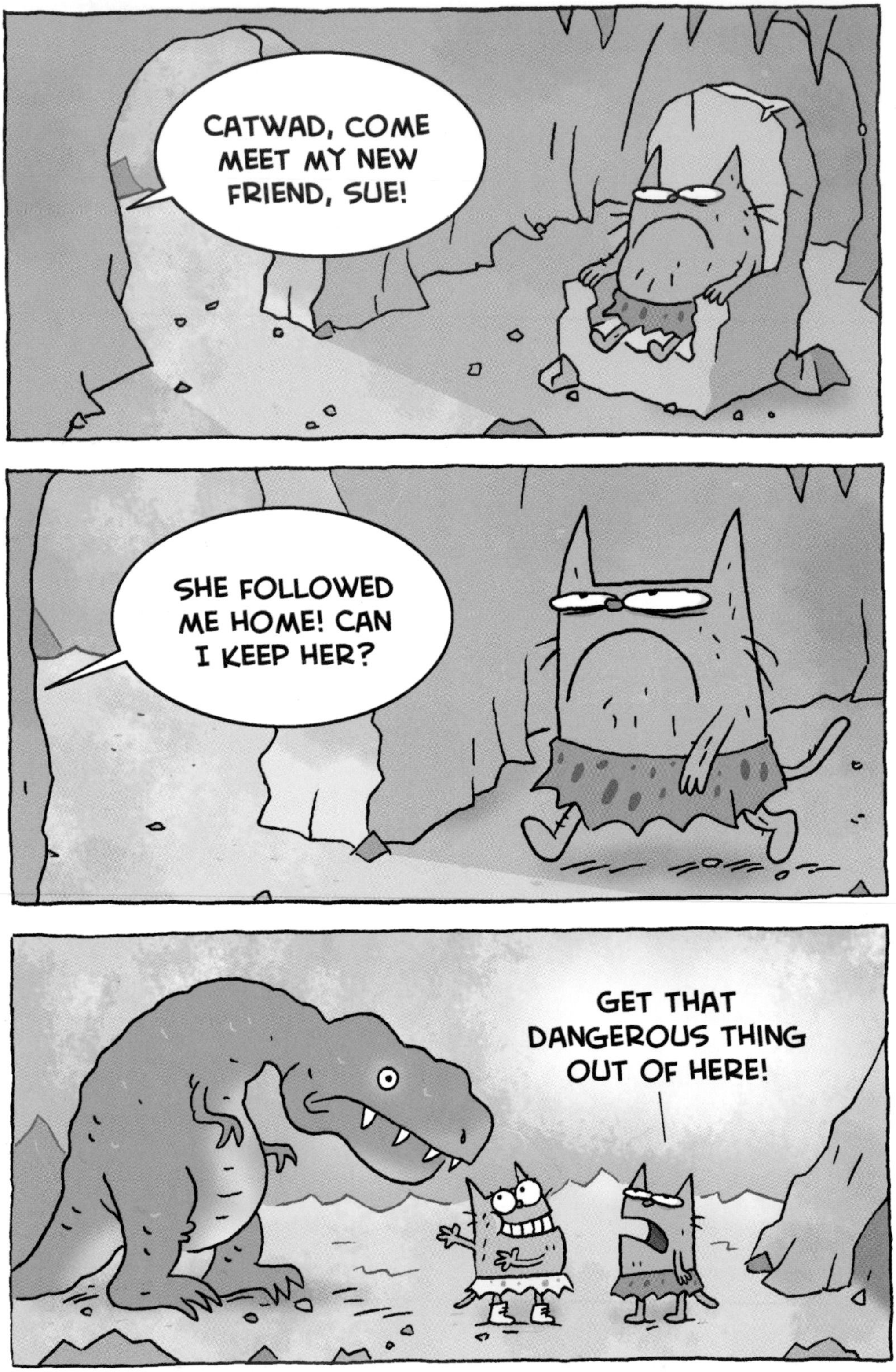
CATWAD, COME MEET MY NEW FRIEND, SUE!
SHE FOLLOWED ME HOME! CAN I KEEP HER?
GET THAT DANGEROUS THING OUT OF HERE!

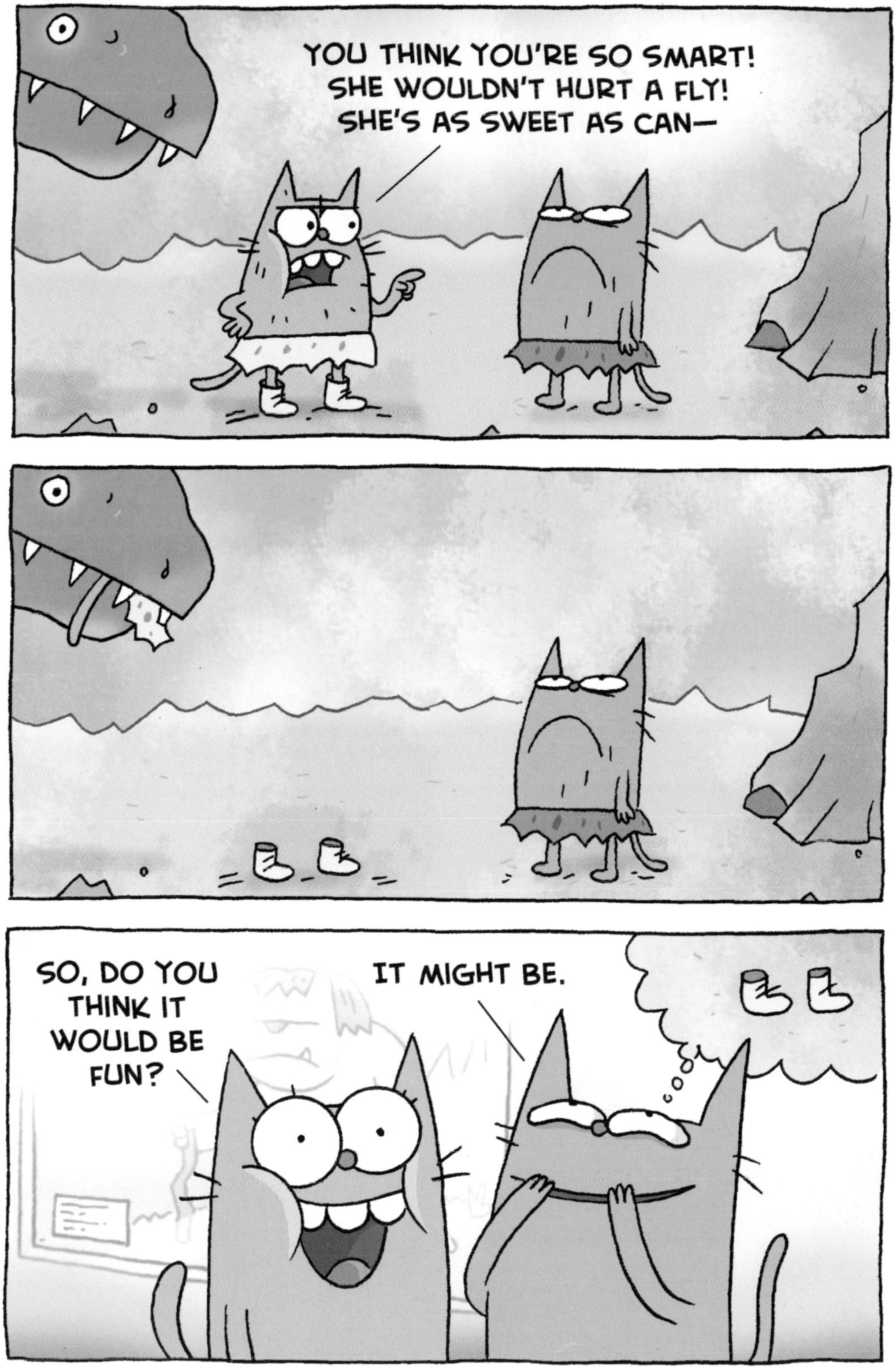
YOU THINK YOU'RE SO SMART! SHE WOULDN'T HURT A FLY! SHE'S AS SWEET AS CAN—
SO, DO YOU THINK IT WOULD BE FUN?
IT MIGHT BE.

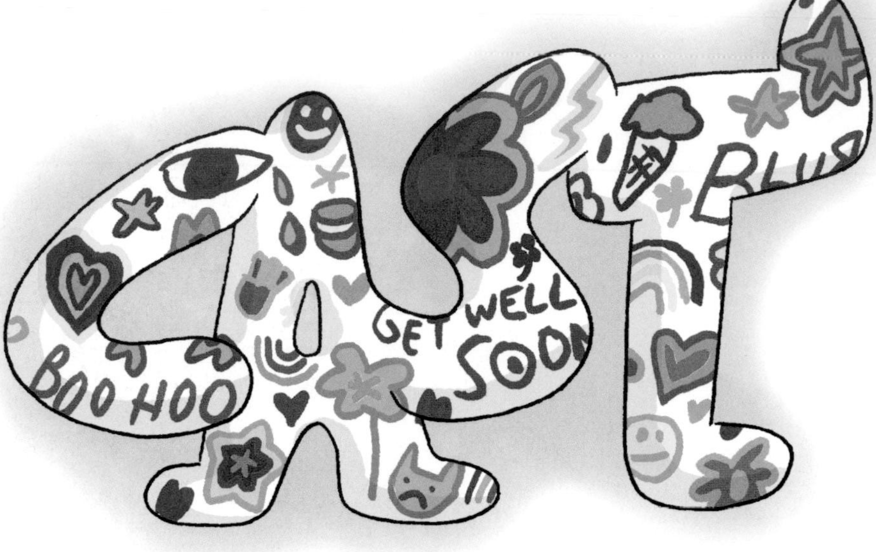
BOO HOO
GET WELL

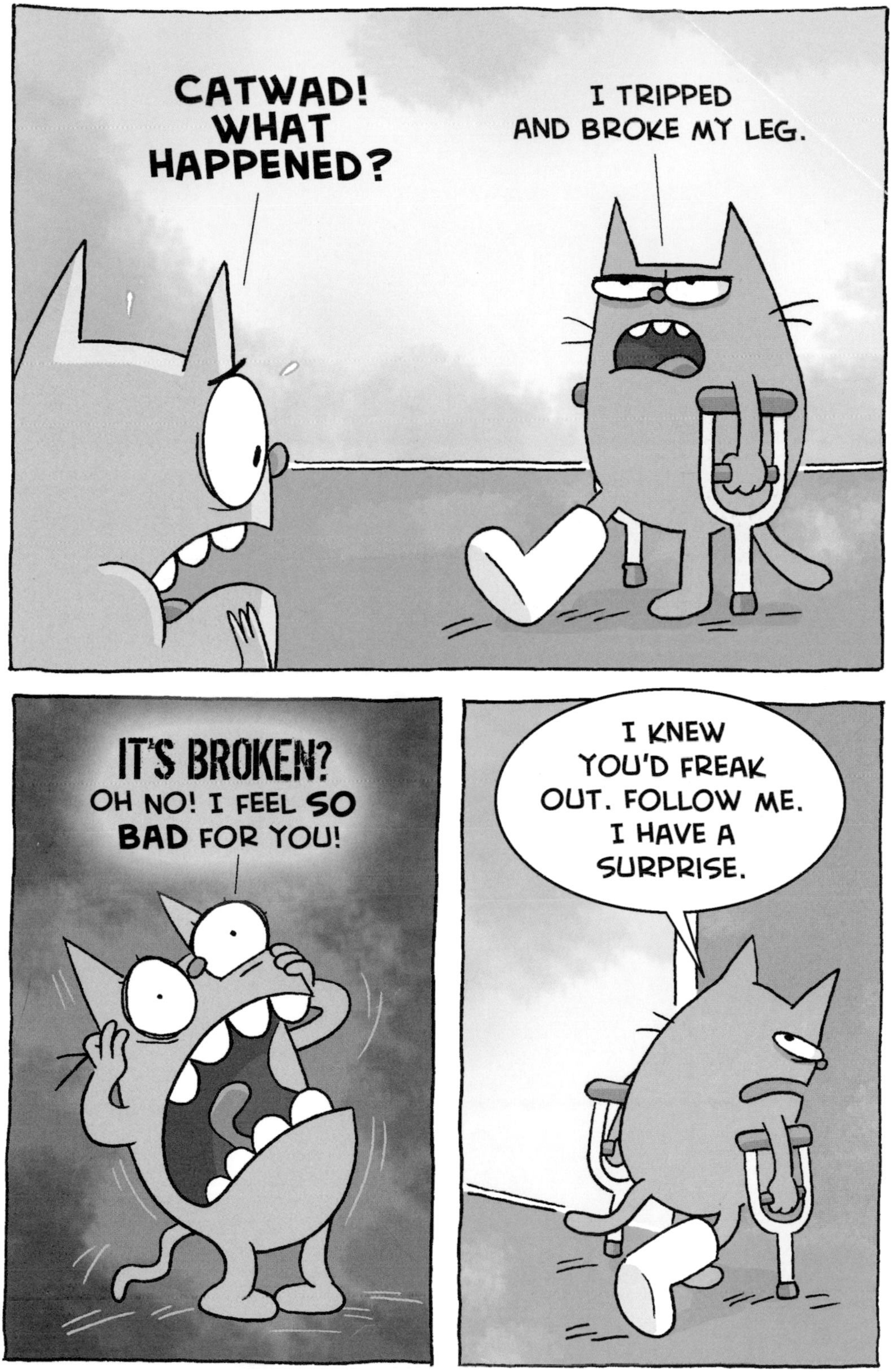
CATWAD! WHAT HAPPENED?
I TRIPPED AND BROKE MY LEG.
IT'S BROKEN? OH NO! I FEEL SO BAD FOR YOU!
I KNEW YOU'D FREAK OUT. FOLLOW ME. I HAVE A SURPRISE.

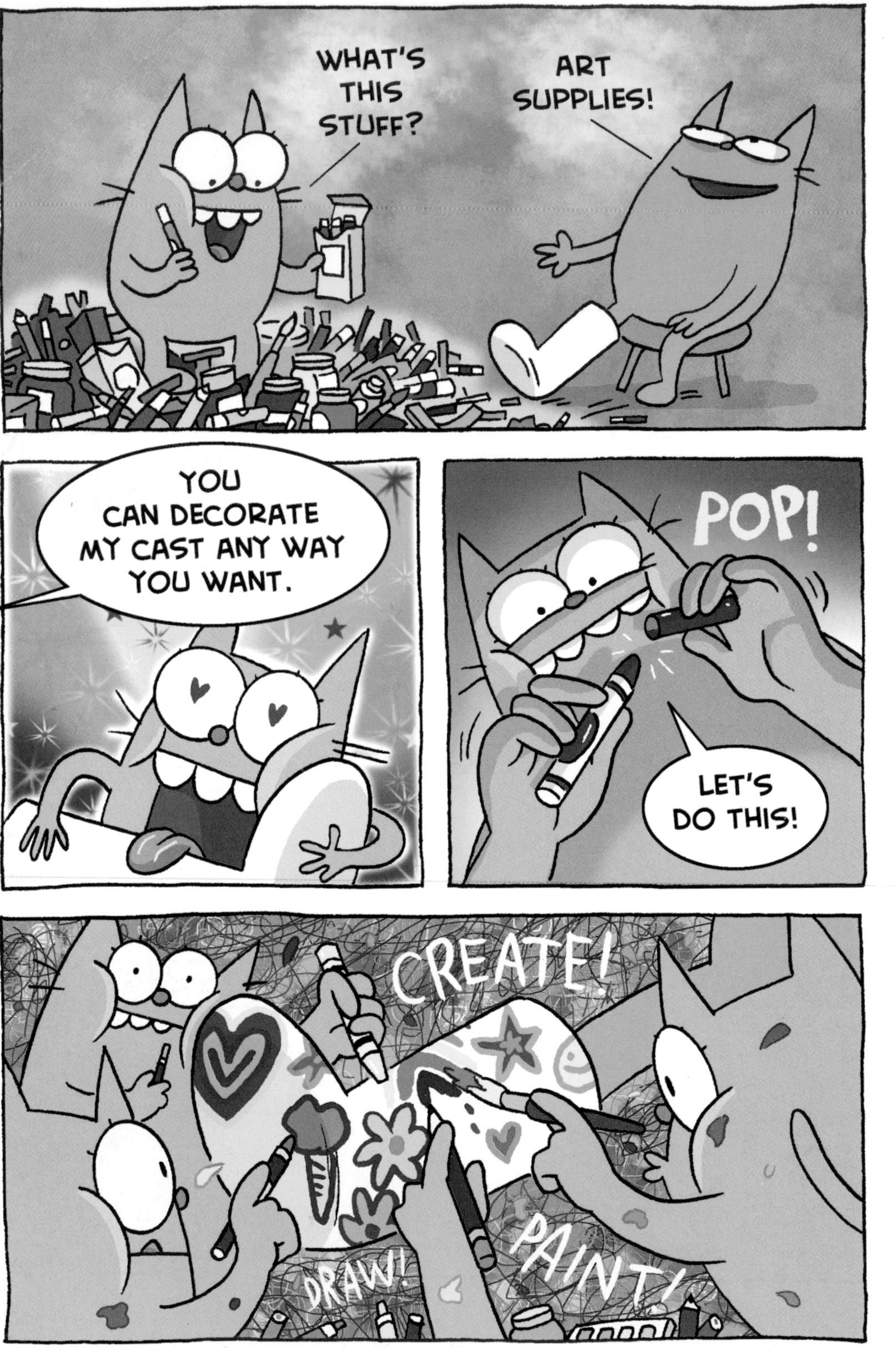
WHAT'S THIS STUFF?
ART SUPPLIES!
YOU CAN DECORATE MY CAST ANY WAY YOU WANT.
POP!
LET'S DO THIS!
CREATE!
DRAW!
PAINT!

I FILLED UP THE WHOLE CAST!

I GUESS THAT MEANS YOU'RE DONE.

AWW! BUT THAT WAS SO MUCH FUN!

CHEER UP. I'M SURE THERE'S ANOTHER CAST FOR YOU TO DECORATE RIGHT AROUND THE CORNER.

OKAY.

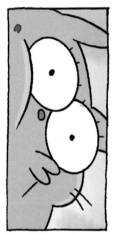

CATWAD ALWAYS HAS THE BEST IDEAS!

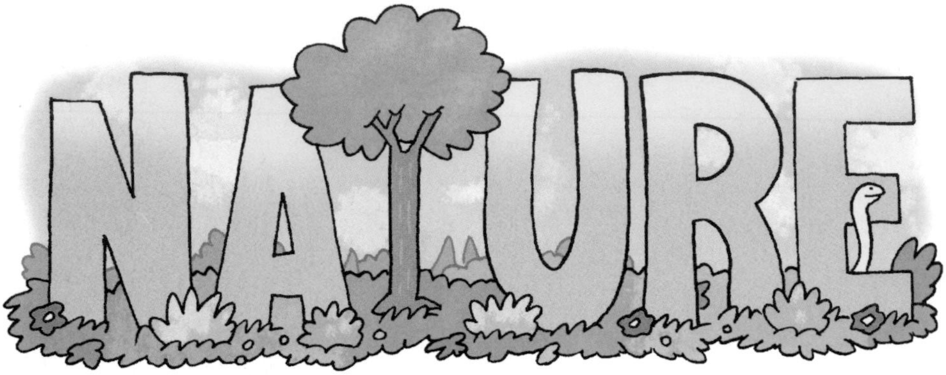
NATURE

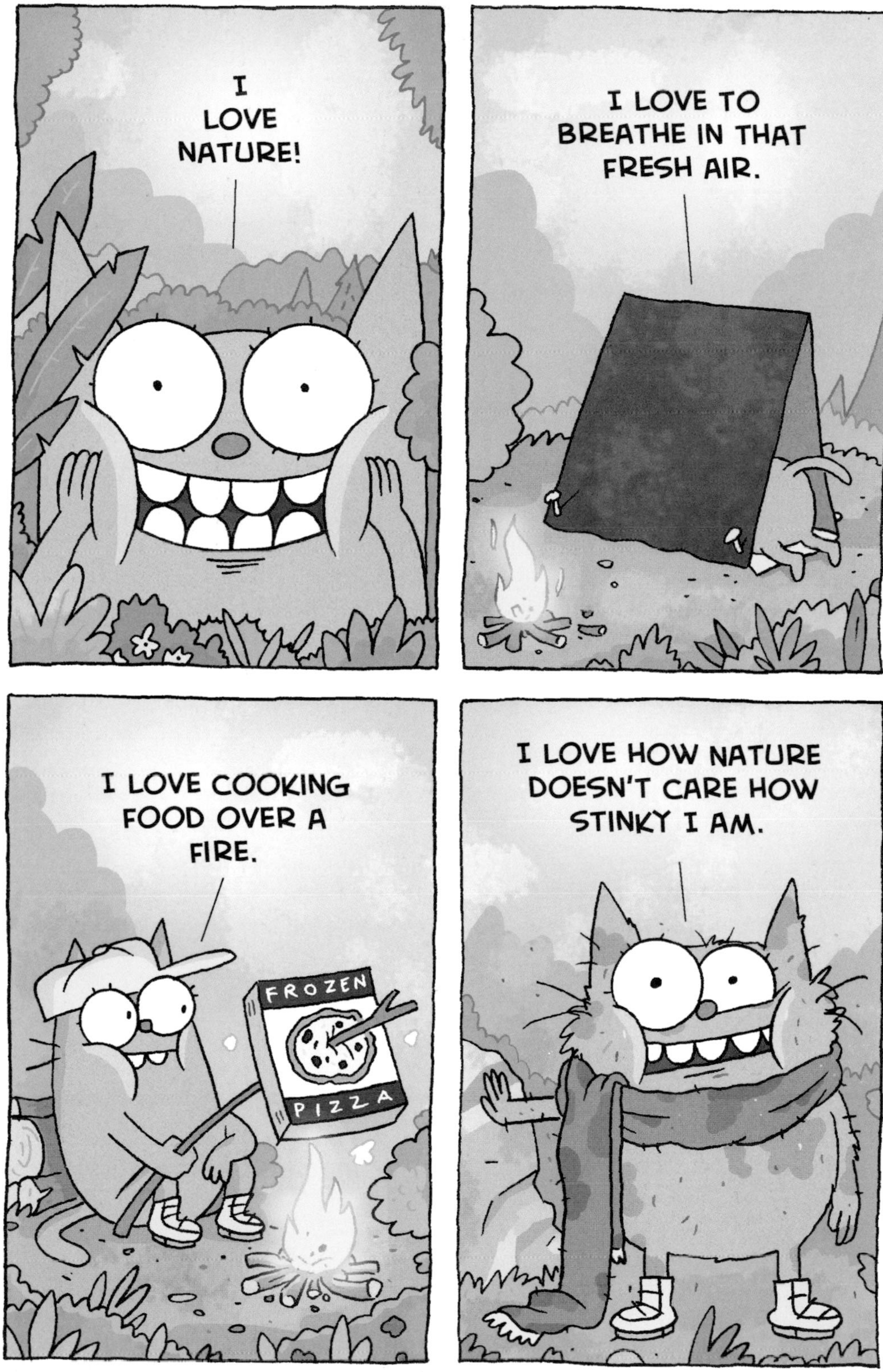
I LOVE NATURE!
I LOVE TO BREATHE IN THAT FRESH AIR.
I LOVE COOKING FOOD OVER A FIRE.
FROZEN
PIZZA
I LOVE HOW NATURE DOESN'T CARE HOW STINKY I AM.

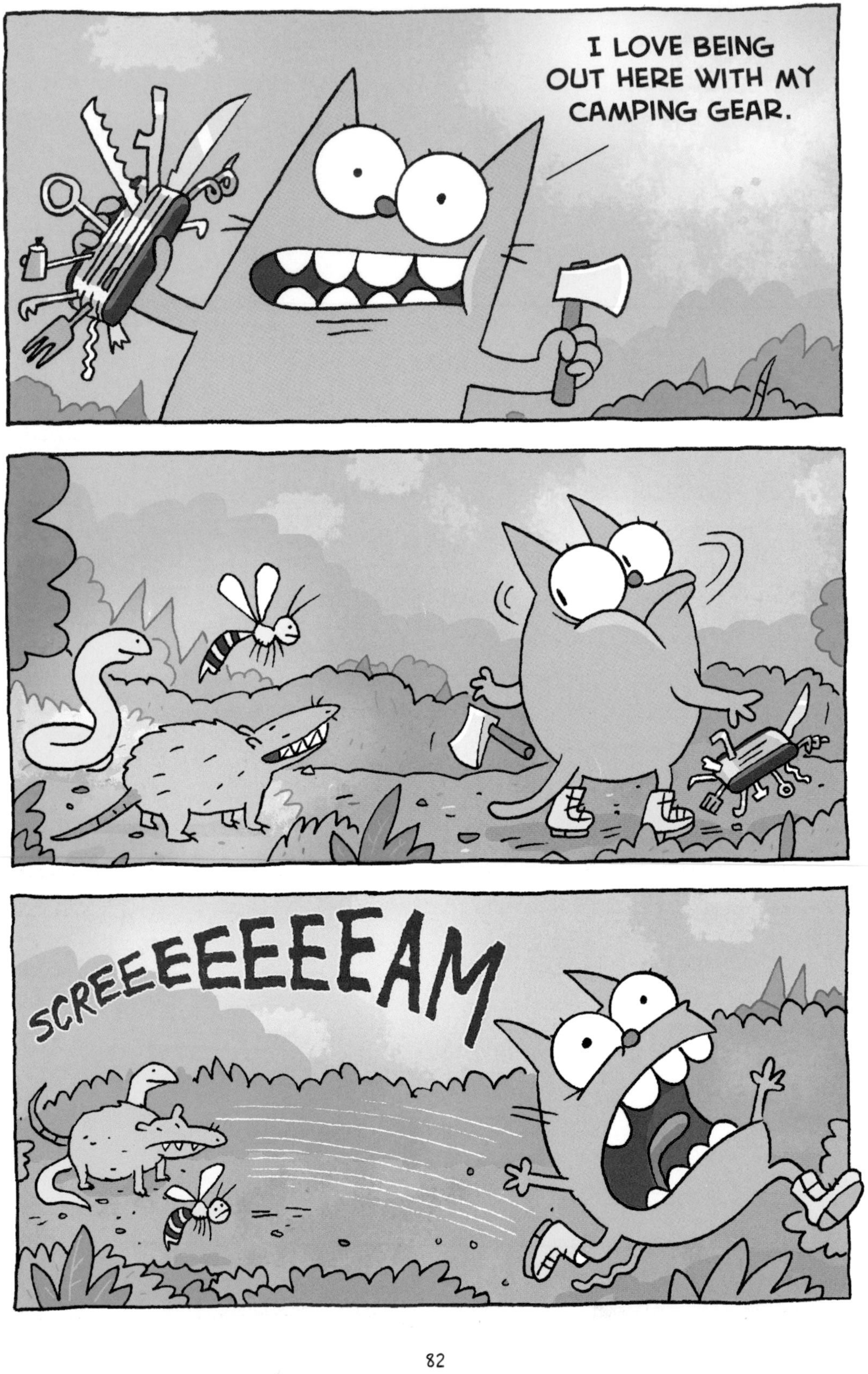
I LOVE BEING OUT HERE WITH MY CAMPING GEAR.
SCREEEEEEEEEAM

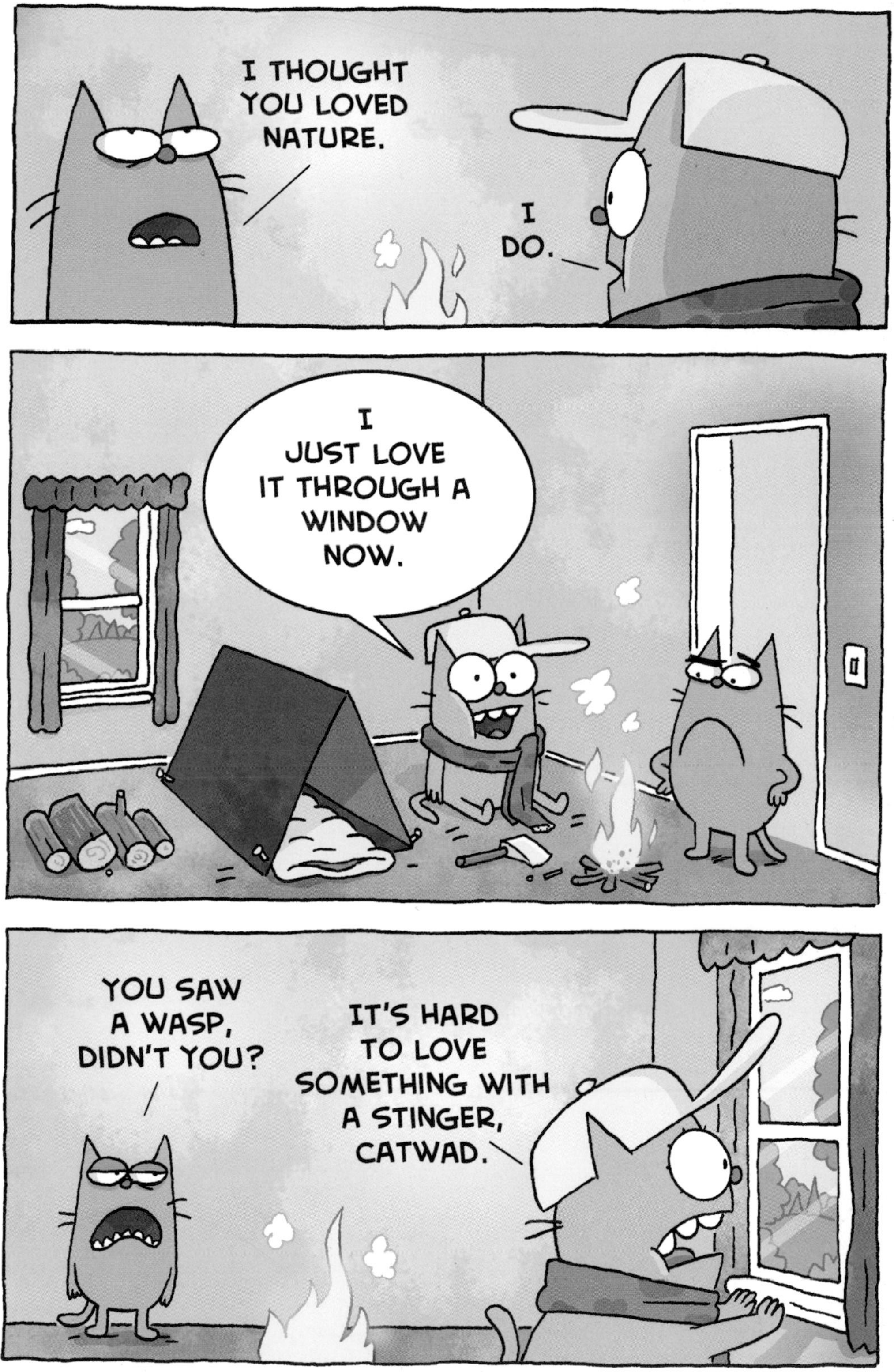
I THOUGHT YOU LOVED NATURE.
I DO.
I JUST LOVE IT THROUGH A WINDOW NOW.
YOU SAW A WASP, DIDN'T YOU?
IT'S HARD TO LOVE SOMETHING WITH A STINGER, CATWAD.

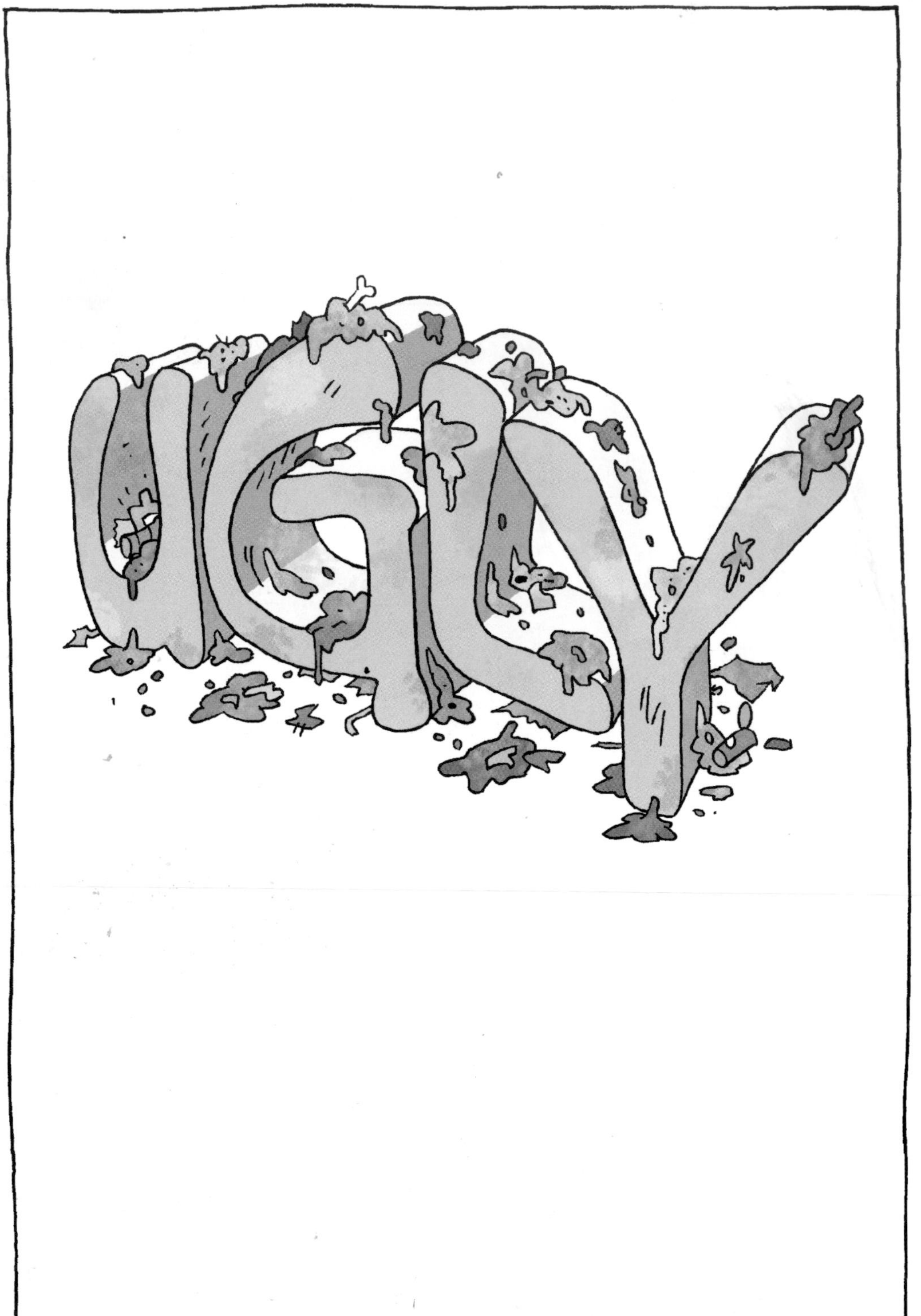
UGLY

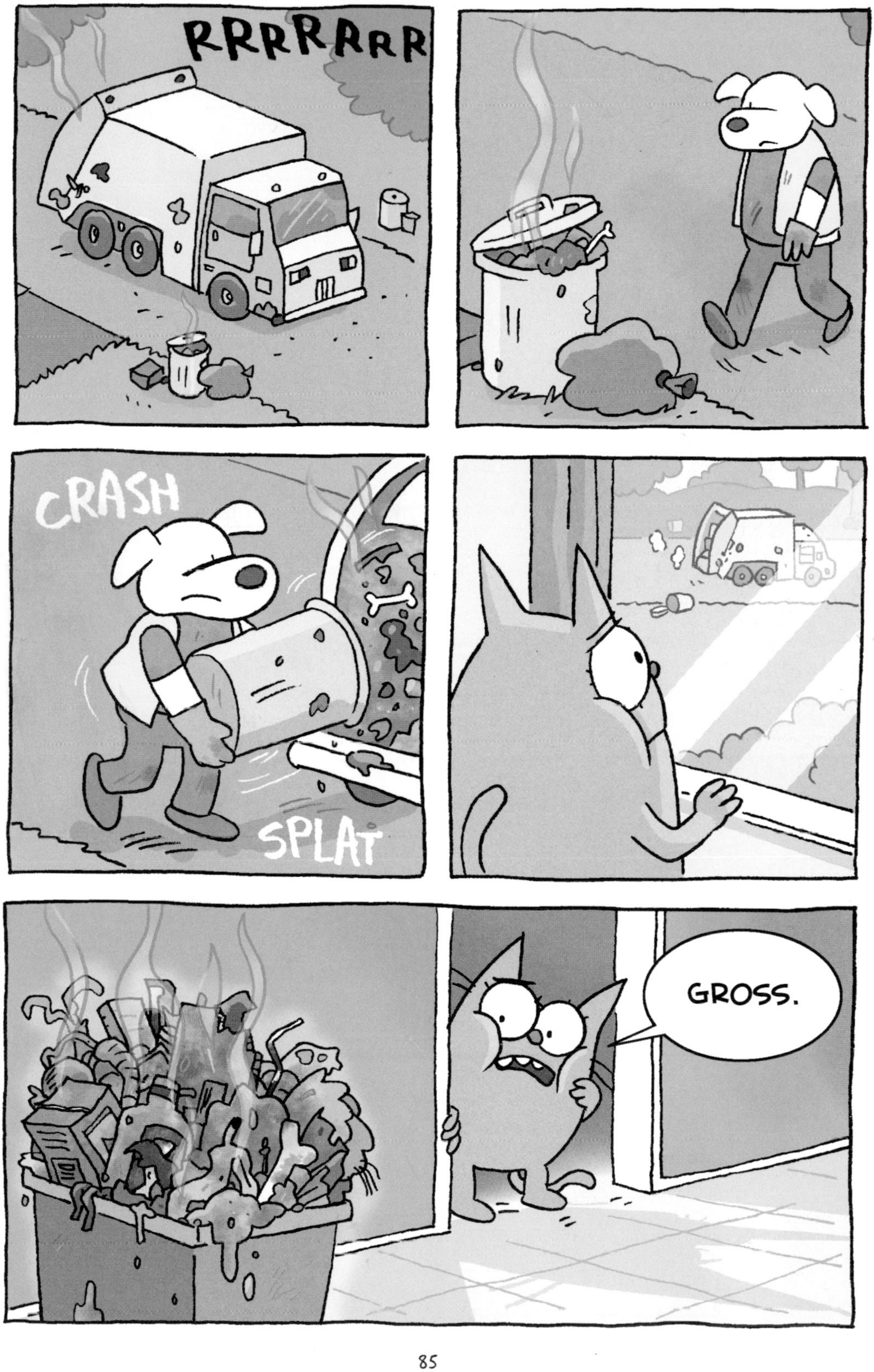
RRRRRRR
CRASH
SPLAT
GROSS.

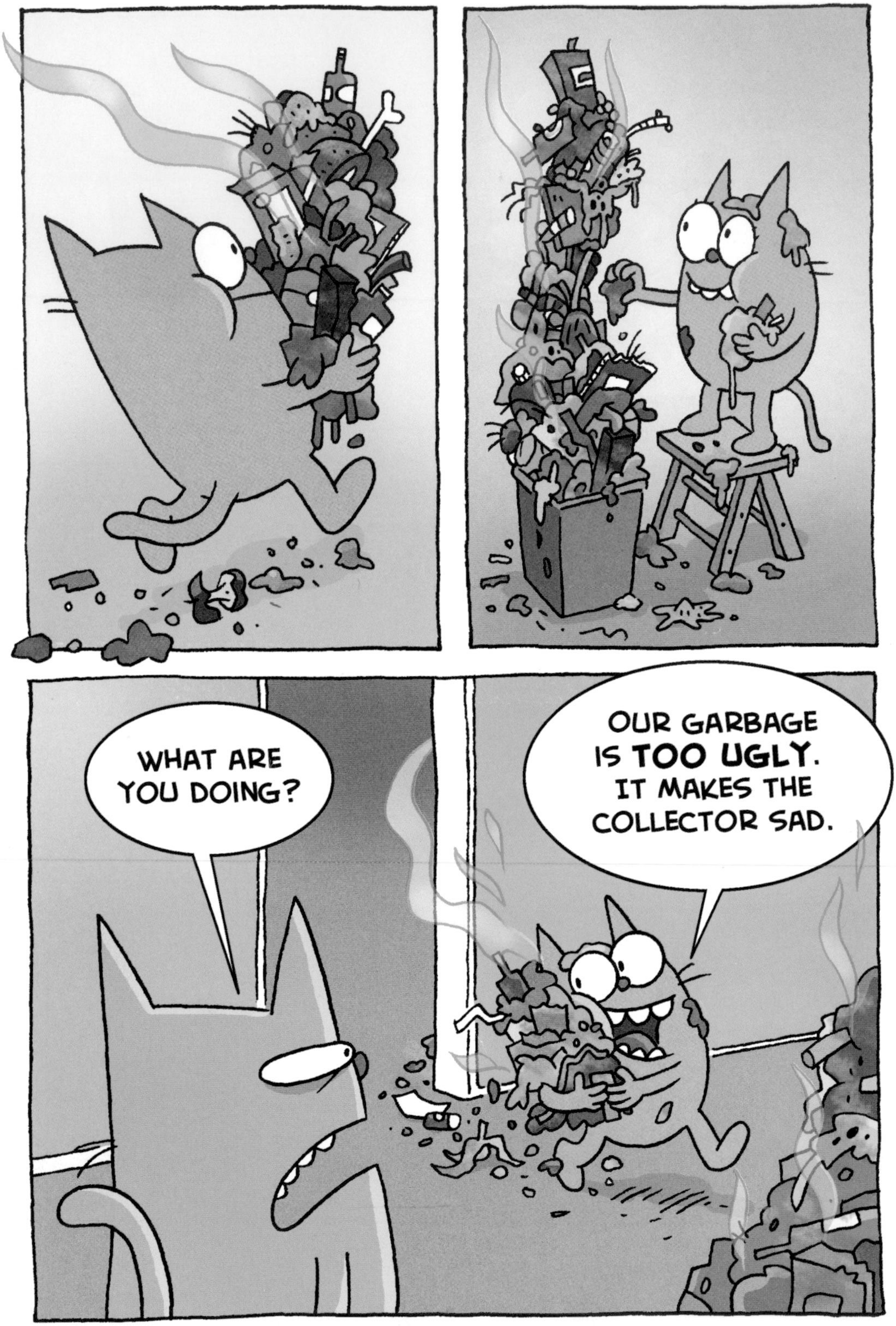
WHAT ARE YOU DOING?
OUR GARBAGE IS **TOO UGLY**. IT MAKES THE COLLECTOR SAD.

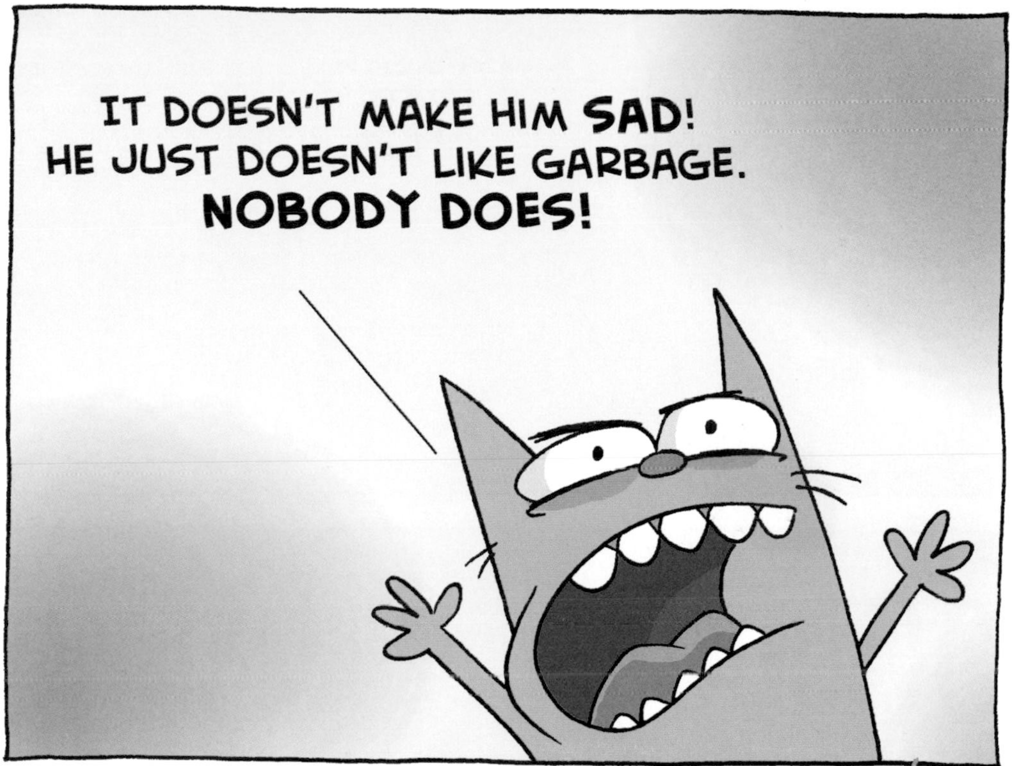
IT DOESN'T MAKE HIM SAD! HE JUST DOESN'T LIKE GARBAGE. NOBODY DOES!

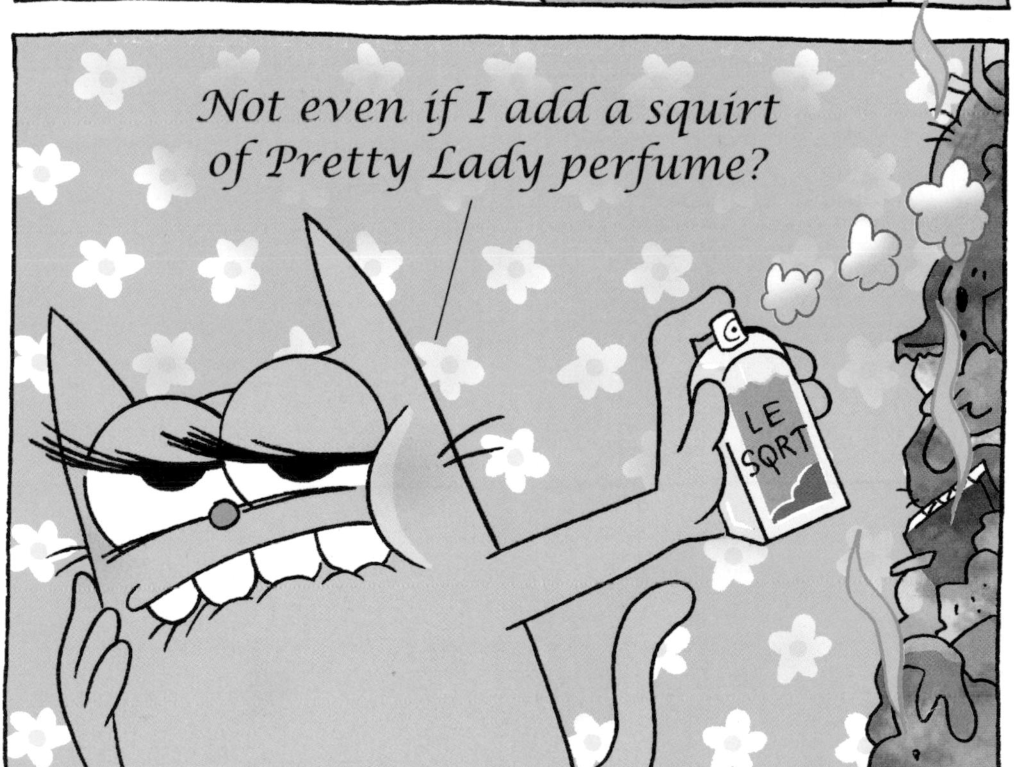
Not even if I add a squirt of Pretty Lady perfume?
LE SQRT

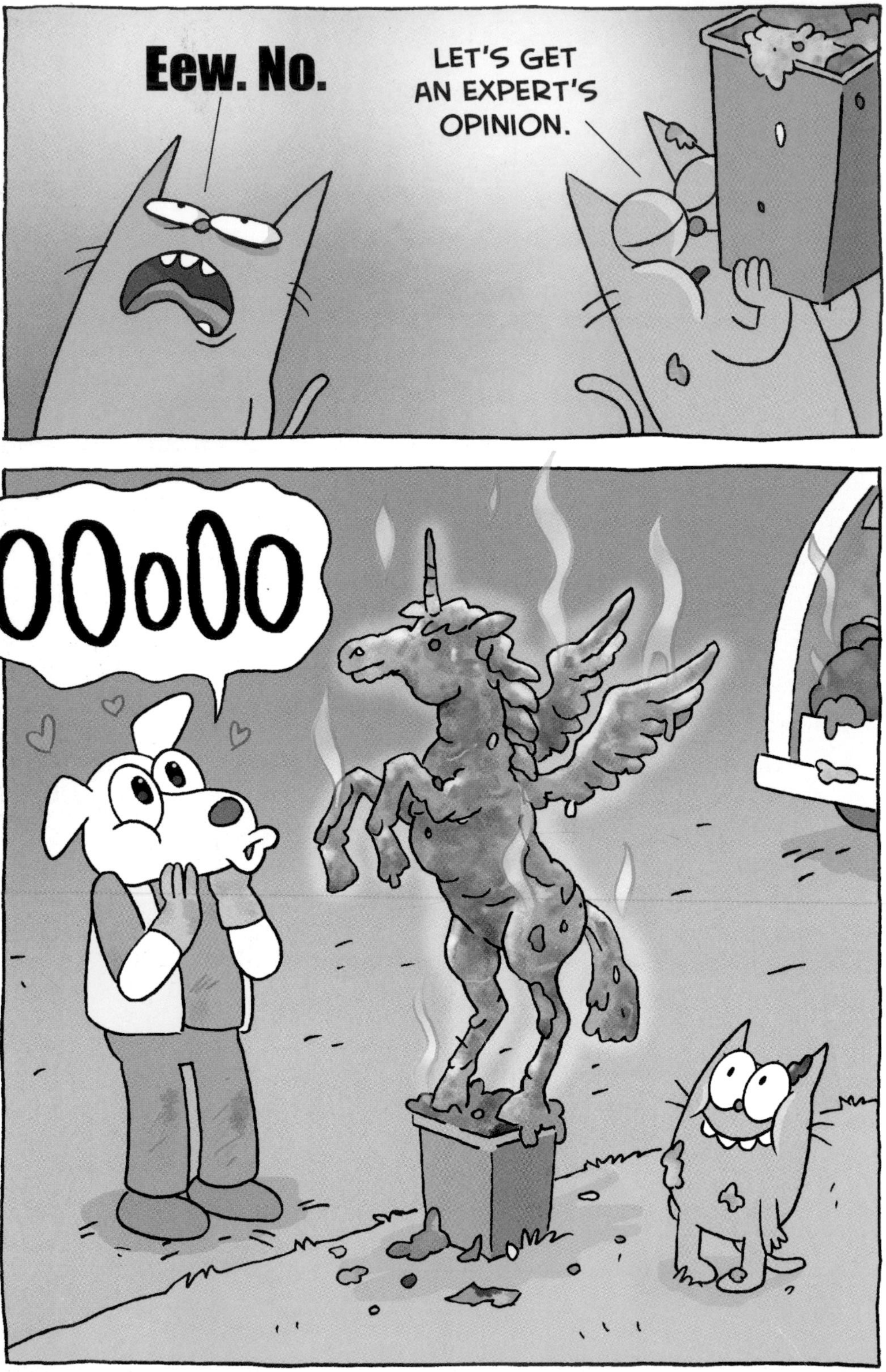
Eew. No.
LET'S GET AN EXPERT'S OPINION.
OOoOO

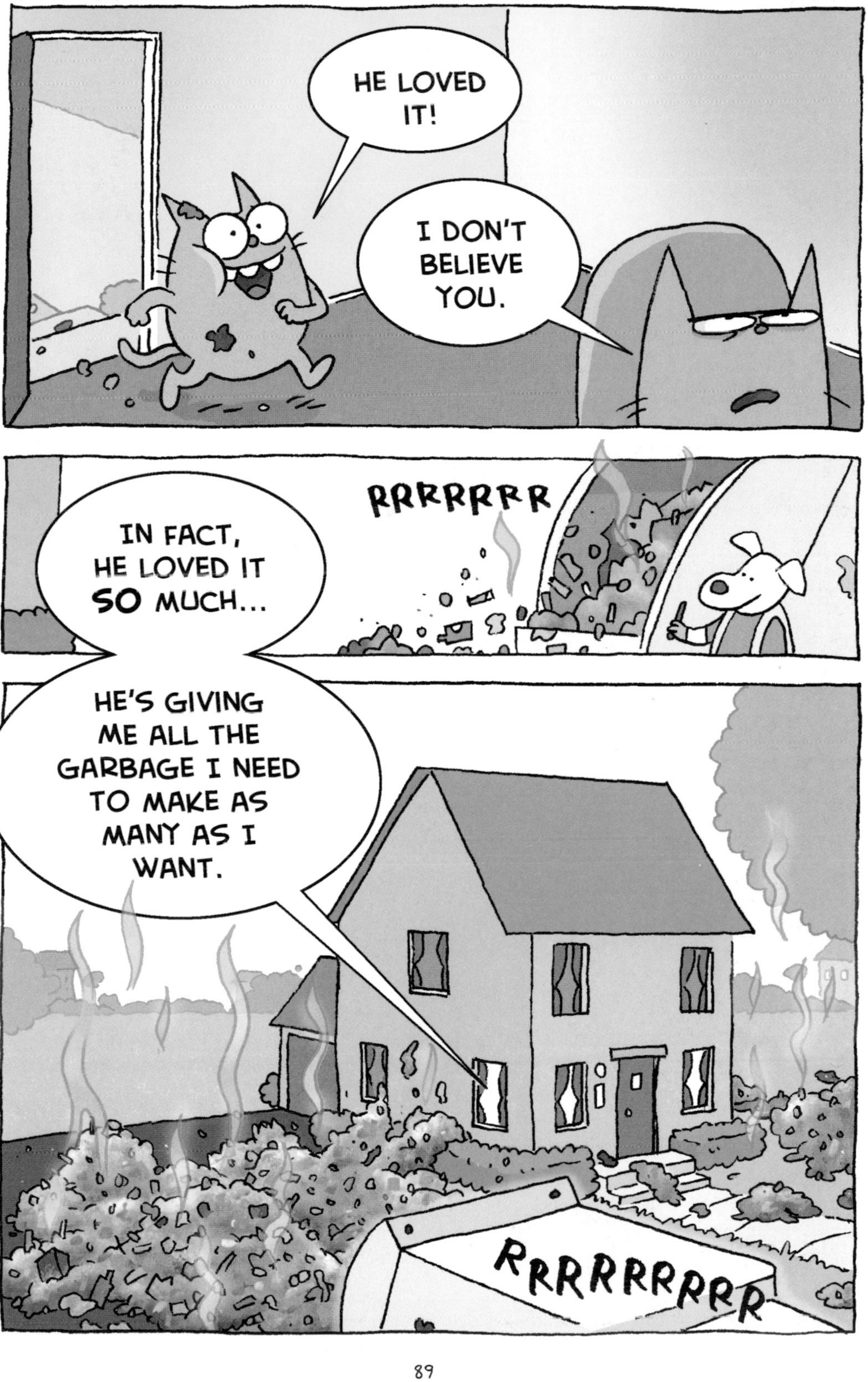
HE LOVED IT!
I DON'T BELIEVE YOU.
RRRRRRR
IN FACT, HE LOVED IT **SO** MUCH...
HE'S GIVING ME ALL THE GARBAGE I NEED TO MAKE AS MANY AS I WANT.
RRRRRRRRRR

UPSIDE DOWN

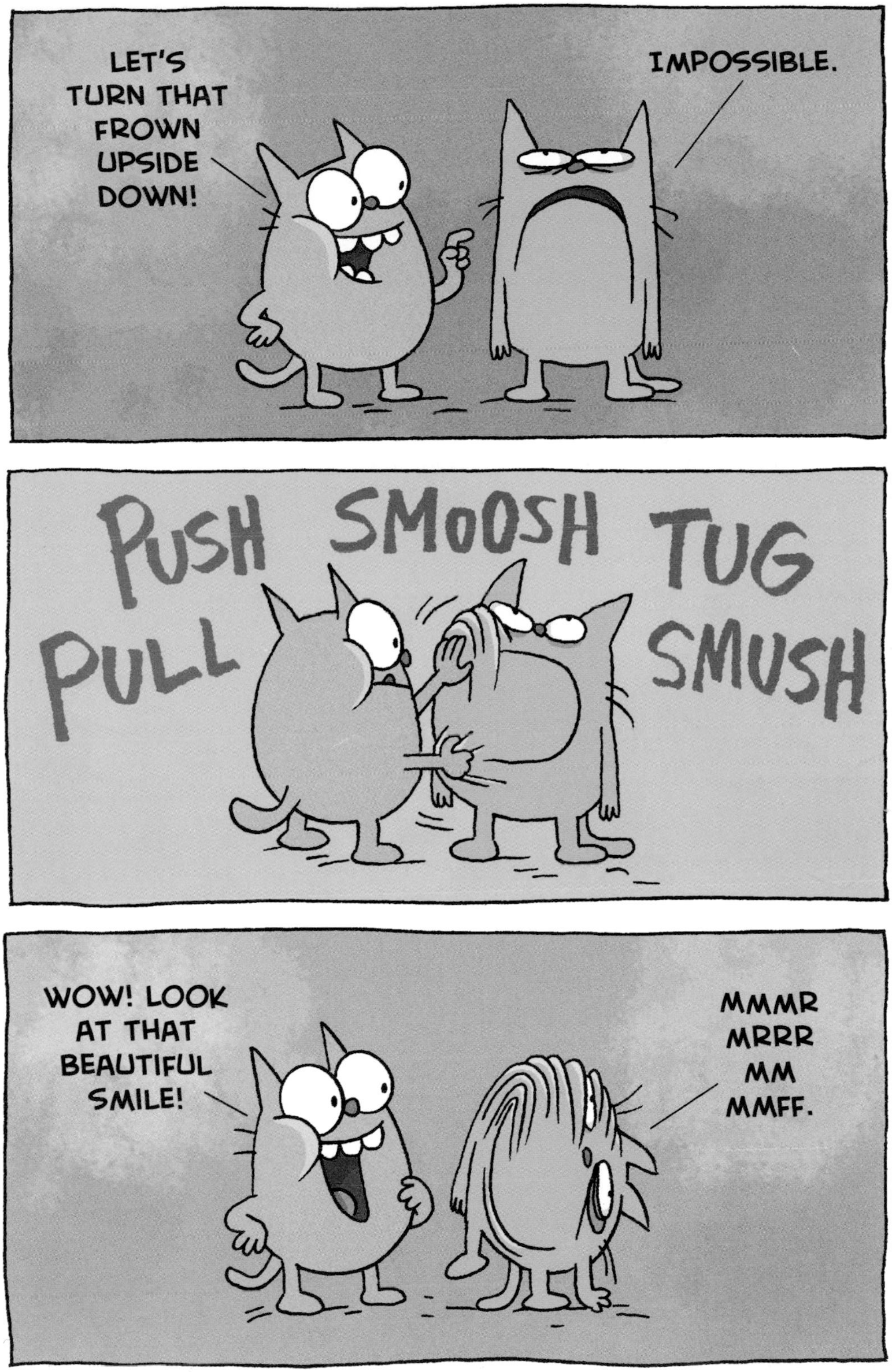
LET'S TURN THAT FROWN UPSIDE DOWN!
IMPOSSIBLE.
PUSH
SMOOSH
TUG
PULL
SMUSH
WOW! LOOK AT THAT BEAUTIFUL SMILE!
MMMR MRRR MM MMFF.

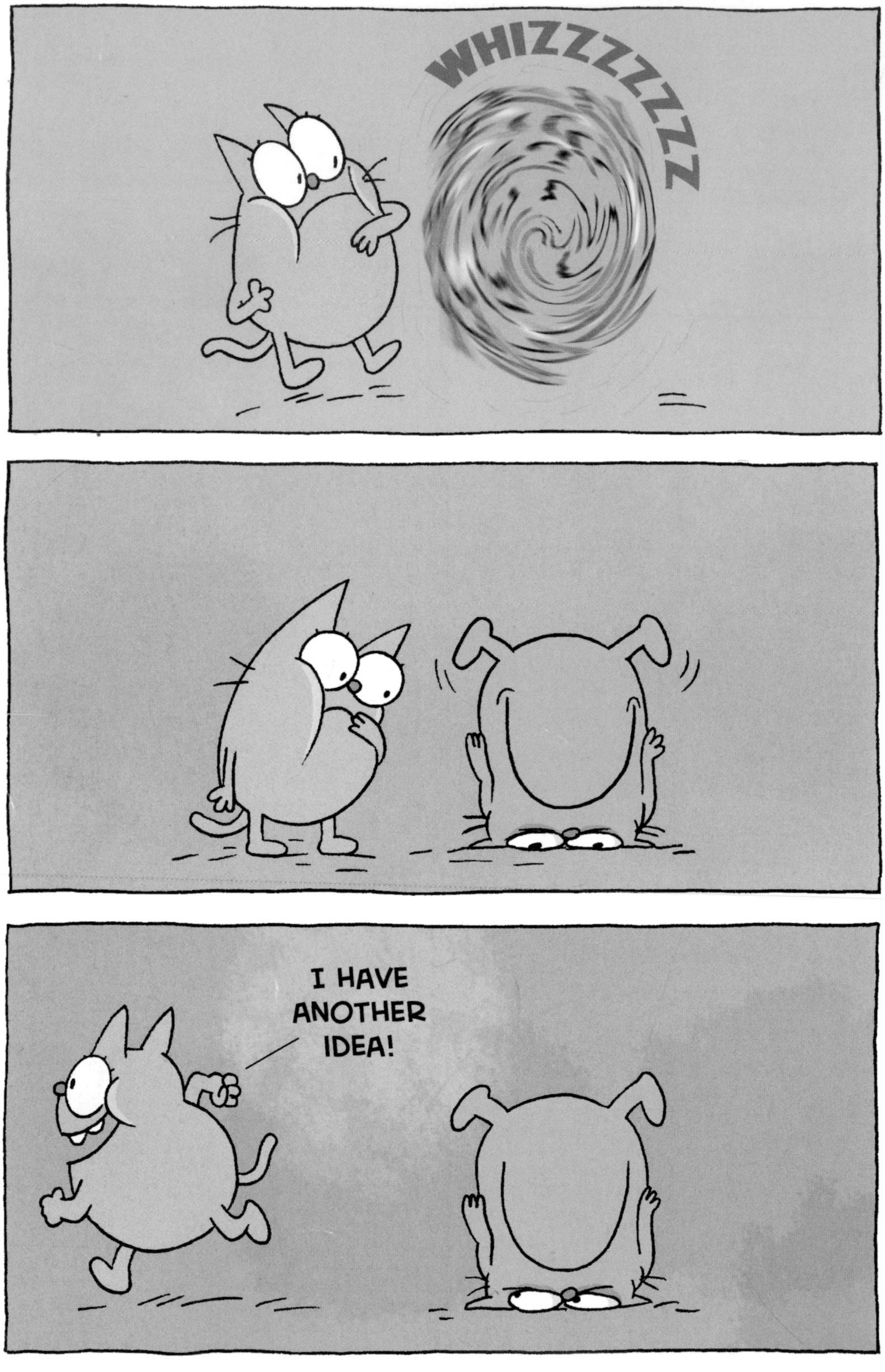
WHIZZZZZZZ
I HAVE ANOTHER IDEA!

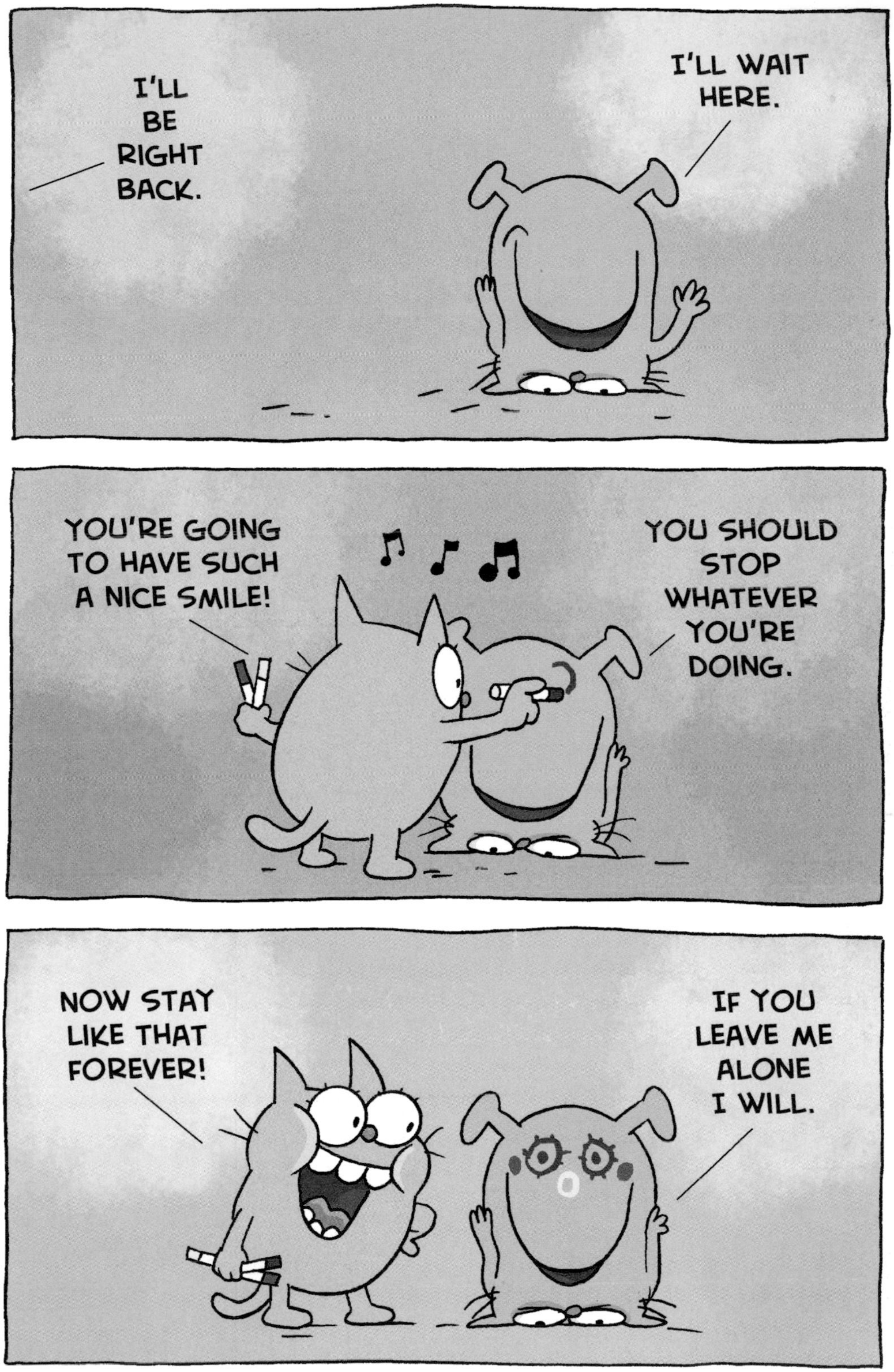
I'LL BE RIGHT BACK.
I'LL WAIT HERE.
YOU'RE GOING TO HAVE SUCH A NICE SMILE!
YOU SHOULD STOP WHATEVER YOU'RE DOING.
NOW STAY LIKE THAT FOREVER!
IF YOU LEAVE ME ALONE I WILL.

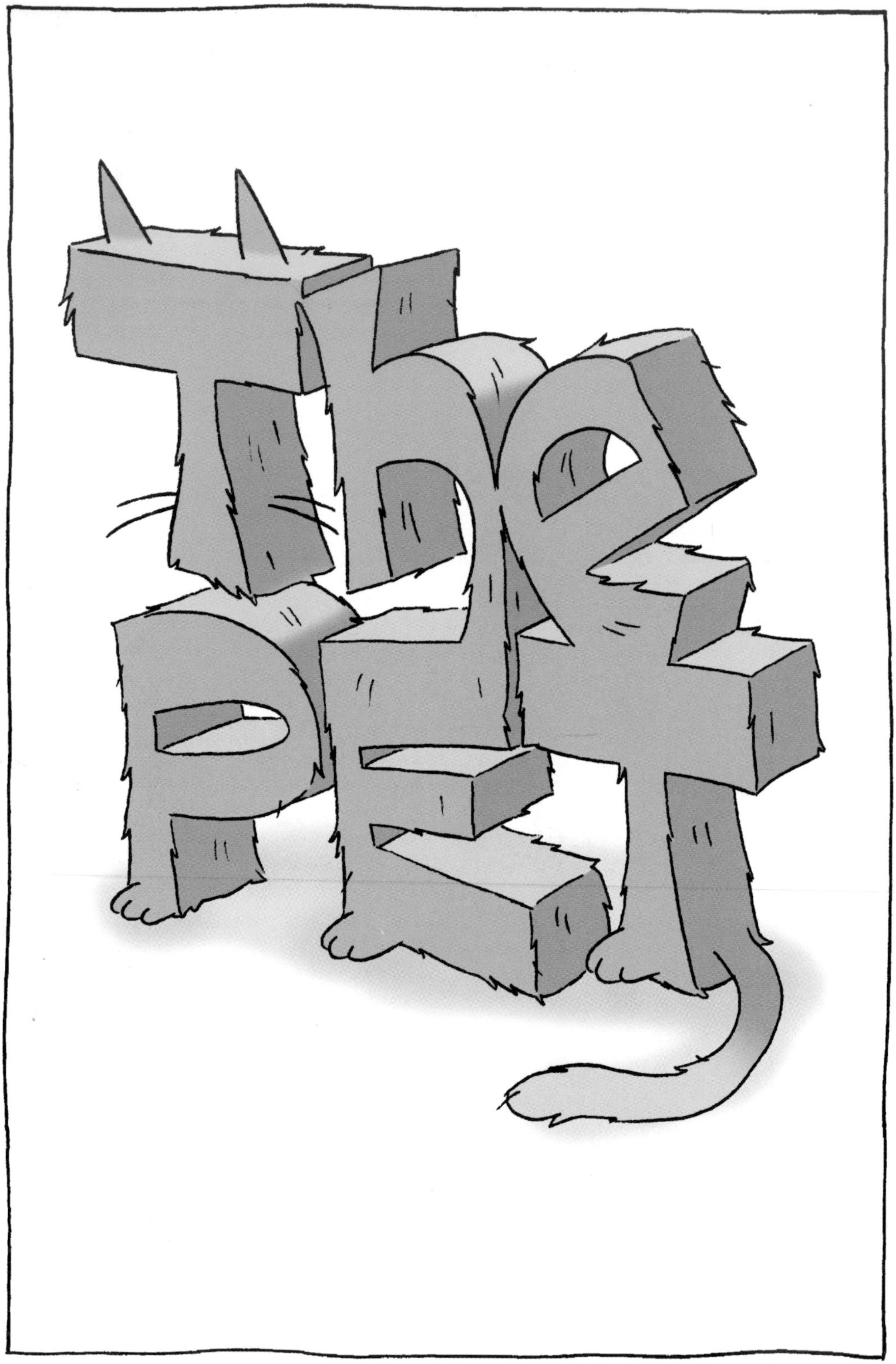
The pet

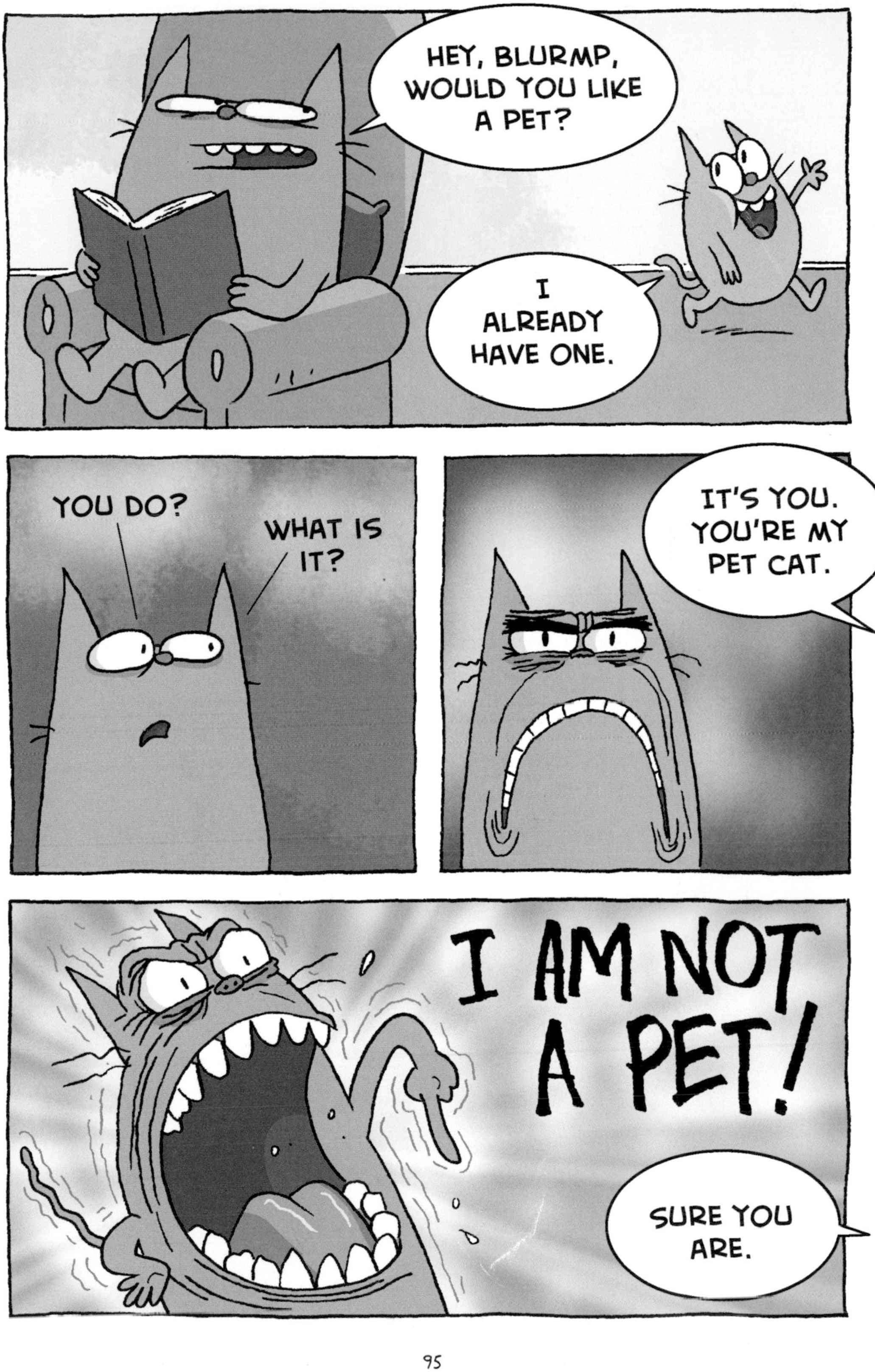
HEY, BLURMP, WOULD YOU LIKE A PET?
I ALREADY HAVE ONE.
YOU DO?
WHAT IS IT?
IT'S YOU. YOU'RE MY PET CAT.
I AM NOT A PET!
SURE YOU ARE.

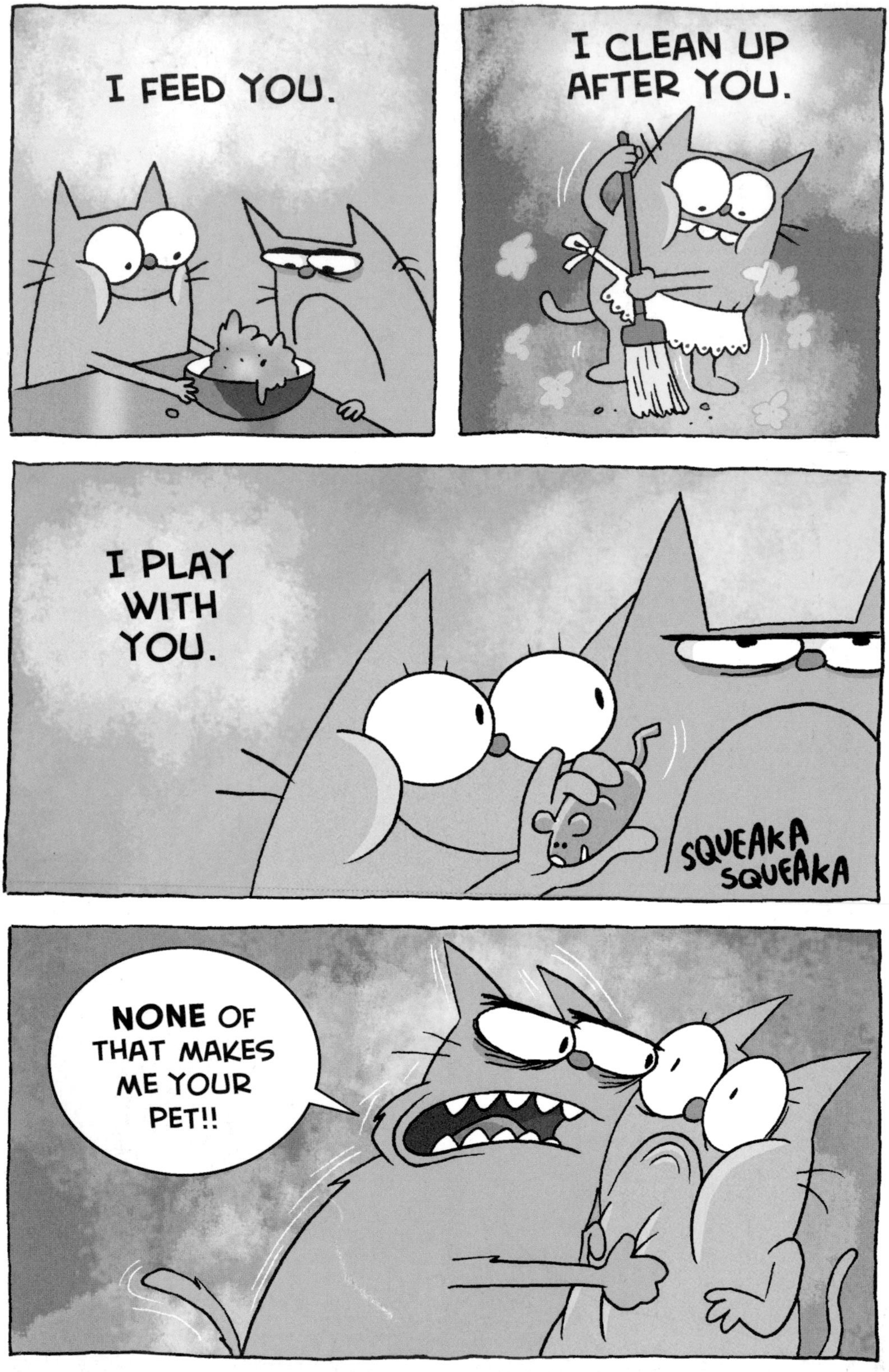
I FEED YOU.
I CLEAN UP AFTER YOU.
I PLAY WITH YOU.
SQUEAKA SQUEAKA
NONE OF THAT MAKES ME YOUR PET!!

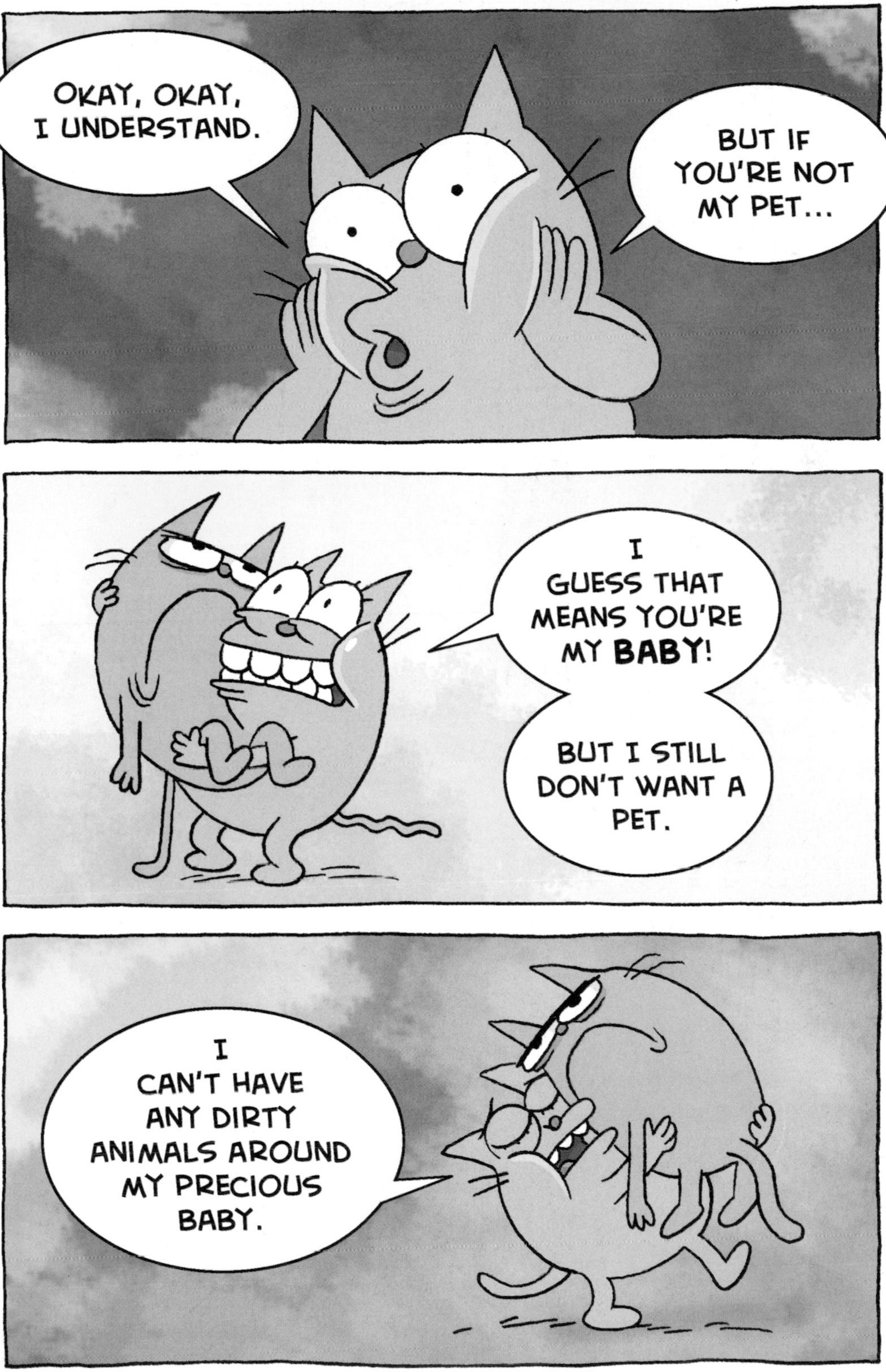
OKAY, OKAY, I UNDERSTAND.
BUT IF YOU'RE NOT MY PET...
I GUESS THAT MEANS YOU'RE MY BABY!
BUT I STILL DON'T WANT A PET.
I CAN'T HAVE ANY DIRTY ANIMALS AROUND MY PRECIOUS BABY.

THE TO-DO LIST

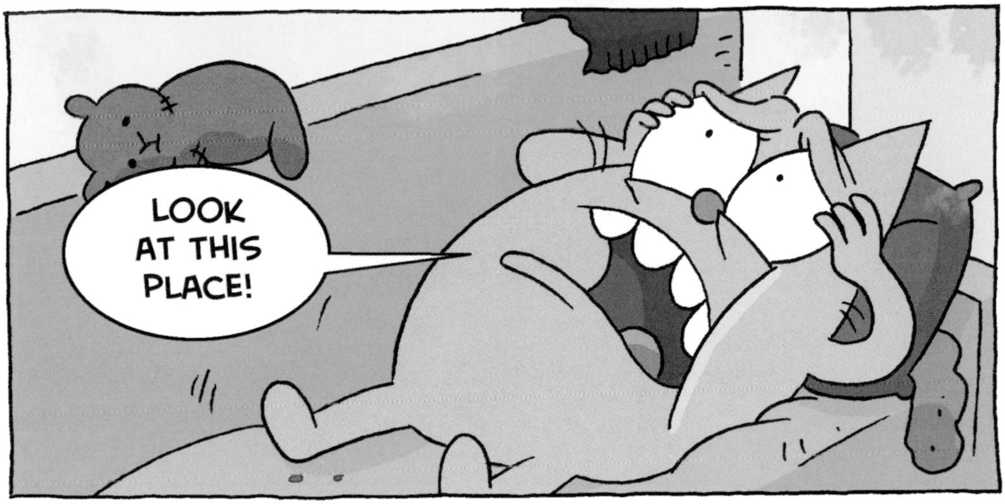
LOOK AT THIS PLACE!

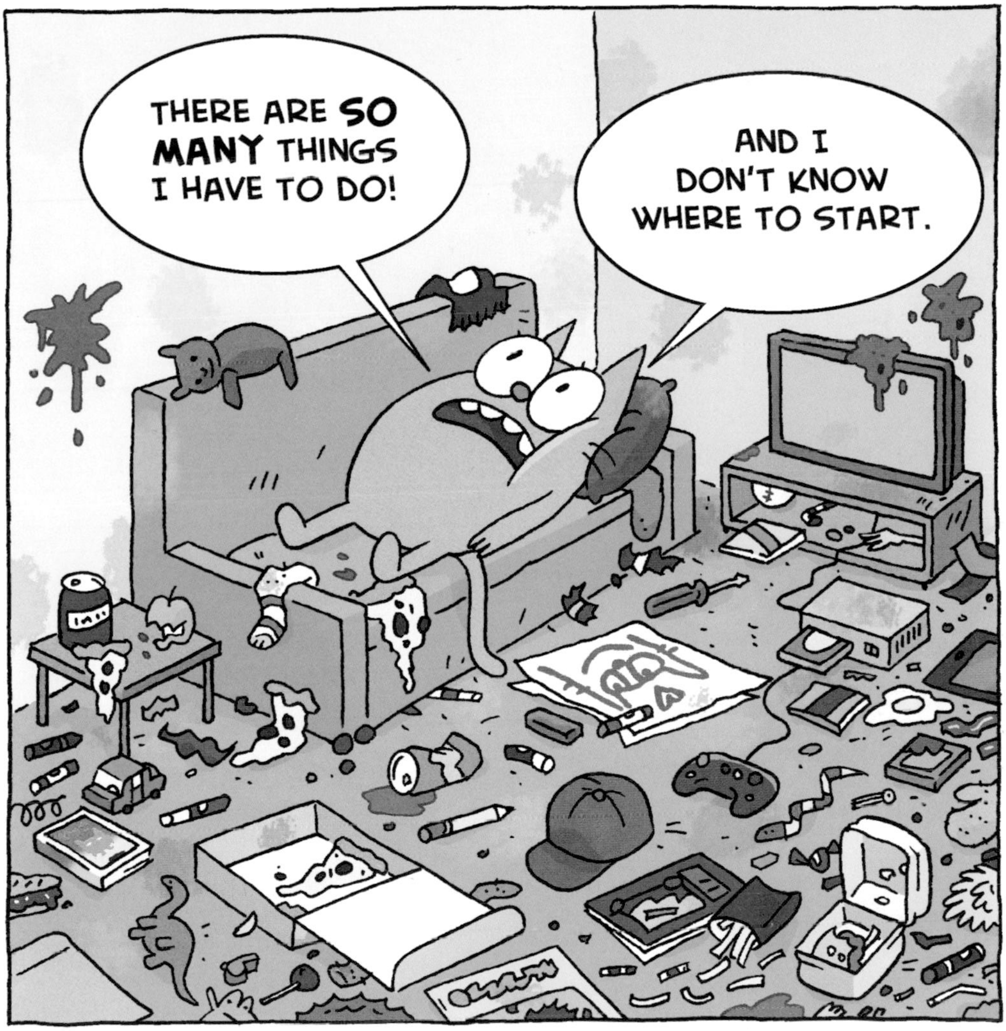
THERE ARE **SO MANY** THINGS I HAVE TO DO!
AND I DON'T KNOW WHERE TO START.

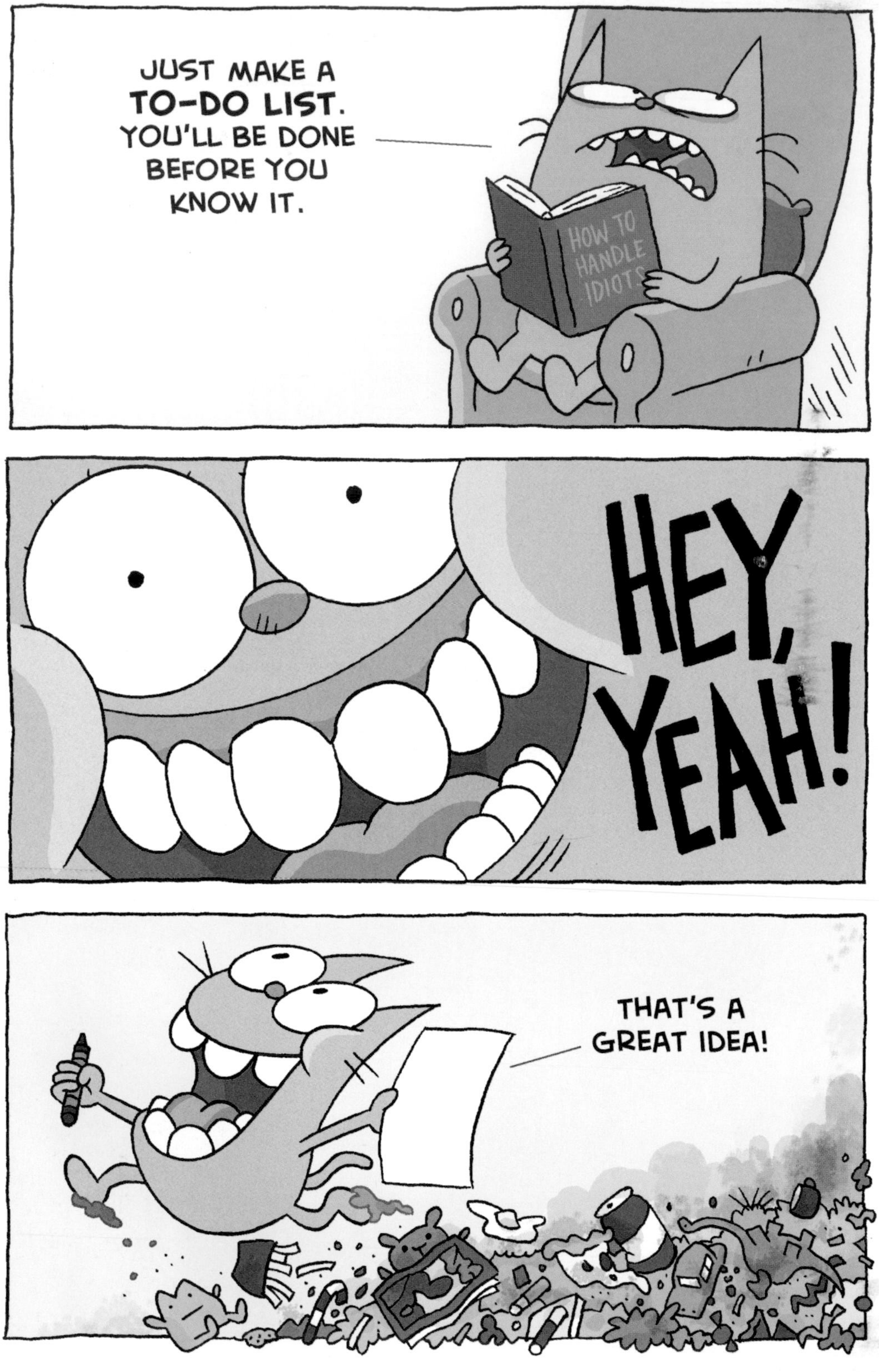
JUST MAKE A **TO-DO LIST**. YOU'LL BE DONE BEFORE YOU KNOW IT.
HOW TO HANDLE IDIOTS
HEY, YEAH!
THAT'S A GREAT IDEA!

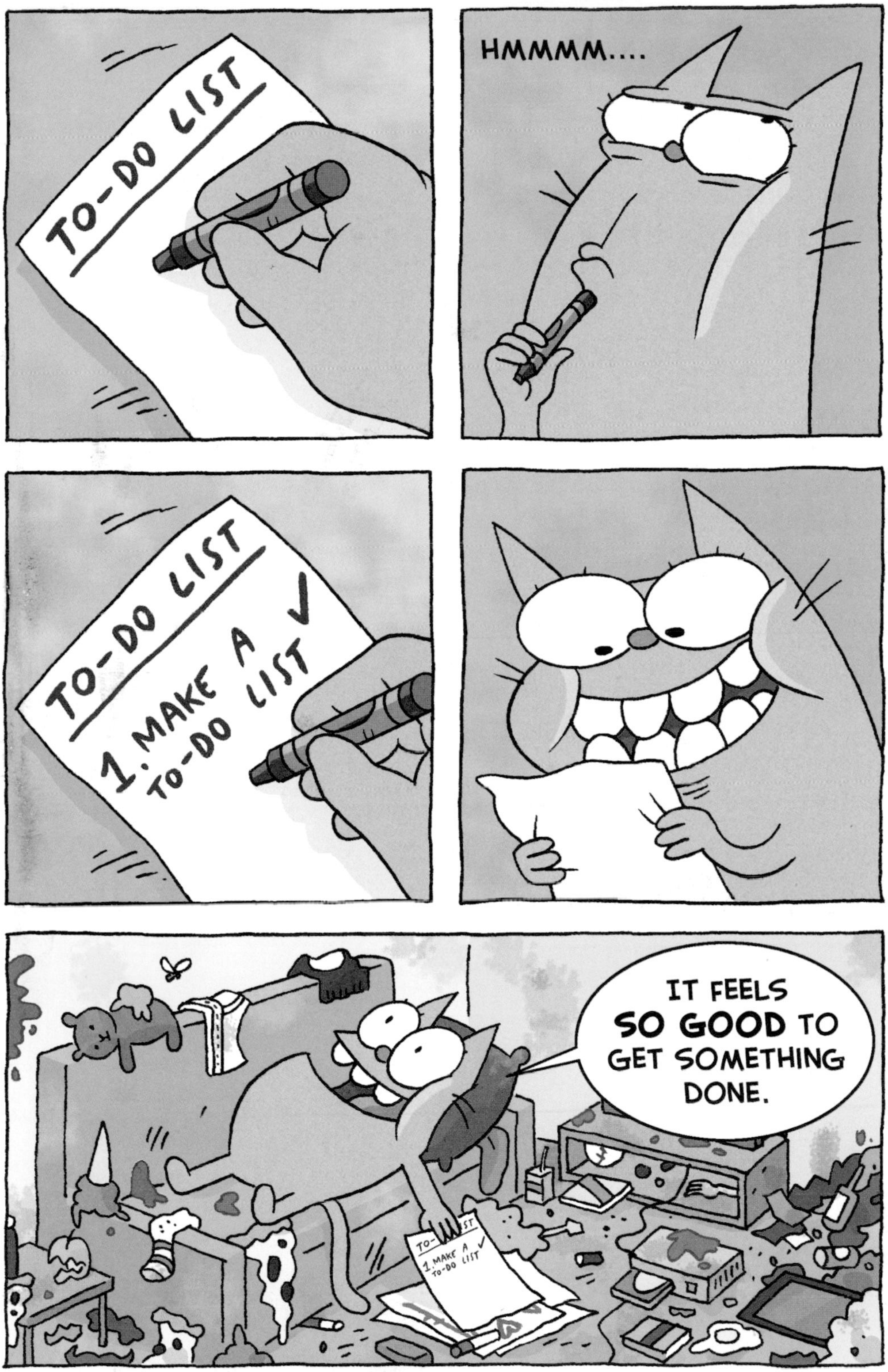
TO-DO LIST
HMMMM....
TO-DO LIST
1. MAKE A TO-DO LIST ✓
IT FEELS SO GOOD TO GET SOMETHING DONE.
TO-
1. MAKE A ✓
TO-DO LIST

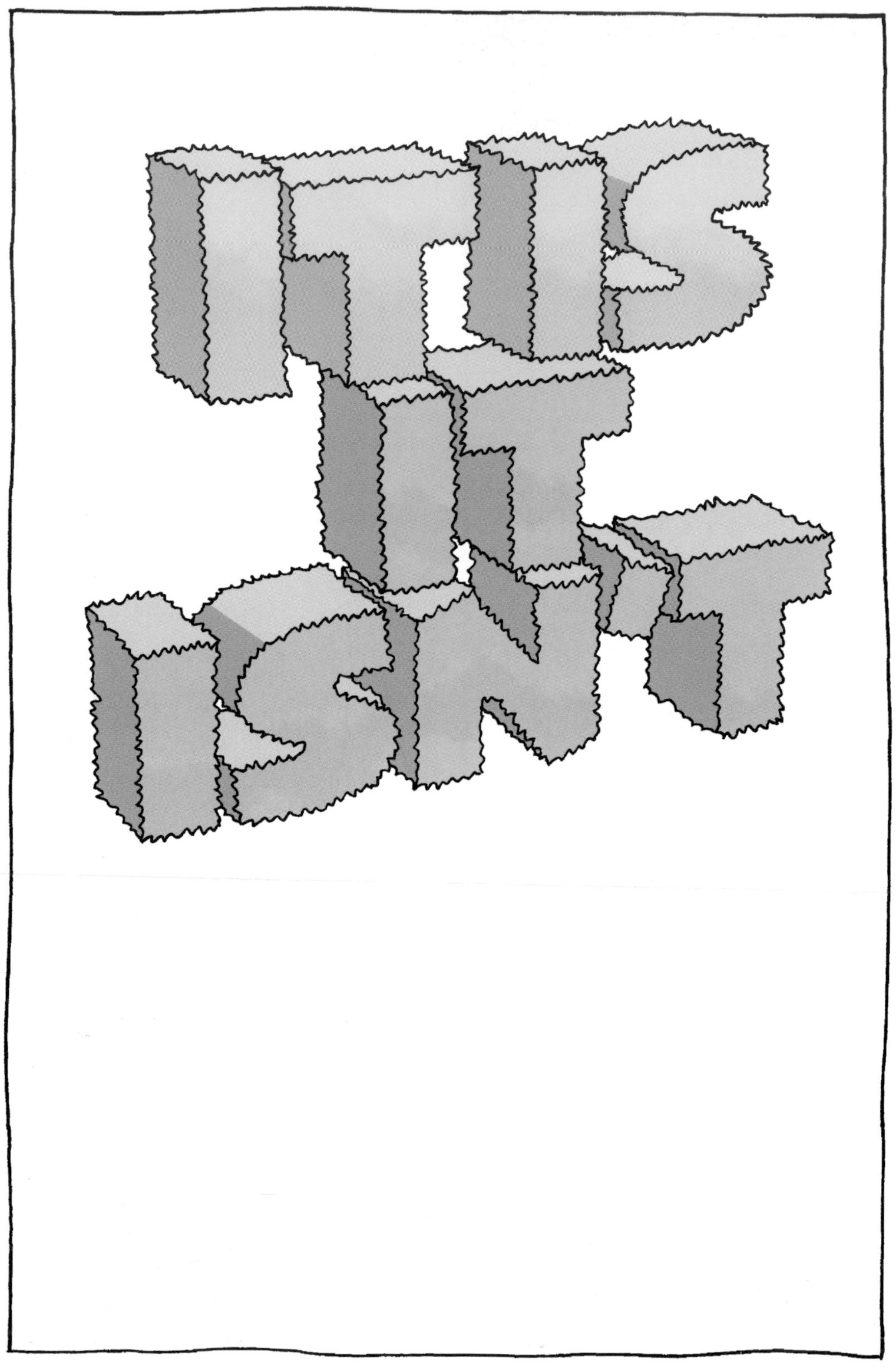
IT IS
IT
ISN'T

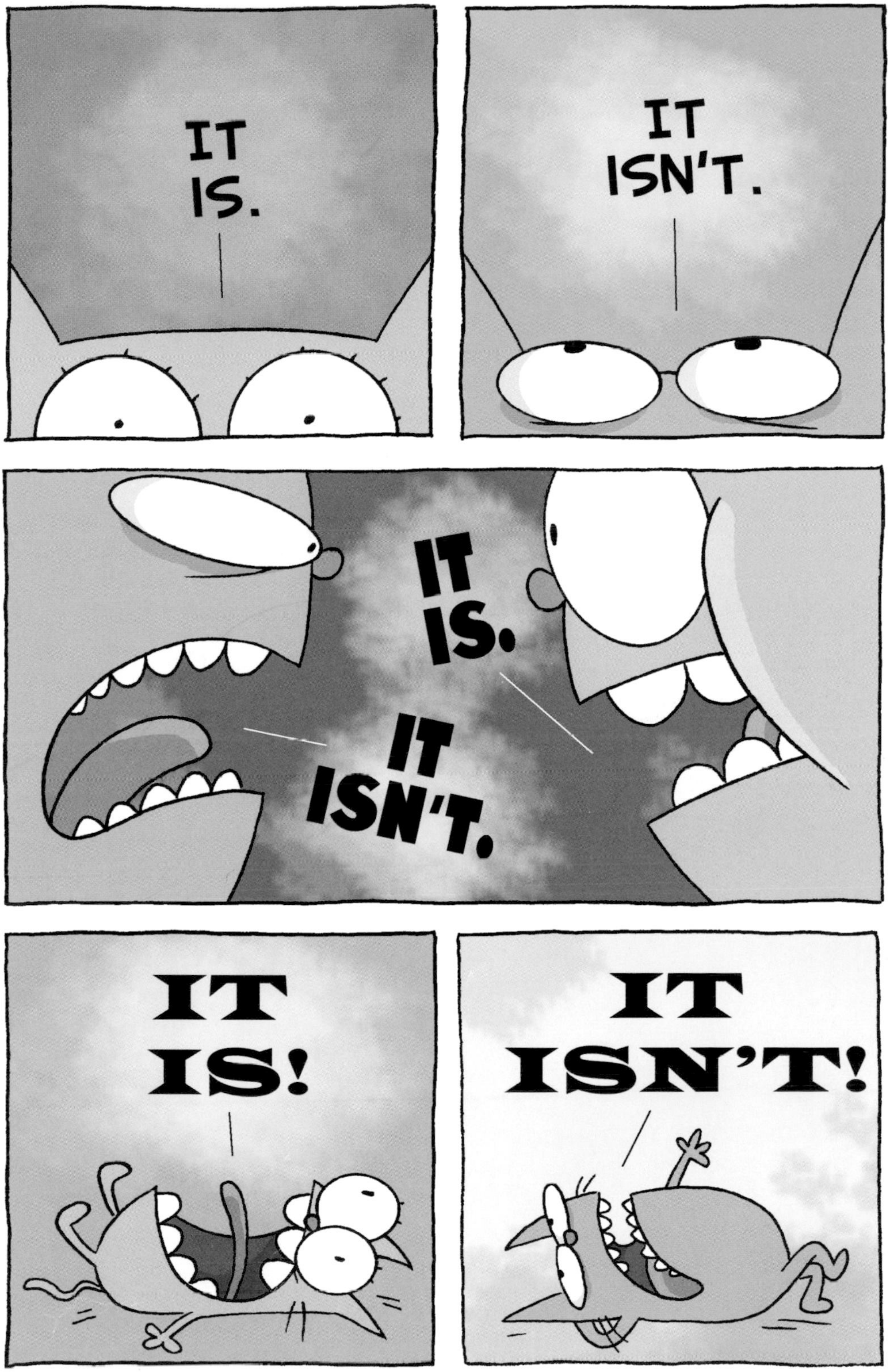
IT IS.
IT ISN'T.
IT IS.
IT ISN'T.
IT IS!
IT ISN'T!

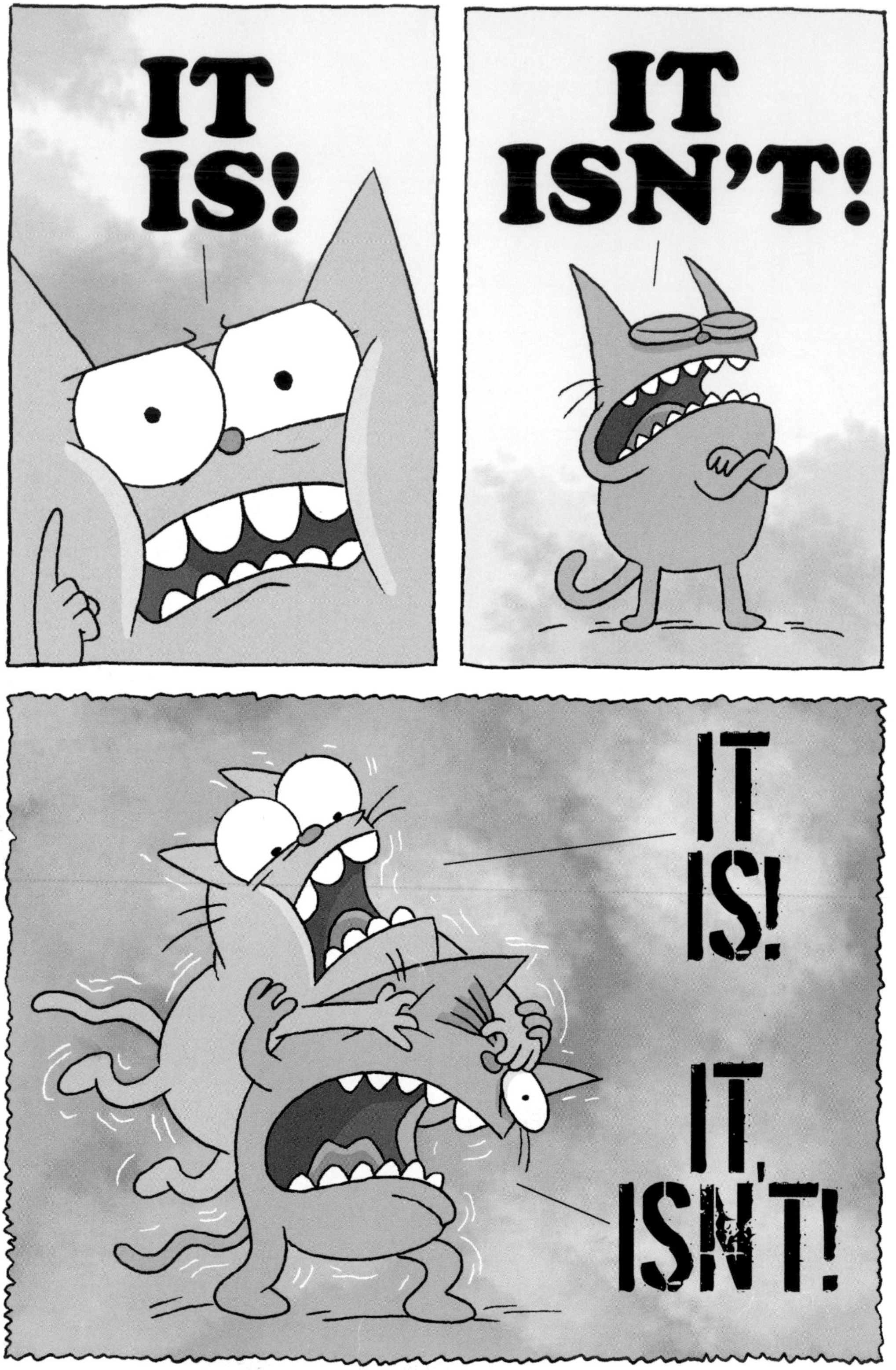
IT IS!
IT ISN'T!
IT IS!
IT, ISN'T!

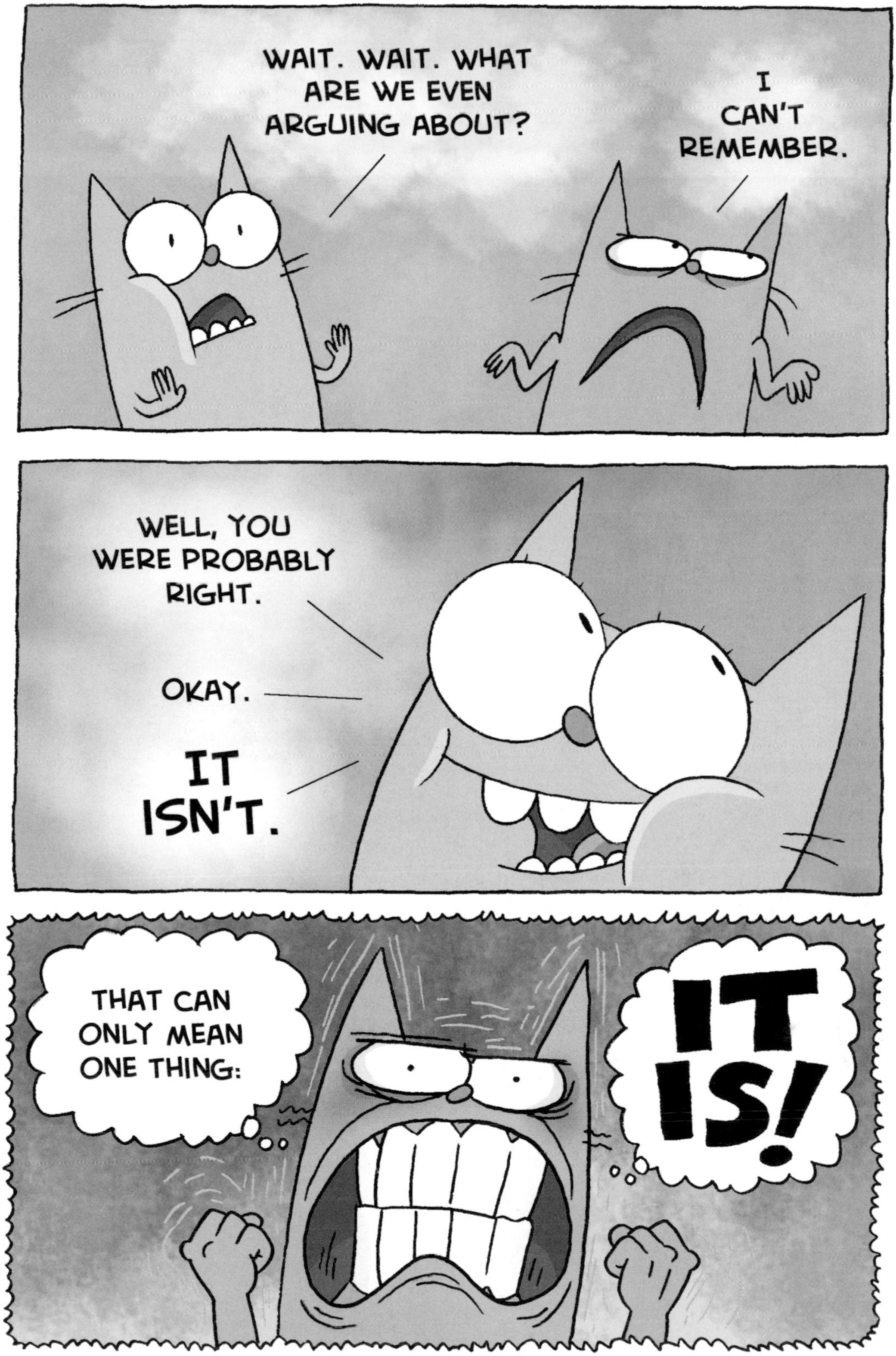
WAIT. WAIT. WHAT ARE WE EVEN ARGUING ABOUT?
I CAN'T REMEMBER.
WELL, YOU WERE PROBABLY RIGHT.
OKAY.
IT ISN'T.
THAT CAN ONLY MEAN ONE THING:
IT IS!

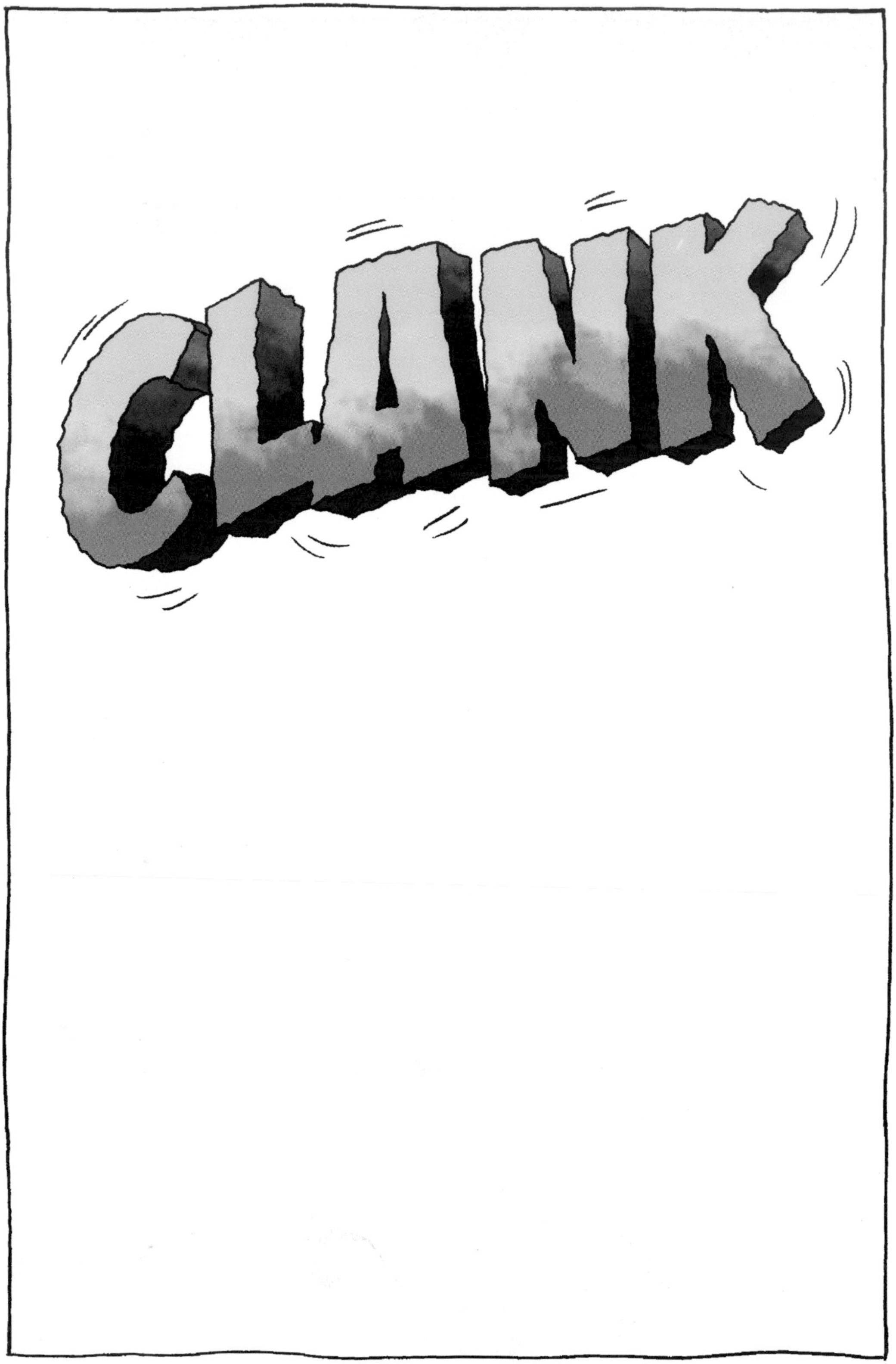
CLANK

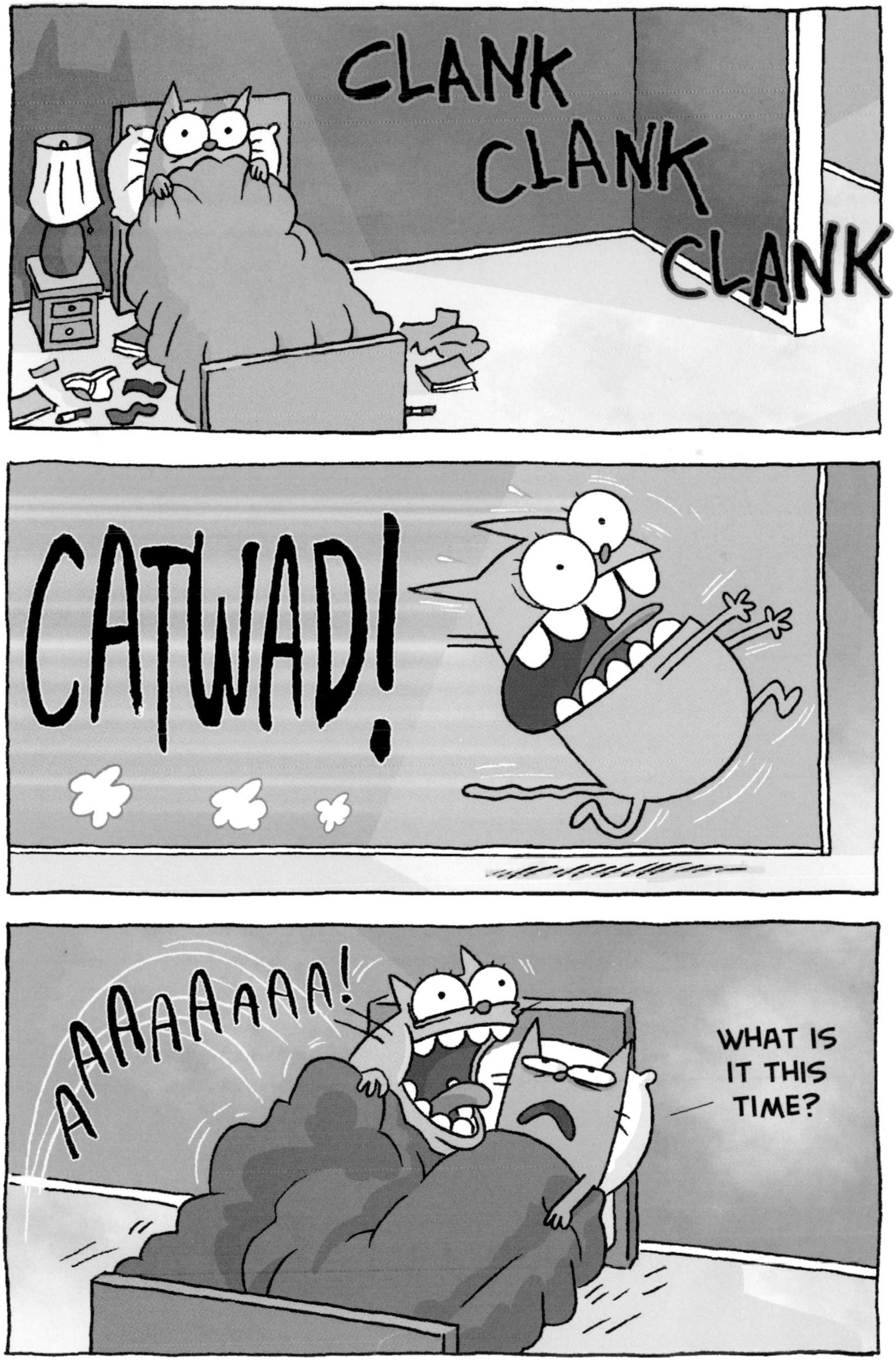
CLANK
CLANK
CLANK
CATWAD!
AAAAAAAA!
WHAT IS IT THIS TIME?

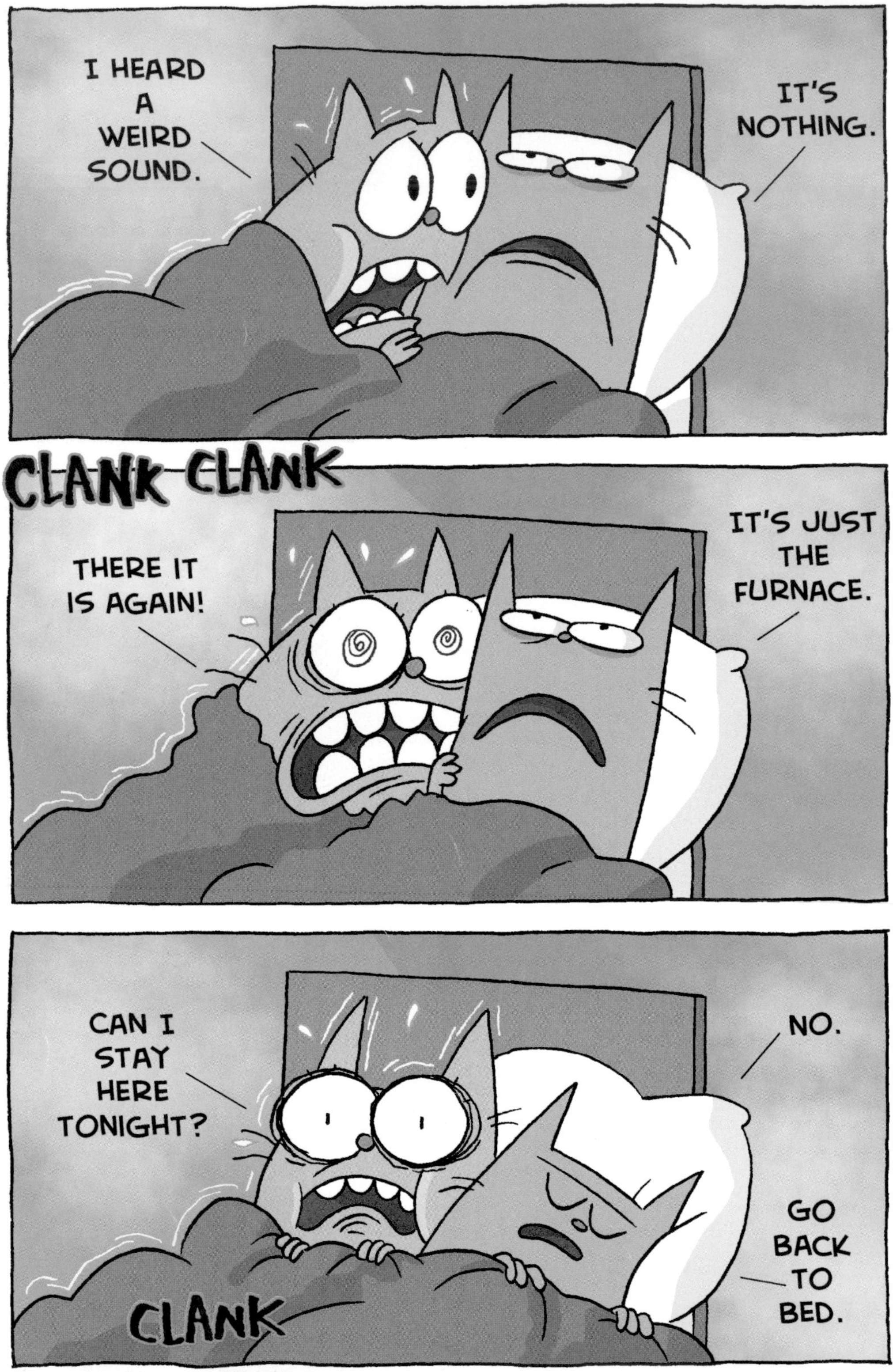
I HEARD A WEIRD SOUND.
IT'S NOTHING.
CLANK CLANK
THERE IT IS AGAIN!
IT'S JUST THE FURNACE.
CAN I STAY HERE TONIGHT?
NO.
GO BACK TO BED.
CLANK

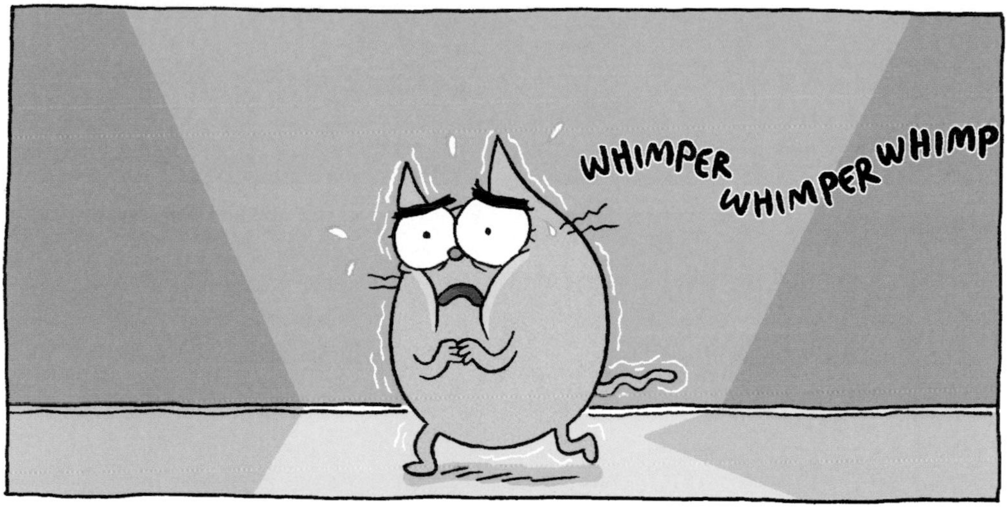
WHIMPER
WHIMPER WHIMP

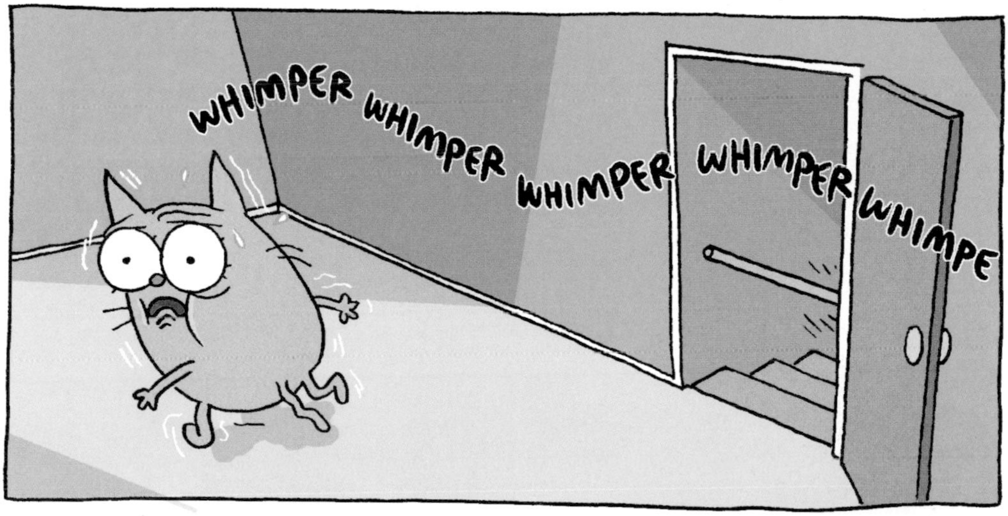
WHIMPER WHIMPER WHIMPER WHIMPER WHIMPE

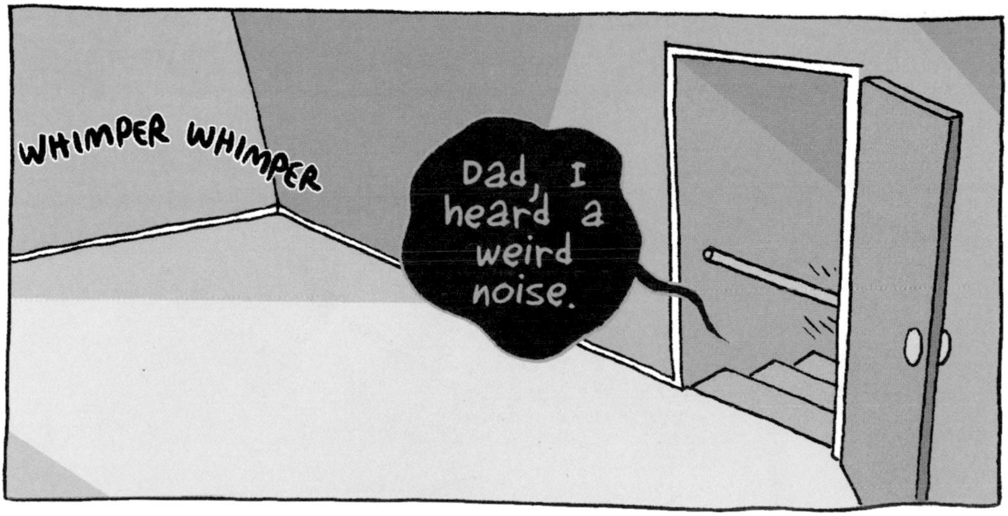
WHIMPER WHIMPER
Dad, I heard a weird noise.

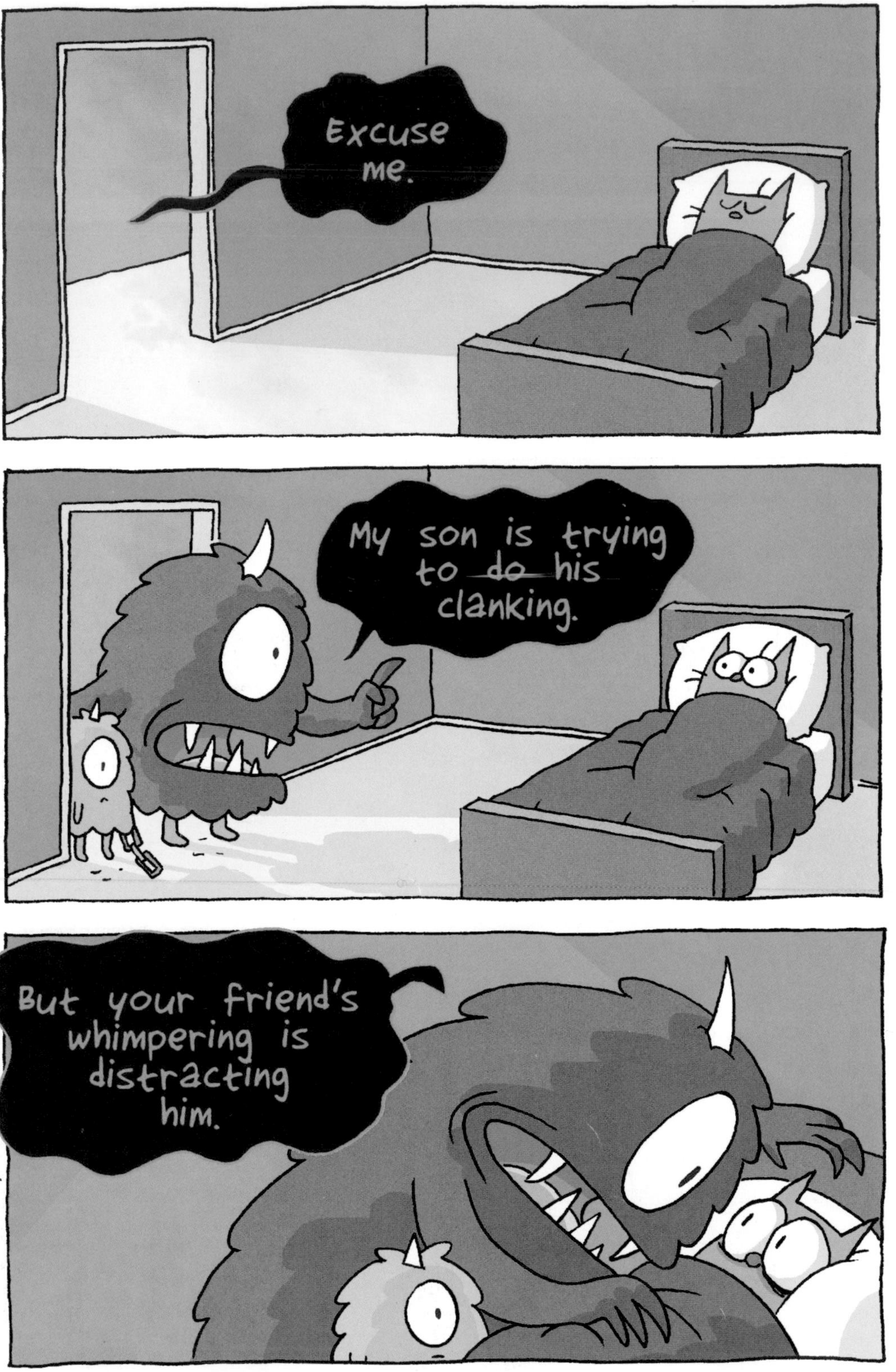
Excuse me.
My son is trying to do his clanking.
But your friend's whimpering is distracting him.

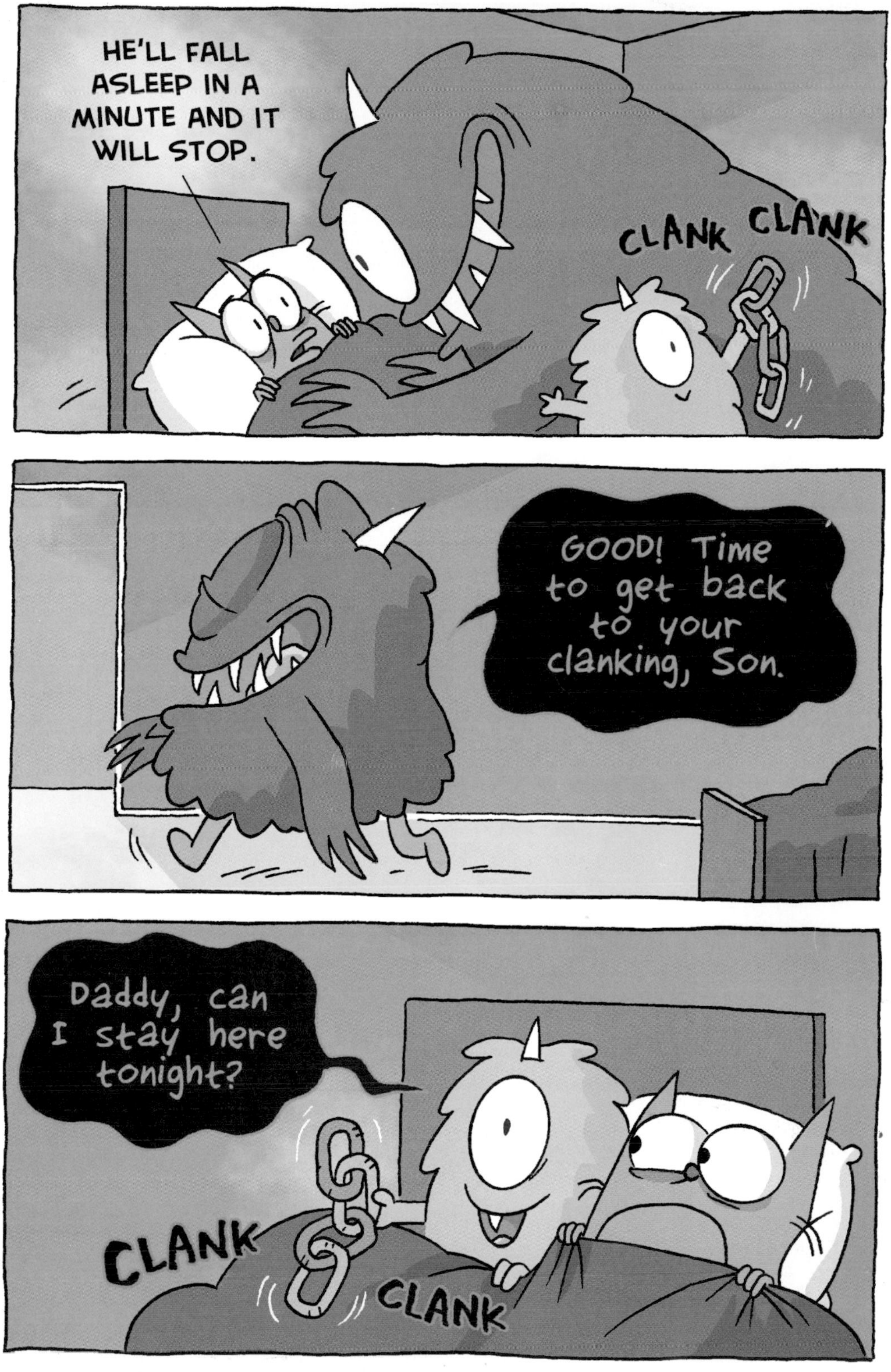
HE'LL FALL ASLEEP IN A MINUTE AND IT WILL STOP.
CLANK CLANK
GOOD! Time to get back to your clanking, Son.
Daddy, can I stay here tonight?
CLANK
CLANK

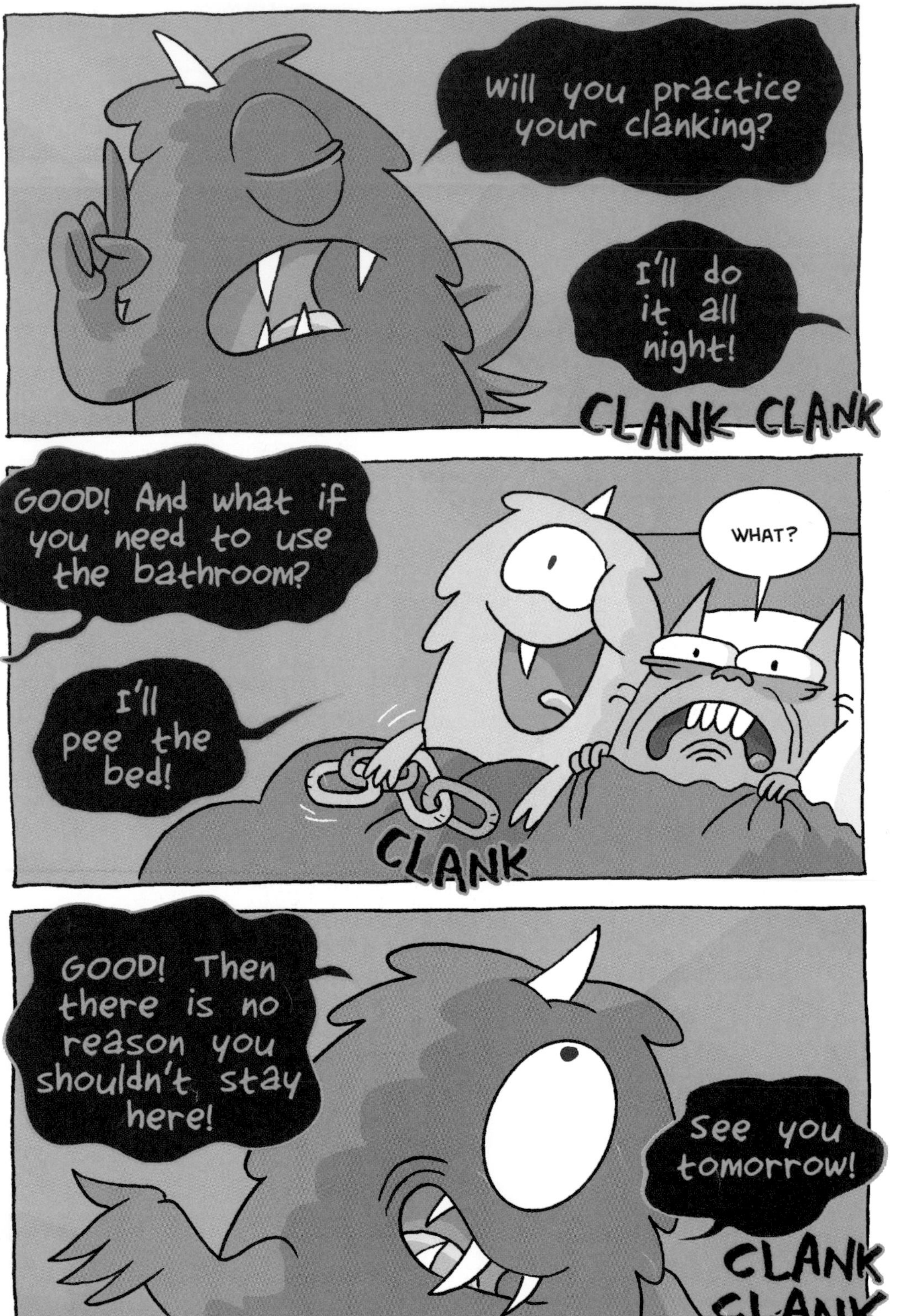
Will you practice your clanking?
I'll do it all night!
CLANK CLANK
GOOD! And what if you need to use the bathroom?
WHAT?
I'll pee the bed!
CLANK
GOOD! Then there is no reason you shouldn't stay here!
See you tomorrow!
CLANK CLANK

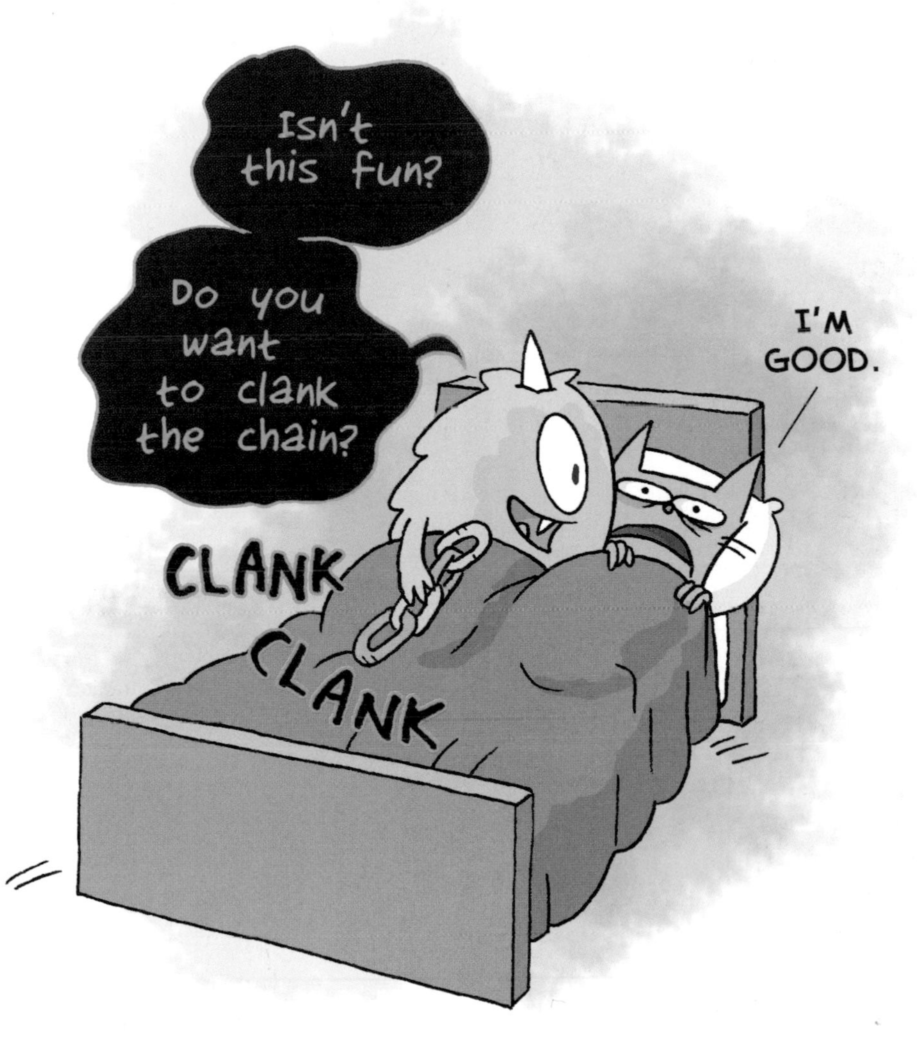
Isn't this fun?
Do you want to clank the chain?
CLANK
CLANK
I'M GOOD.

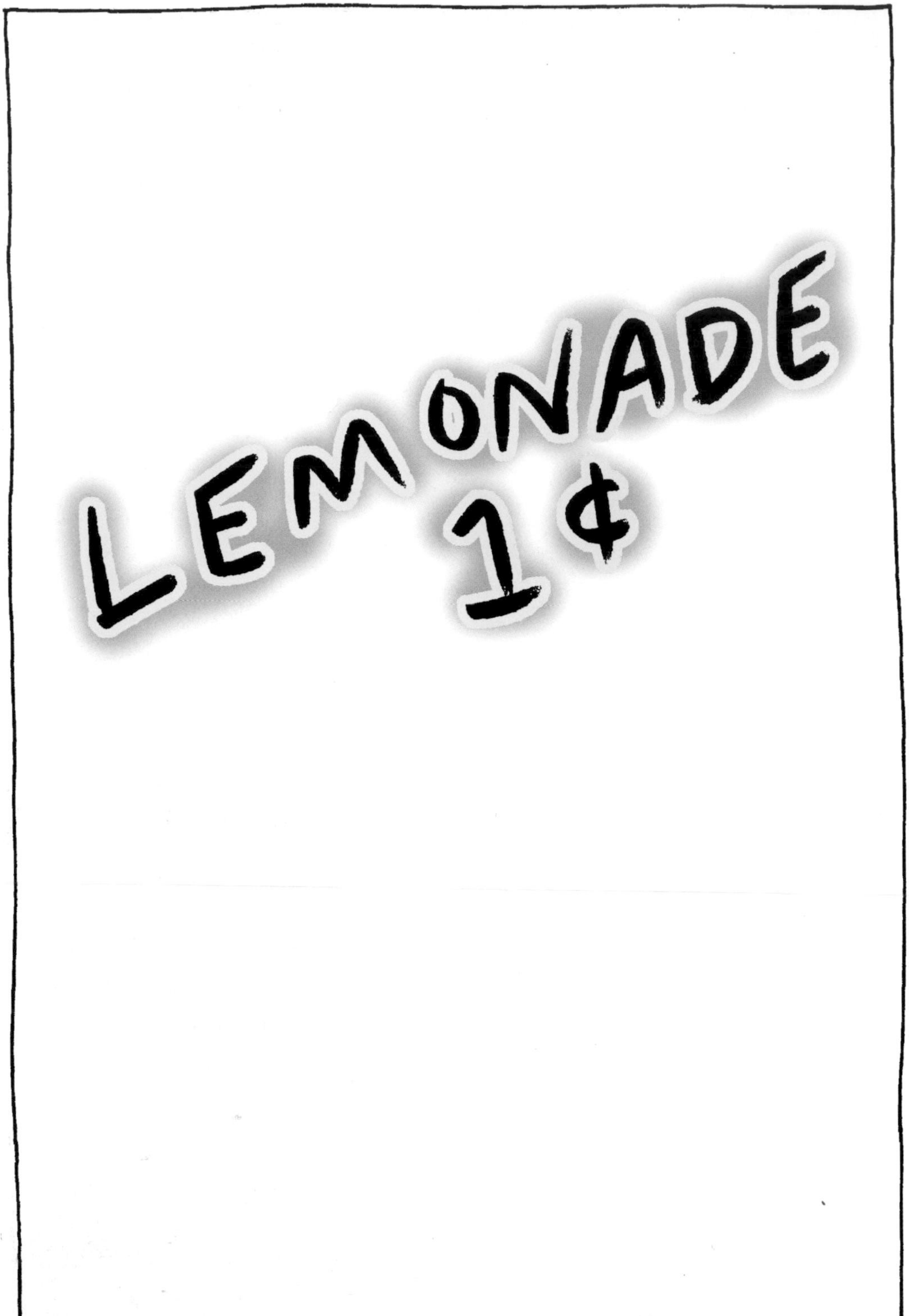
LEMONADE
1¢

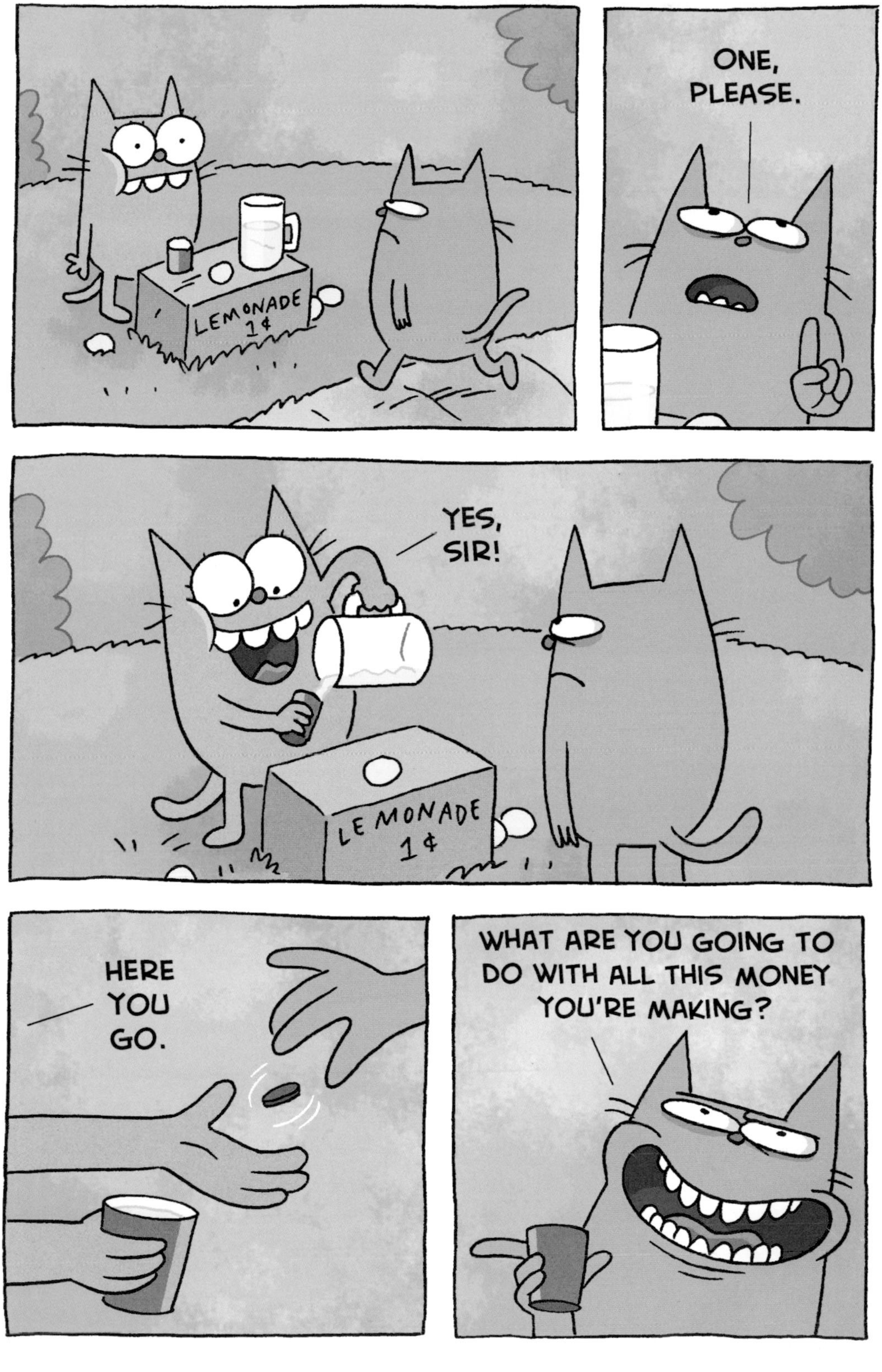
LEMONADE 1¢
ONE, PLEASE.
YES, SIR!
LEMONADE 1¢
HERE YOU GO.
WHAT ARE YOU GOING TO DO WITH ALL THIS MONEY YOU'RE MAKING?

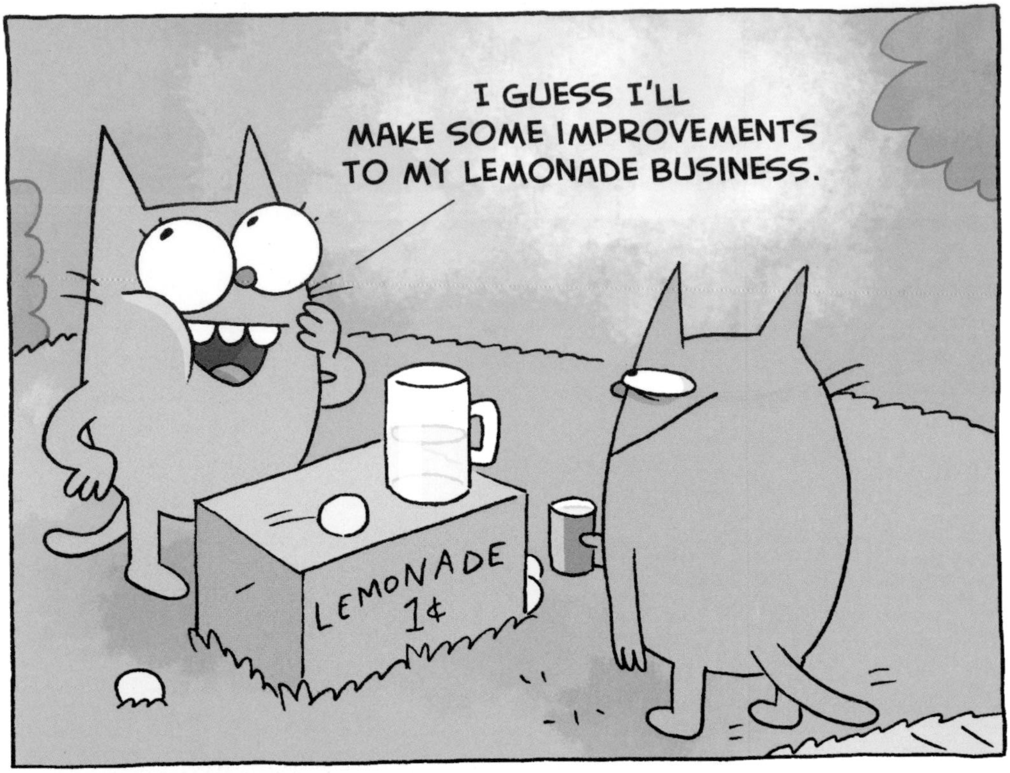
I GUESS I'LL MAKE SOME IMPROVEMENTS TO MY LEMONADE BUSINESS.
LEMONADE 1¢

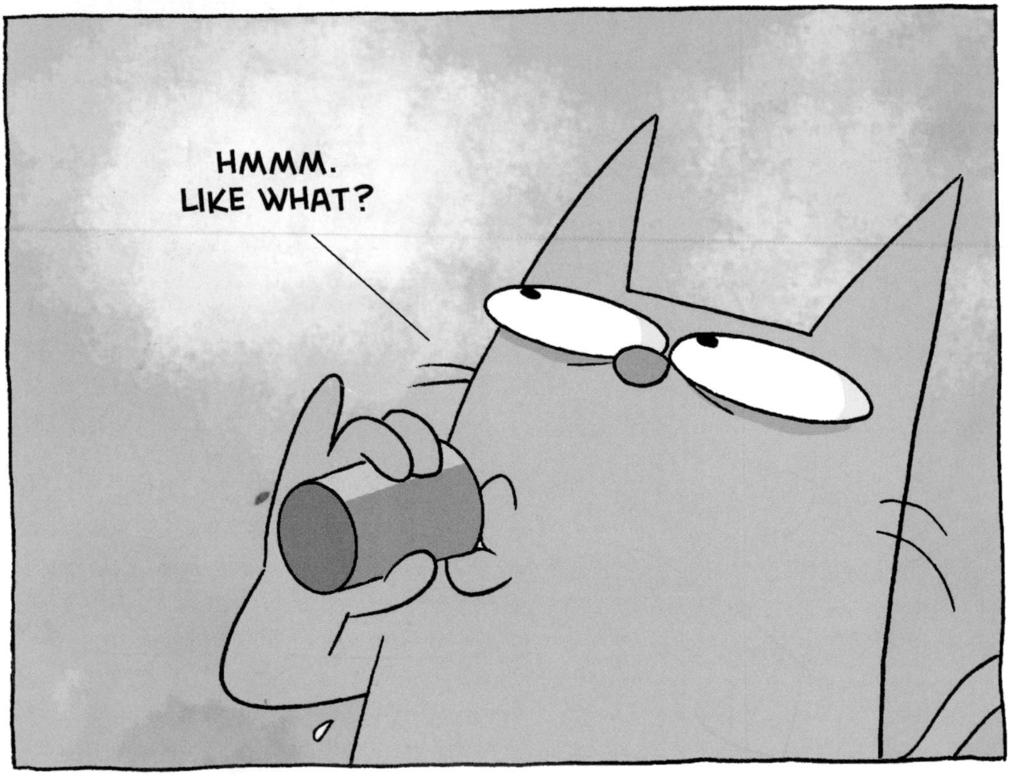
HMMM. LIKE WHAT?

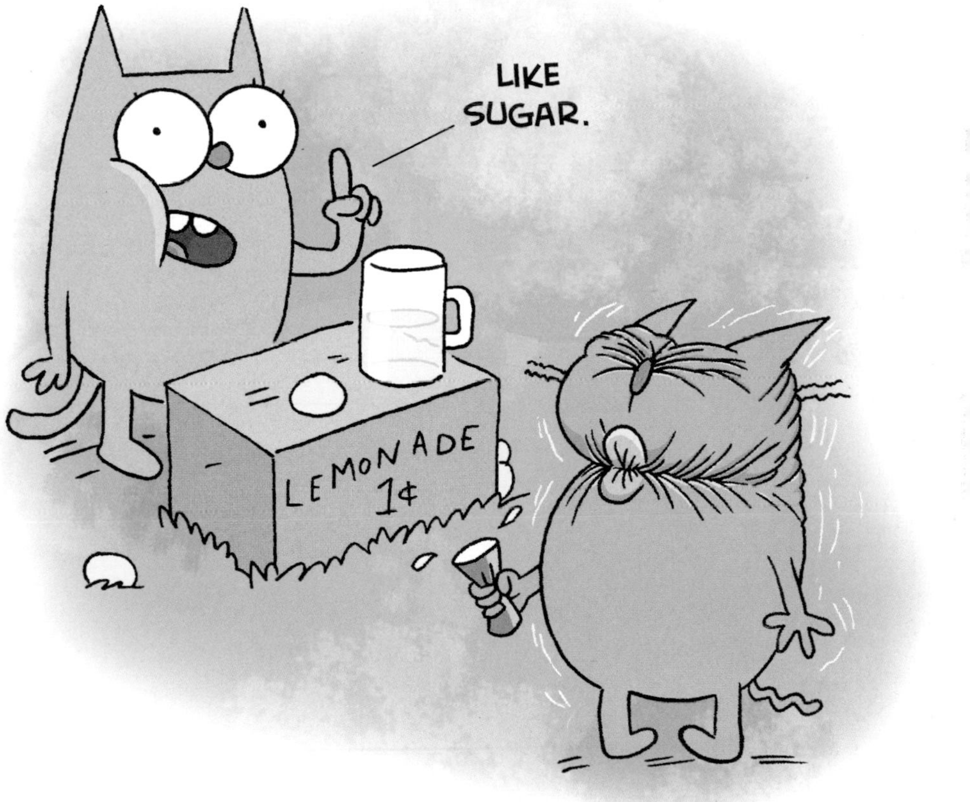
LIKE SUGAR.
LEMONADE 1¢

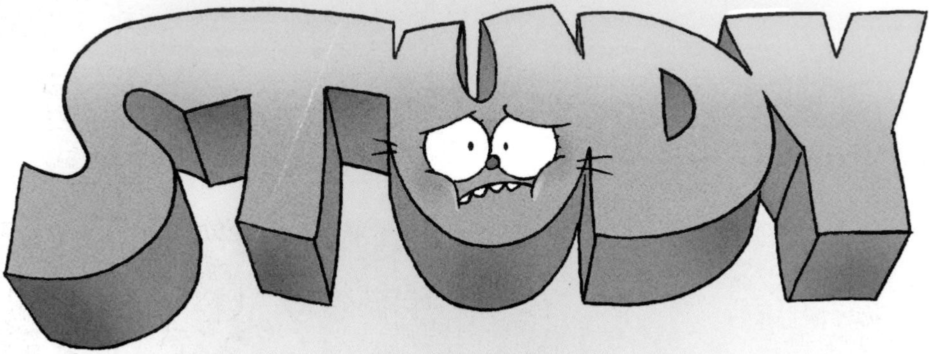
STUDY

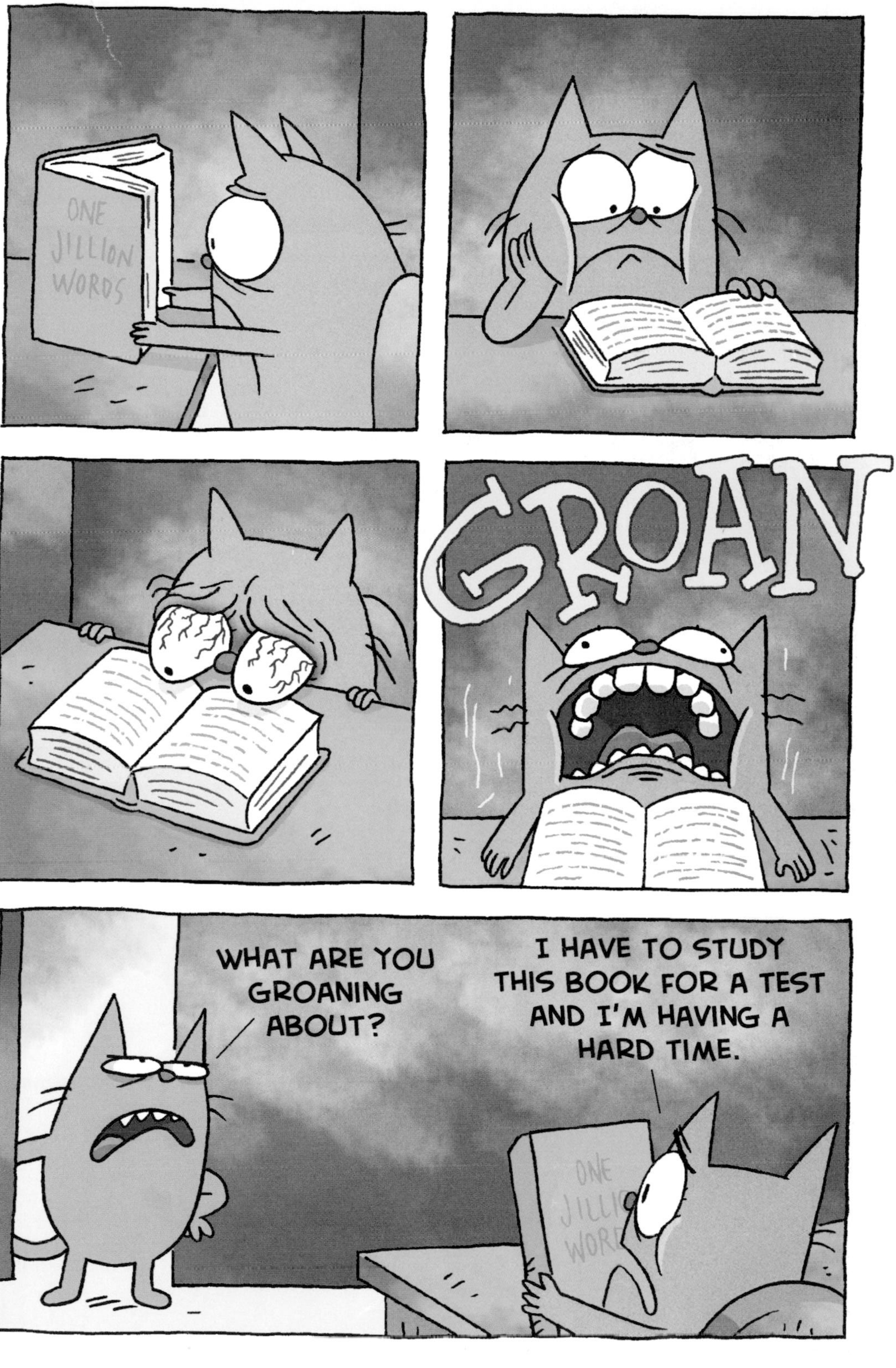
ONE JILLION WORDS
GROAN
WHAT ARE YOU GROANING ABOUT?
I HAVE TO STUDY THIS BOOK FOR A TEST AND I'M HAVING A HARD TIME.

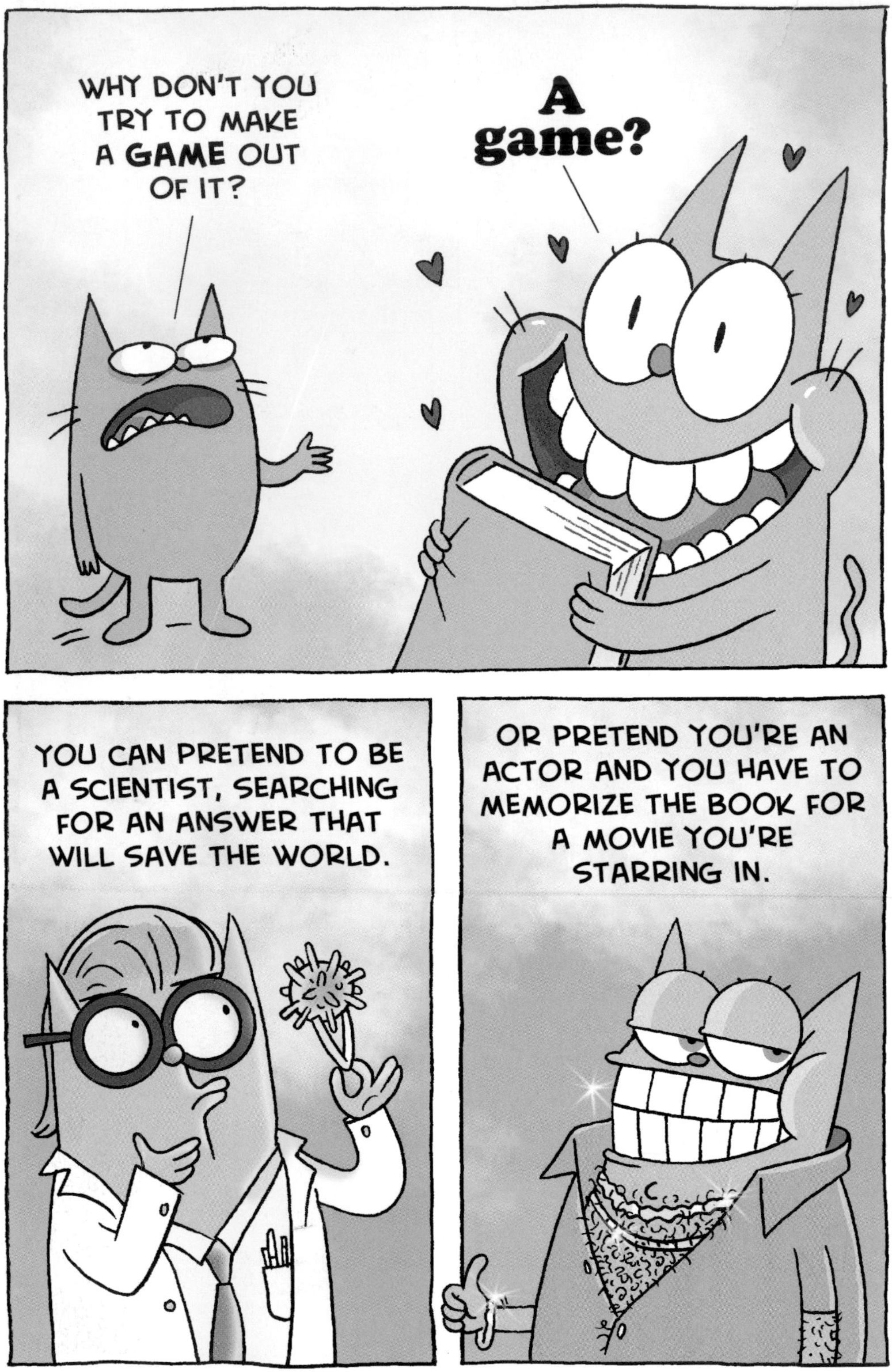

WHY DON'T YOU TRY TO MAKE A GAME OUT OF IT?
A game?
YOU CAN PRETEND TO BE A SCIENTIST, SEARCHING FOR AN ANSWER THAT WILL SAVE THE WORLD.
OR PRETEND YOU'RE AN ACTOR AND YOU HAVE TO MEMORIZE THE BOOK FOR A MOVIE YOU'RE STARRING IN.

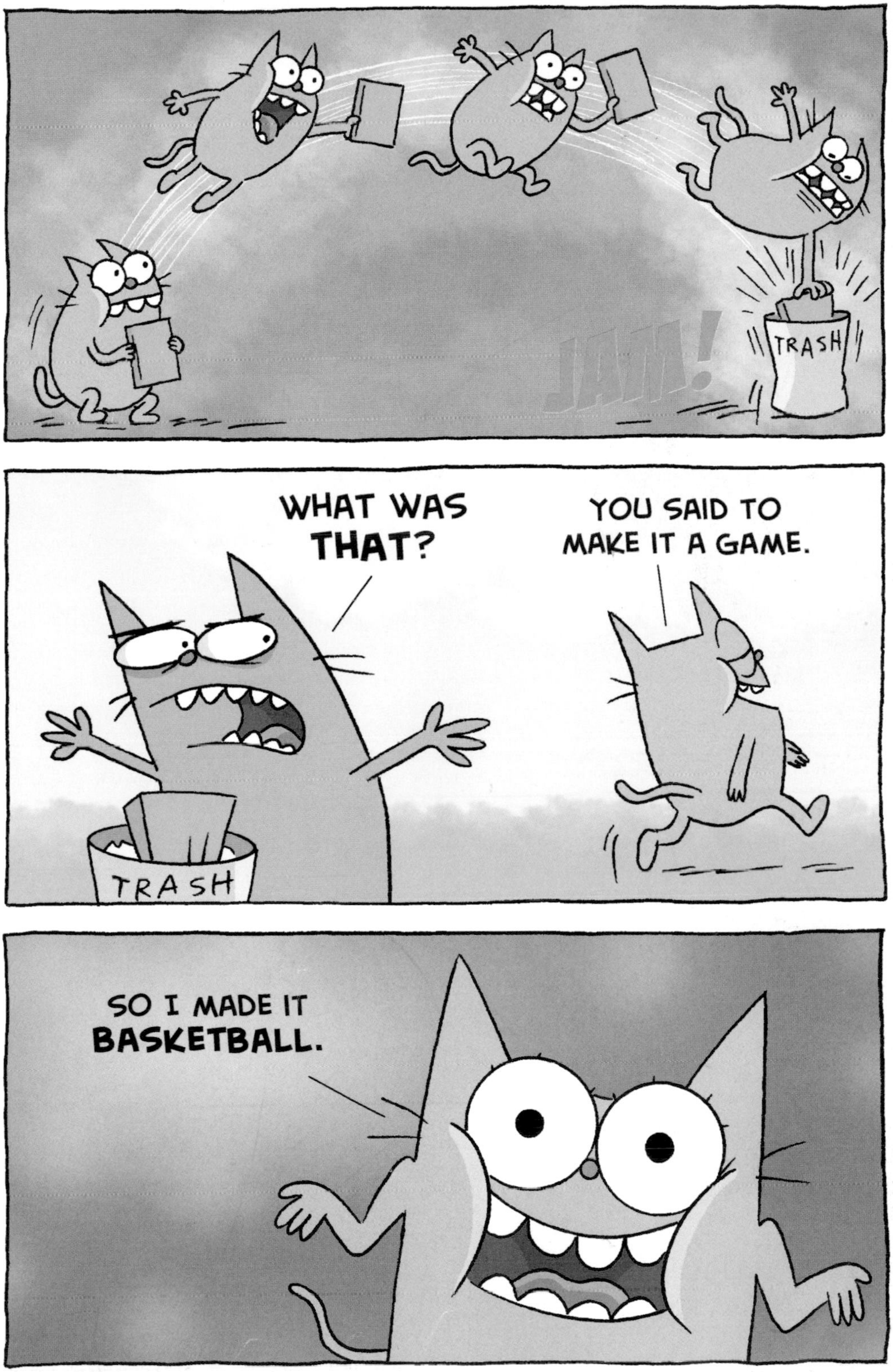
JAM!
TRASH
WHAT WAS THAT?
YOU SAID TO MAKE IT A GAME.
TRASH
SO I MADE IT BASKETBALL.

THE STYLIST

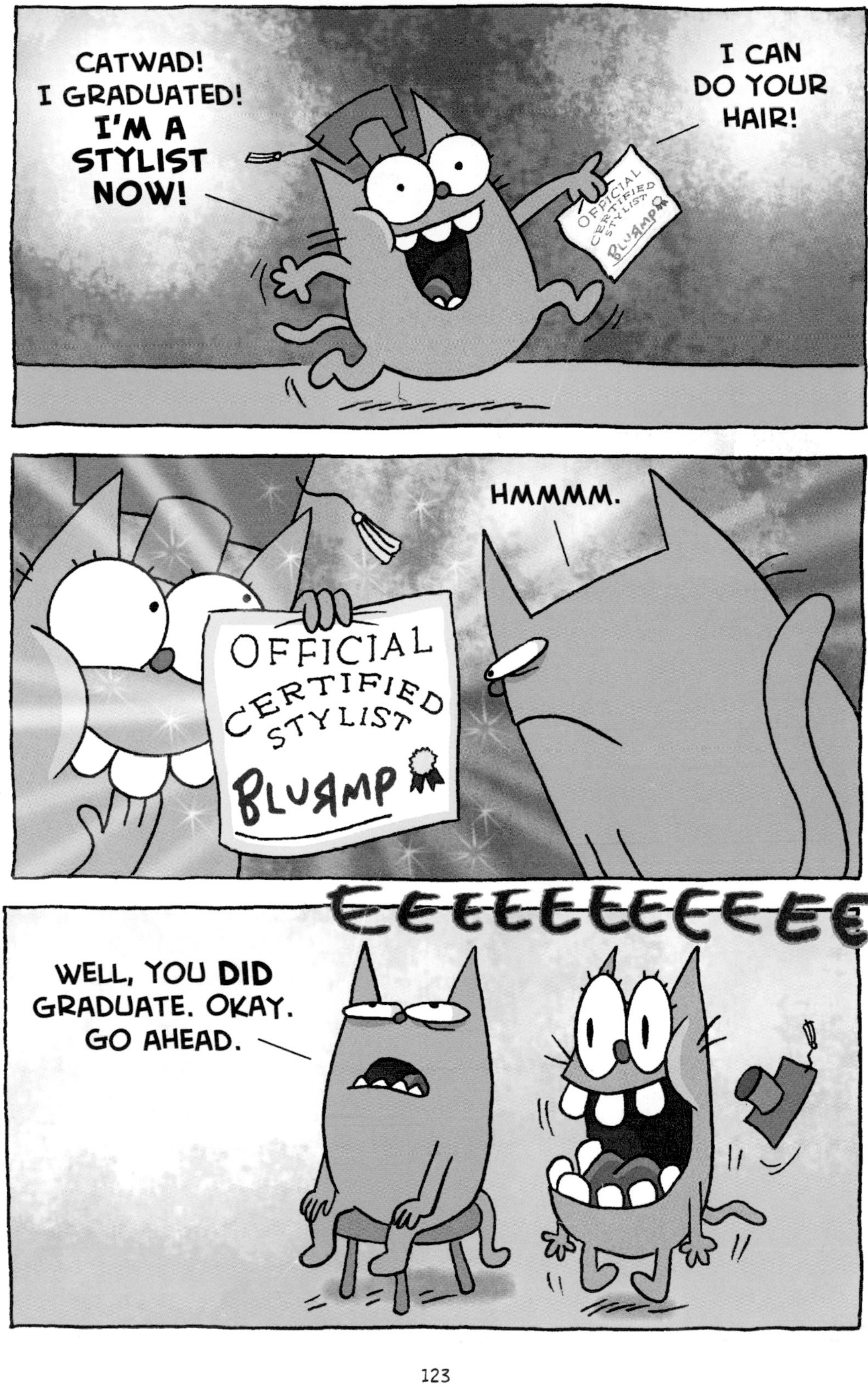
CATWAD! I GRADUATED! I'M A STYLIST NOW!
I CAN DO YOUR HAIR!
OFFICIAL CERTIFIED STYLIST
BLUЯMP
HMMMM.
OFFICIAL CERTIFIED STYLIST
BLUЯMP
EEEEEEEEEEEE
WELL, YOU DID GRADUATE. OKAY. GO AHEAD.

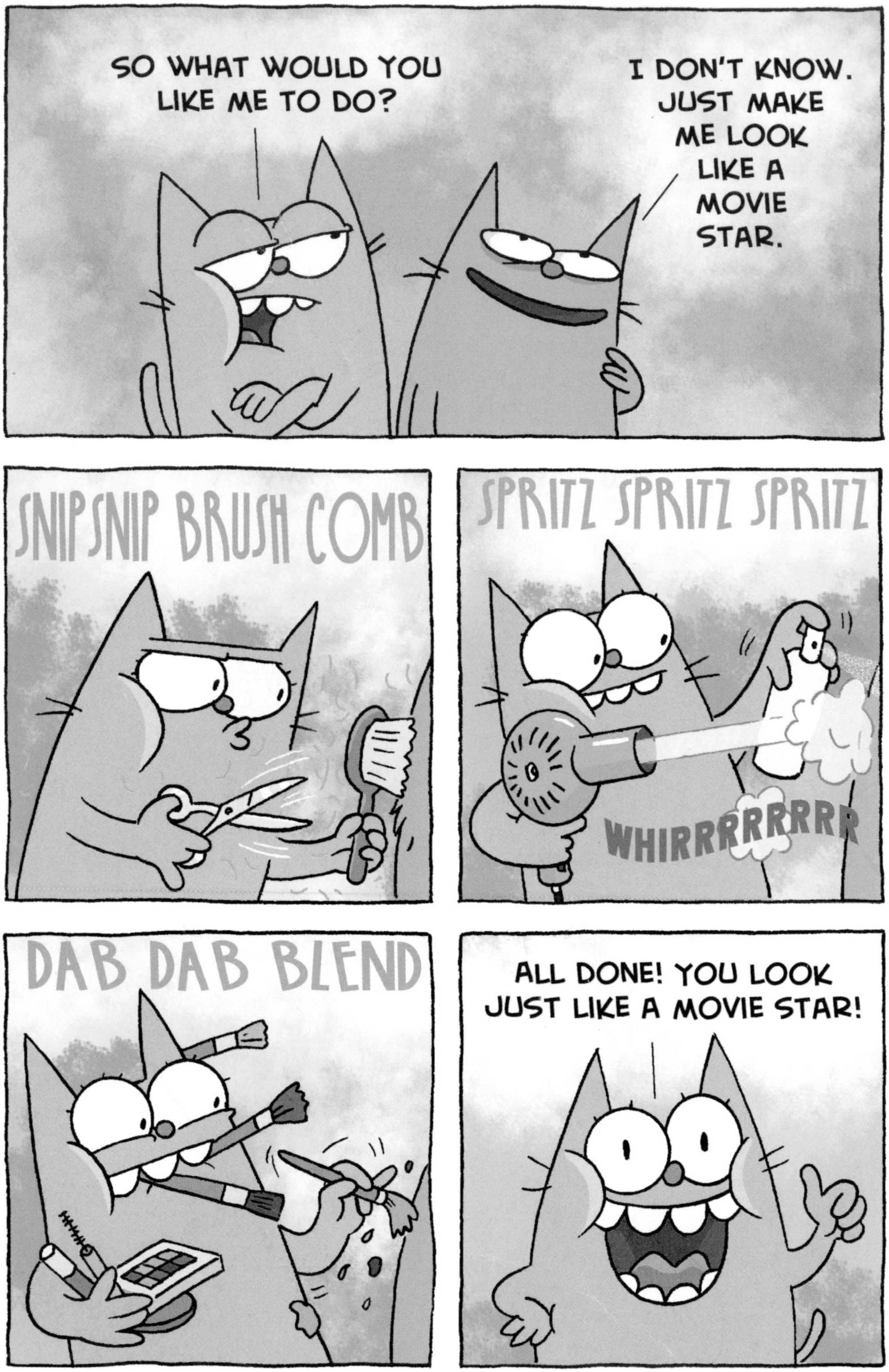
SO WHAT WOULD YOU LIKE ME TO DO?
I DON'T KNOW. JUST MAKE ME LOOK LIKE A MOVIE STAR.
SNIPSNIP BRUSH COMB
SPRITZ SPRITZ SPRITZ
WHIRRRRRRRR
DAB DAB BLEND
ALL DONE! YOU LOOK JUST LIKE A MOVIE STAR!

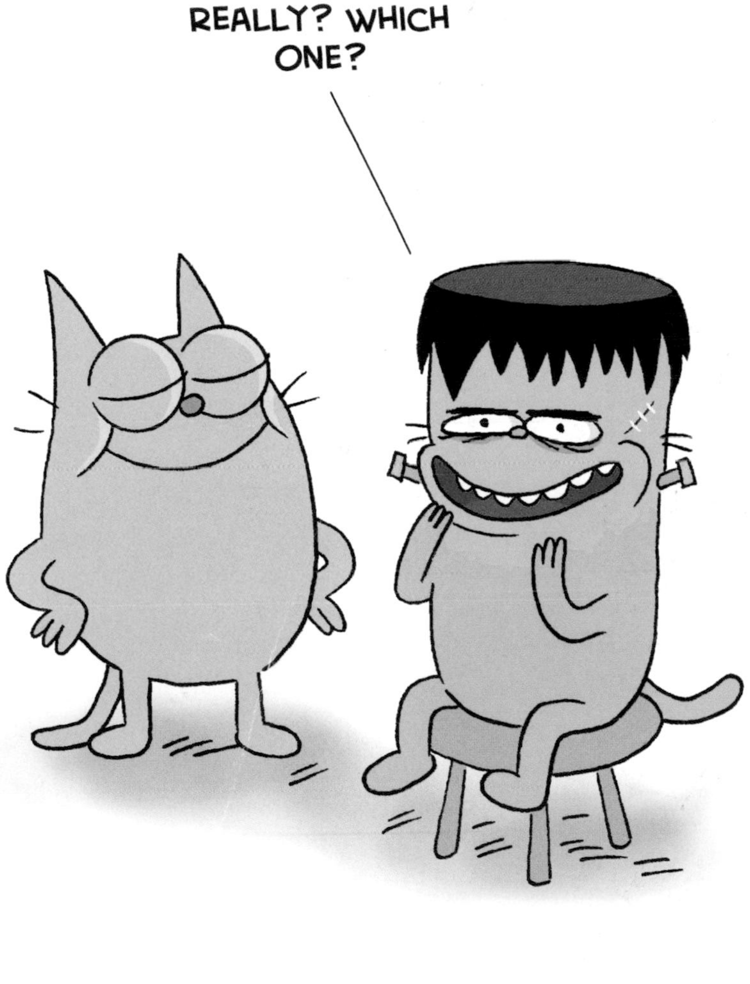
REALLY? WHICH ONE?

BONUS ACTIVITY! THERE ARE 25 DIFFERENCES BETWEEN THESE TWO PICTURES! HOW MANY CAN YOU FIND?

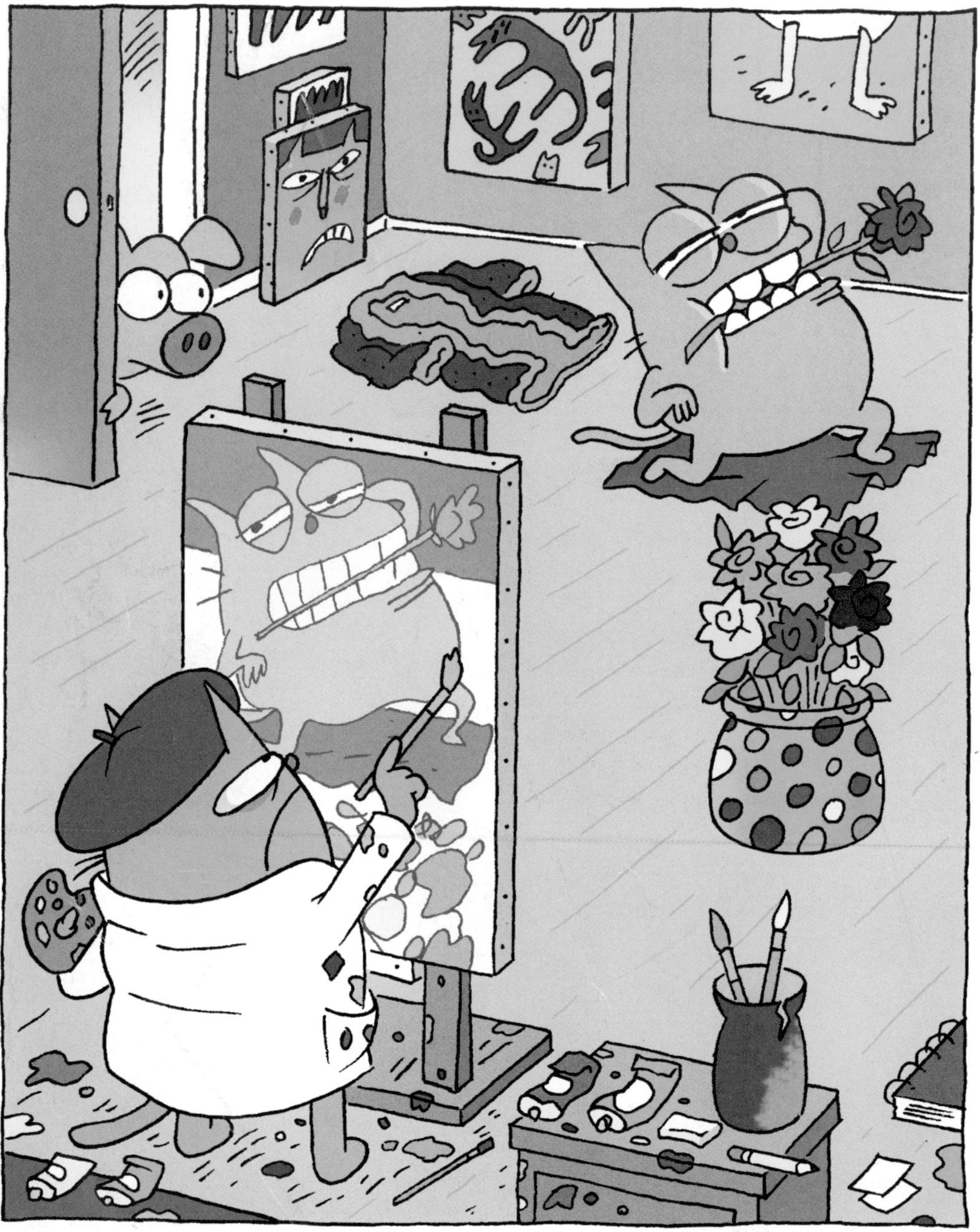

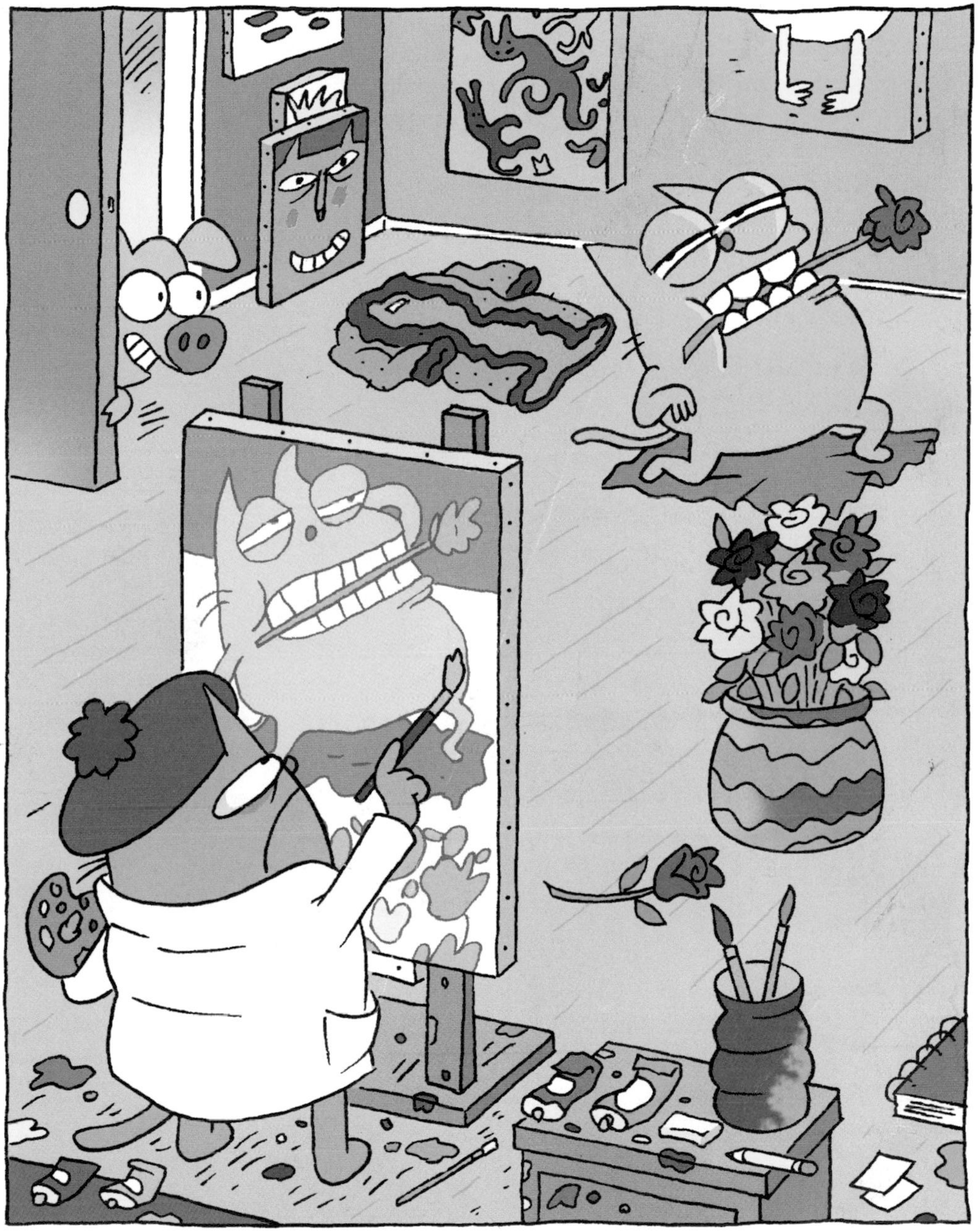

ALSO AVAILABLE!

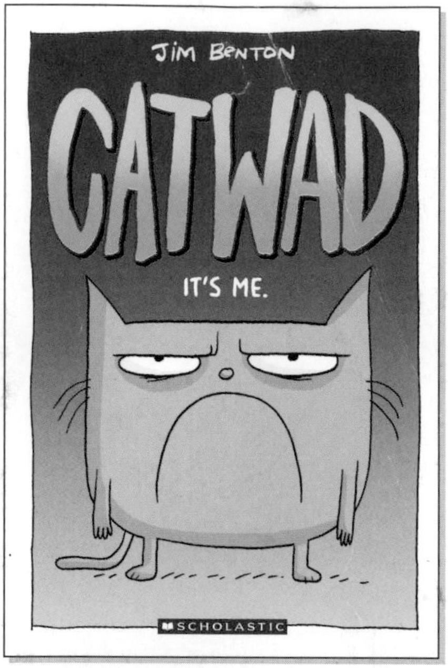
JIM BENTON
CATWAD
IT'S ME.
SCHOLASTIC

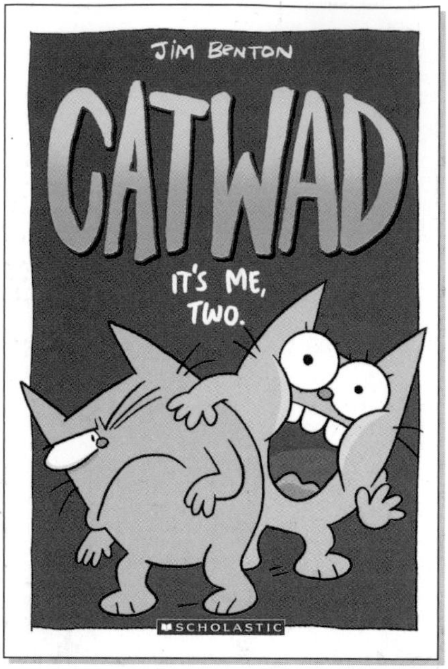
JIM BENTON
CATWAD
IT'S ME, TWO.
SCHOLASTIC

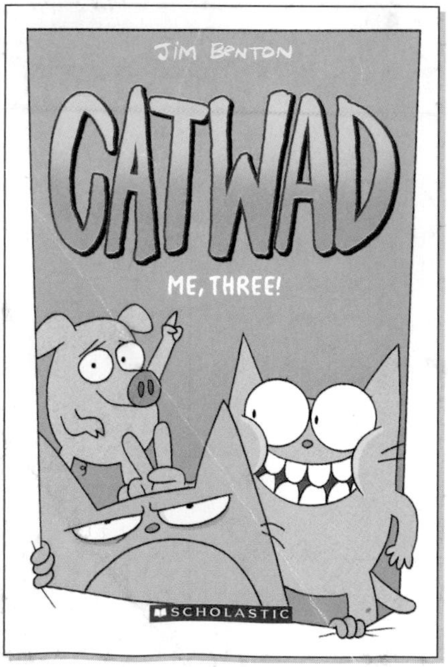
JIM BENTON
CATWAD
ME, THREE!
SCHOLASTIC

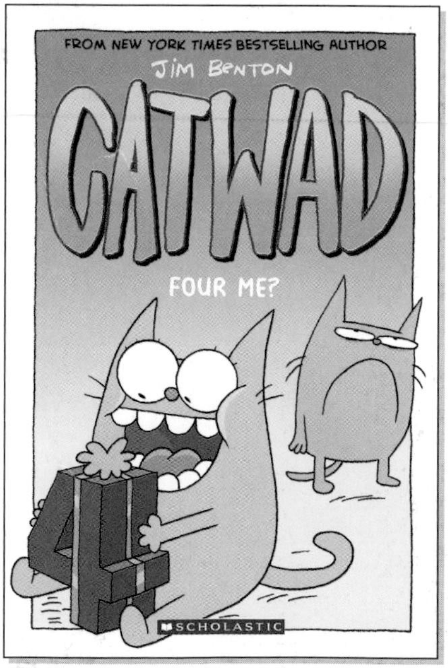
FROM NEW YORK TIMES BESTSELLING AUTHOR
JIM BENTON
CATWAD
FOUR ME?
SCHOLASTIC